Torch

LILA ROSE

This story is for my mum.

*After reading Death, I loved how you rang, asking for Torch's
book every day
because you'd fallen in love with him.*

*I just wish we had more time together... where I could give it to
you now.*

*I'll love you forever, Mum, and I know that while I was
writing this,
you're looking down enjoying your tortured guy!*

PLAYLIST

Save Me
Jelly Roll

Happy People
X Ambassadors, Teddy Swims, Jac Ross

HOPE
NF

Lovely
Billie Eilish and Khalid

When the Party's Over
Billie Eilish

BLURB

Her screams were what drew me in.
Since the night I heard them, I followed her.
She was my obsession.
My addiction.

But I could never have her.
She had to be free.
Had to feel peace.

I was nothing but a mess of darkness.
Even on my good days with my brothers from the Diamond
MC, I was nothing but tainted.

Still, I would end anyone who hurt her.
Especially those who touched her.
Their blood would stain my hands—one way or another.
Because I would torch the world for her.

CHAPTER ONE

*S*he was here. The one who'd been in my head and on my mind since the night I heard her screams. The night she woke yelling for help. The night her cries slid into my chest and wrapped around my beating organ like barbed wire to skin and stayed.

Since then, I wanted to know her.

Since then, I couldn't stop thinking about her.

And since that first time, she'd become my obsession.

My addiction.

A part of my life where I needed to see or hear her every day.

Not that *she* knew.

Wren was what her sister called her.

Wrenley was her full name.

I liked it.

Her name had my lips tipping up. Not many things could do that for me. Except my brothers. My brethren who were my family. My only family. One I didn't come from but stepped into.

They'd accepted me.

They understood pain and the craving I had for blood. The want I had to make people hurt.

Shoving those thoughts away, I blinked down at my obsession, who was currently in my domain. She came toward the area where I hid in the covered darkness. A position where I could admire without judgment or fear from others.

My blood raced through my veins; she was prettier this close.

Stunning.

I was happy for my brother Death that he found his woman, Raya—Wrenley's sister. I glanced to where the couple stood near the door of the compound watching Wrenley as she approached my dog. Death would know I lurked close by. He was a good brother and deserved Raya, but the best part about them two together was that it brought Wrenley into my orbit.

I was surprised he'd agreed that I could meet Wrenley when I first asked, especially as he'd tensed from my question.

He knew me.

Knew I wasn't exactly right in the head at times. But he trusted me.

So, I'd do good by him. I would have anyway since this was *her*.

The screaming beauty of the night.

I fisted my hands at my sides as I watched her drop to her knees and coo at my new dog, who growled low. But she didn't seem to care and kept talking to him in her reassuring, comforting tone.

She's sweet, soft, and gentle.

She was trying to woo him, yet my brothers were scared of my dog.

She cooed again. "What's your name, buddy? I bet you've got a good one. You're such a handsome boy." She ducked her head, and then she called back to Death and Raya, "Yep, he's a boy."

My brother chuckled.

I wanted her attention. I wanted her words.

My dog stopped growling. She'd already won him over. But I knew she would.

Moving out from the shadows, I ran a couple of fingers over my lips. I didn't know what to say. Would she like how I looked? Would she run scared? I pushed my fingers up to tap at my temple. Too many thoughts spazzed me out.

Her voice broke through when she said, "See, you are a good boy. You know I won't hurt you. Yes, you do." She crawled—*crawled*—closer. My dog could have lunged at her, but from his wagging tail, he trusted her.

"Harley," I blurted, tone low.

My obsession jolted from my word and glanced up. Looked right at me.

Fuck.

"Sorry?" she asked.

"His name," I told her.

She gifted *me* with a smile. "Harley?"

I nodded, drinking her in with my eyes.

Pretty.

Blonde curly hair was down around her shoulders, moving in the breeze.

I wanted to be that breeze. I wanted to touch it. Would it be soft?

She shifted her blue eyes away and back down to my dog. He was lucky.

"Harley," she murmured. "That's a good name for you at a biker compound."

I'd thought so too. She reached out to him and rubbed over his head.

When her warm gaze shot up to me again, something hard clenched in my chest. "I'm Wrenley." She pointed over her shoulder. "Raya is my sister. She's with Death."

Knew all of it.

But *she* didn't know that.

"I heard. Just hadn't met you."

Wanted to.

Needed to.

And now that I had, my obsession just grew.

Surprise flickered through me when she sat her ass on the grass-covered ground. Like she wanted to stay around me longer.

More tightness grew in my chest.

She petted my dog over and over, then looked back at me to ask, "Um, is Harley yours?"

Now my gut acted up. I kicked at some rocks to distract that feeling. "Yeah."

Death cleared his throat. "My brother saved me when Harley went to attack me after finding him. Now he's Torch's. They claimed each other."

I didn't do much. His previous owners had hurt him. Made him do things.

Know that fucking feeling.

I bit the inside of my cheek, halting *those* thoughts, and tasted blood.

Wrenley smiled. "You must be a good person."

I wasn't. *I'm not.*

Coldness seeped into my blood, and annoyance surfaced. I shoved my hands in my pockets and looked away.

"No," I said roughly.

"No?" she asked quietly.

I winced.

Fuck me, fuck me, fuck me.

I didn't want to scare her. I didn't want her to go. I didn't want to lose this. Her here with me.

Moving closer, I crouched at Harley's back and petted him before I lifted my gaze to my brother and his woman.

Would they let me have her alone?

Death studied me for a beat. "Wrenley, we're gonna head in for a drink. You want—"

She didn't turn to them but waved over her shoulder. "I'll stay with Harley for a little longer."

My gaze swung down to her. My lips tugged up at the corner. She wanted to stay. She knew I was here with Harley and wanted to be here even with me around.

My body shuddered.

"You got it, kid," Death called. "Just don't be too long. Torch, ten, yeah?"

Ten. I could do that. Without looking away from Wrenley, I nodded.

I'd do anything just to have her alone.

But fuck, what did I say? What did we talk about? Would she think me awkward? Stupid? A monster?

I *was* a monster. I liked to hurt people. I liked to kill. Even now, as the thought crossed my mind, I wanted to draw blood and watch it drain from someone who deserved it.

But Wrenley didn't deserve any pain.

She needed to be taken care of.

She was sweet, soft, and gentle.

I had to be careful with her. I couldn't hurt her.

"See you soon," Raya said. Her tight tone told me she was a little worried about leaving her sister with me. I couldn't blame her.

"Got it," my pretty girl called back, lifting her eyes to me so I could see her roll them.

She thought her sister was being silly. She wasn't, but I liked that she wanted to share that moment with me.

I wanted to say something, but what?

I lifted my free hand and pressed my knuckles into my temple. *Fuckin' work, brain.* Usually, it worked fine around the brothers. I could hold a conversation—unless we had a job. Then I lost words more. Was my brain not working because I was nervous? At least, with the way my stomach flopped around, I thought I was nervous. Sometimes I had trouble working out the exact emotion.

Shit, shit, shit. I was going to lose my chance.

"Death called you Torch. I guess that's your club name?"

"Yeah." Did she like it? Should I ask her? That was a question.

She gave me a soft smile. "Cool." Under the back light, I saw color hit her cheeks.

"You're blushing."

The color darkened even more. She laughed. "You're not supposed to point it out."

I cocked my head to the side. "Why?"

She shrugged and glanced around. "It's so I don't get embarrassed even more."

I shook my head. "No. Why did you blush?"

There'd been no cause for it. I hadn't said or done anything as far as I knew, only agreed my name was Torch.

"Oh," she whispered, and the red spread down her neck. "I can't remember why." She bit her bottom lip, and that action made me think she was lying.

How long had we been sitting here?

I didn't want to get her back to Death and Raya late. I didn't want them to think I was doing something wrong. I wouldn't.

But I wanted to.

Not in the harmful way. I would never ever hurt her. I just wanted to touch her, and that'd be wrong in their eyes. I wasn't good for Wrenley. She needed someone smart. Someone good. Someone who didn't have so much blood soaked into his skin.

I stood and flicked my hand to the back door. "You better go."

She needed to stay away from me.

I saw her tense before she slowly got to her feet after patting Harley one more time.

If she stayed away, I could allow myself to watch her from afar. To protect her. I'd make sure nothing harmed her again. Nothing new that could cause her to wake in the middle of the night screaming like she did after her dad killed her mom.

"I'll take you to your sister," I told her and clenched my jaw to keep myself from saying more. I wanted to tell her she didn't need to worry, that I'd keep an eye out for her. That she looked real pretty, and that I wished I could stare at her all the time.

But that shit was weird to say out loud.

Creepy.

I didn't want her to worry I'd be a problem.

No one would. Not even me.

"Thanks, Torch."

When she turned to face the compound, giving me her back, I closed my eyes for a second to take in her words. To freeze the moment for a beat because she'd said my name in such a nice way. Without fear, without disgust or anything horrible.

As she made her way back inside, I silently followed her.

I'd follow her anywhere, really.

Not that she knew. And she never would because then I'd worry that I'd see true fear in her pretty, pretty eyes.

Especially if she found out exactly what I was like.

Broken, beaten, and bloodthirsty.

FOR THE REST of the night, I stayed near but just out of sight. Wrenley wasn't in any trouble at the compound, but I couldn't stop watching her.

My brothers were good. The only ones I hadn't liked were long gone.

Dead Duck.

I'd enjoyed killing him.

He'd insulted Wreck.

He'd hurt Dusty, and she was important. She was the president's old lady, so Duck's blood was worth spilling.

My obsession listened to her sister as she talked with a bright smile on her face. She was happy. She loved her sister, and I could tell she liked Death for Raya when her eyes got soft after Death walked up to curl his arm around Raya.

I was glad she had her sister. Raya would take care of her in ways I couldn't. I heard how Raya stepped up when my Wrenley witnessed their dad kill their mom. It was why they moved in together, so they could have each other's backs.

That was how siblings were supposed to be.

Like my brothers were.

But the more I watched and listened to Wrenley, the more I believed there was something hidden in her gaze that sang to my tortured soul. But it was something that I didn't like seeing in her blue depths. I wasn't sure her sister knew, but I sensed my Wrenley was dealing with another situation, more than just the aftereffects of her murdering father.

She has a secret.

I clenched my jaw when sweet Wrenley suddenly tensed. Her smile dimmed a little as she pulled out her cell to only quickly place it back in her pocket.

There.

Her gaze dulled before she tried to hide it from her sister with a smile.

Wrenley's attention was drawn away from Raya to Courtney, State's old lady, but I saw Raya's lips thin as she stared at her sister before she glanced up at Death.

Maybe they did know something.

Who'd been on the phone?

Who texted her and dulled her shine?

Whoever it was had ruined her mood. Her shoulders slumped and tightness coiled her body.

I needed to find out who it was.

Should I talk to Death about it first?

If I did, he could stop me.

If he stopped me, then whoever cast that cloud over Wrenley would get away with doing it again.

I couldn't allow that.

I'd already promised myself I'd do anything to protect her, which meant that if I had to go behind people's backs, I would. But it'd be for the right reasons.

She had to be safe.

If I lost my obsession, I'd torch the fucking world around me.

CHAPTER TWO

TORCH

When Wrenley left with Death and Raya, I knew she'd be safe getting home with them at her side. Which was why I didn't leave right after. Instead, I made my way to Tech's room.

"What?" my computer-freak brother called when I knocked.

Opening the door, I paused. I'd wanted to talk to Tech alone, but Blaze was there. He was a new club person, who I was still getting used to. He seemed like an okay guy, but he'd been into shit my prez didn't like, so I wasn't going to trust him easily.

"Bonjour, Torch." I glanced to the side where the couch was, and there sat Henri, Blaze's man and Dusty's boss. He was a cool guy. Never feared me. Then again, he was dating a man who could be classed scarier than me.

"Henri." I nodded.

He smiled up at me while he flicked to a new page in his magazine. "I'm bored, Torch. Tell me you have something I can do."

"Henri," Blaze warned.

Grinning, I liked the fact that Blaze obviously didn't trust me either.

Maybe we'd work on it. Maybe we wouldn't. It was no skin off my nose.

Henri sighed and dropped his magazine beside him. His man hadn't even turned from the computer he tapped away on. Tech sat at another desk beside him, typing just as fast.

"They are like this all the time." Henri waved a hand toward the two men. "Work, work, work. If my Blaze is not careful, I will find someone else to warm my body—"

"Like fuck," Blaze snarled, swinging around in his seat.

Henri cackled.

Tech sighed and stretched. "I guess we're finishing this shit another day?" He spun in his chair to face our way.

Blaze stood and stalked over to Henri, picked him up, and flung him over his shoulder. It was lucky Henri laughed because my hand twitched to stop Blaze's movement. Anger tried to surface, but I reminded myself that Henri was okay.

I didn't like anyone being touched without wanting it.

It brought the bad memories forward.

"Torch?"

I swung my gaze to Tech. His attention flicked down to my hand and back up to me. I realized I'd pulled my knife without even a thought. Memories had triggered the movement to keep me safe.

I slipped away the blade and nodded to Tech and then

chanced a glance to Blaze just as Henri smacked his ass. "What's the holdup?" he asked, not knowing Blaze was eyeing me as if I was going to be a problem.

I wasn't.

"All good," I told him and grinned.

Blaze narrowed in on my smile. Shit, maybe I shouldn't have.

He grunted, and I moved from the doorway in time for him to strut out while Henri waved back at us. "Au revoir."

Snorting, I shook my head. That guy was cool.

I turned to Tech as he asked, "What can I do for you, brother?"

Walking over, I took the seat Blaze vacated. "Need a favor."

He rocked side to side in his swivel chair and raised a brow at me. "You know the deal. Tell me what it is first before I agree."

Nodding, I tapped a couple of fingers to my knee. "You know who Wrenley is?"

His other brow shot up with the first. "Brother—"

"Wait. Hear me out. I ain't lookin' at hookin' up or anythin'. She's too...." *Sweet, soft, and gentle. Not for me.*

When Tech clasped me on my shoulder, I brought my head up. "Brother, I didn't mean anythin' by that. You deserve happiness, Torch. I'm not sayin' you can't go for Wren. All I was gonna say is good luck tryin' to get through Death to have somethin' with her."

Smirking, I shook my head. "Nah, I don't want anythin'."

He leaned back in his chair. "You sure?" When I nodded, he added, "Then what's this favor?"

If I didn't get it out quickly, he'd say no straightaway, so I blurted fast, "Need you to hack her phone to see who's texting her because there's someone on there she doesn't like. It dulls her eyes. It makes her tense. She needs help."

His jaw clenched as he studied me. Groaning, he ran a hand over his face. "Brother, this is a fuckin' pickle. If I help you, then I'm invading her privacy, and not only would she be after me, but Raya and Death would come for me too."

I waited.

He had a sister. A twin. I knew he wouldn't like that Wrenley was being hassled.

"Jesus Christ," he bit out, turning toward the computer. "If I do this, don't tell anyone it came from me."

I grinned. "My lips are sealed."

He rolled his eyes. "Right, give me time. I'll call you when I'm done. Probably tomorrow since I'm not super-human and need sleep."

"Thanks, brother." I stood and made my way to the door still grinning.

"Torch," Tech called, and when I faced him, he said, "I'm going to make the choice if you need to intervene from what I find out."

"Fair." I trusted Tech.

"*And* if I think it needs your attention, you can't go off like a damn bomb, brother. You need to keep your head, and I'll be helpin' if there's a situation."

I stretched my neck from side to side. "I'll try to stay calm. And I'll accept your help."

"Shit," Tech drew out as he watched me. "If it's also needed, we tell Country."

"If I don't agree to that, will you not look into it?"

"I won't."

I tipped my chin up. "Okay."

Tech nodded once before he spun back around, and I left. It wasn't like I didn't trust Country. I did. Completely. He'd helped me after…. Still, there was a chance he'd stop me from finding whoever made sweet Wrenley sour. I wasn't sure I'd be able to listen to Country or Tech if they tried to hold me back.

We'd soon see.

Tech was smart with computers. It wouldn't take him long, and even if it did take him until tomorrow, it still impressed me. I didn't understand much about technology, and when I had to learn for jobs at Death's security business or the escort agency, it sometimes took the brothers a few goes explaining before it sank in.

They were patient, though. Always had been. Which was good since I liked to work at both places when I could. But I preferred the security office.

As I walked through the common area, I nodded to the brothers who caught my attention but otherwise left them alone. It was a party night. Most were busy drinking, hanging with their partner for the night or their claimed other half.

When I was younger and had become a full member, I used to drink. Used to smoke pot too. But both messed with my head too much. I also ended up in more fights than normal. Not with any of the brothers. I respected them too much to throw my bullshit at them. But if I was away from the club and some guy did something that pissed me off, yeah, I hadn't held back. Back then, I triggered quicker when it came to fucked-up situations.

Now, though, I was called in when rough circumstances needed my kind of crazy. Still, my brothers loved me no matter what I was thinking or what mood I was in. They were there for me if I needed them. Like I would always be for them.

I pushed open the front door and made my way to my vehicle. I wasn't taking my ride. It made too much noise. I wanted to be unheard and unseen.

Would Wrenley be in bed by now?

Could Raya be at Death's, leaving Wrenley alone in the house?

If it weren't weird, I would have asked Death what his plans were with his old lady, where they would sleep. But that'd also give away that I was up to something. So far, he hadn't found my nightly hidden spot, and I wanted to keep it that way.

Parking a block away, I grabbed my thicker jacket and got out of the car. The night still held a slight breeze to it, but it wasn't too bad. I could handle it. I'd dealt with worse before.

Fuck, don't think about that. I couldn't go there. My throat thickened as anger rose, my past flashing in my mind. It happened more and more recently.

Grumbling under my breath, I put the jacket on and pulled up the hood. It was late, so the streets were quiet. Though, this whole area was a peaceful place to be in at night. No doubt it was why Death picked this spot in the first place.

Stuffing my hands in my pockets, I glanced around before I ducked down the side of a random house and then into their backyard that fitted onto the rear of Raya and

Wrenley's home. I was lucky their neighbors didn't have a dog, or they'd be barking up a storm from me creeping around.

I jumped the fence and ducked low. The shadows covered me and kept me out of the view of the cameras Death had set up. I knew where they were pointed from the times I worked at his security business. Death always had a couple of brothers or employees watching all the screens back at the office. They also covered the clients who'd hired him, plus the other businesses the club owned.

Eyeing the house, I noticed there weren't any lights on. I slunk through the shrubbery until I reached the side of the house where Wrenley's room lay. Leaning back against the fence, I shifted on my ass to get comfortable between two bushes. Long ago, I'd found the best position to give me the perfect view of her window. Her curtains were closed, like always, and there was nothing but darkness inside.

My sweet girl was already in bed, but was she asleep? It didn't matter; either way, I'd stay where I was to keep watch.

Bending my knees, I wrapped my arms around them and eyed her window.

I hoped she had a peaceful sleep.

I prayed that whoever texted her hadn't forced unease on her so she wouldn't be able to rest.

Scrubbing a hand over my face, I listened to the night. In the distance there was music from a party. Close by, leaves rustled, cars drove, houses creaked. But not the house that was in front of me. All was quiet in there.

I stilled.

Footsteps sounded.

Pulling my blade free, I silently moved into a crouch.

"Brother?"

Sighing, I cursed inwardly.

"How long you been doin' this?"

I glanced up at Death, who had his head over the fence. They had been next door, leaving Wrenley alone. Annoyance settled inside of me, and I clenched my jaw.

"Torch?"

Straightening, I pressed a finger to my lips before I waved him back. When he stepped out of sight, I pocketed my knife, grabbed the fence, and jumped it.

"Back deck," Death ordered. I followed him with my hands in my pockets and head down.

My gut clenched. My chest hurt.

He'd tell me to stay away.

I couldn't.

Someone had to watch her. Didn't he understand she was to be protected from everything?

She was soft, sweet, and gentle.

All good things that needed to be cherished.

Climbing the steps to the deck, I pulled my hands free and wiped them over my hips.

"Torch?"

He wouldn't like my answer.

He'd ask me to stop.

I couldn't.

"Brother?"

Unlocking my jaw, I said, "Since the night I heard her screams."

Death cursed. "That was months ago. You tellin' me you've been sittin' out under her window at night for months?"

I wouldn't meet his gaze, kept my head down. But I nodded.

"Even in the rain?"

I nodded again.

He stayed silent. I didn't fucking like the silence. It made my gut eat at my organs.

"Why?"

She was my obsession. My addiction. Mine.

But I couldn't have her beauty, her softness, her sweetness.

Should I tell him the truth about what I heard in those screams? Would she want me to?

"Brother, you gotta give it to me. You get that, yeah? Wrenley's sister is my woman. Meanin' Wrenley is a part of my family. I need answers, Torch, and once you give them, I'll let you know if you can still keep doin' what you're doin'."

Rocking back and forth on my feet, I rubbed two fingers against my temple.

I had to tell him.

Fuck.

She could get angry at me for telling him. Or maybe he'd keep it a secret.

"Her screams."

"Yeah?" Death prompted.

"They're not only from what she's seen. Or maybe they are." I shook my head. "But not all of them. A part of her nightmares could be from what her dad did, but somethin' else happened. Before it, maybe."

"The texts."

My head shot up.

Death grunted. "I've seen her gettin' some texts that make her stress." He waited a beat and added, "From your reaction, you've noticed too." I nodded, and he queried, "Tonight?" I tipped my chin up. His upper lip rose for a beat before he bit out, "Fuck." Death ran a hand at the back of his neck.

I glanced to the left just before his back door slid open and Raya stood here in a robe. "Leland?"

She used my brother's birth name, not his club one.

I cocked my head to the side. I hated the name I'd been given at birth. It reminded me too much of my past, so I hadn't thought of it in a long time and was surprised I'd even remembered it. I doubted I'd ever share it freely with someone, though. Not when it could trigger me into losing my shit.

"I'll be in soon, darlin'."

"Okay. Hey, Torch."

I waved and smiled. She returned it. At least she wasn't wary of my smile like Blaze had been.

When the door closed and she was out of sight, Death turned back to me. "You think we need to take charge and investigate those texts? Find out what exactly is goin' on?"

Shit. Fuck. I had to tell him more. No doubt he'd tell Country. Then they'd both be on my back to leave her be. I'd lose her. They wouldn't like me looking and listening to her.

I fisted my hands and sighed. "Asked Tech for a favor tonight. He's gonna hack her phone and let me know if it needs more attention. He was gonna help me. Not leave me to it. He'd tell Country if it was bad, and then we'd all deal with it."

Deal with it while the brothers kept an eye on me, so I didn't go loco.

"Shit, brother. Wren's gonna be pissed we went behind her back." He ran a hand through his hair.

"It was me. Not you. Blame me." If she got pissed at just me, it wouldn't matter since I couldn't have her.

"Nah, brother." He shook his head. *Nah? Why?* He went on, "You saw somethin' I missed in my woman's sister. You won't take the fall. You're usually spot-on with what you sense. I shoulda done somethin' before now. Raya and I saw her get a text a while ago that made her shut down. I didn't realize until tonight that it'd continued to happen. Raya and I already spoke about it. We were gonna sit Wrenley down and have a chat with her." He glanced to the back door and then me again. "I'm gonna get Raya to hold off on that chat. I'll talk to Tech, too, let him know I want to be informed of what he learns. From that, we'll figure out if we step in or leave it for Wrenley to handle on her own."

My jaw clenched.

Death snorted. "I see you don't like that idea. Let's discuss things once we have answers, yeah?"

"Got it."

He reached out, hand to my shoulder, and squeezed. "Appreciate you lookin' out for her, brother."

"She won't be mine. I-I-I..." I dropped my head. "I just want to watch out for her."

"You don't want to date her?"

My chest ached.

What I wanted wasn't dating.

I'd own her.

But she'd own me back.

Still, I couldn't.

"No."

"Torch—"

"No," I snarled darkly.

"All right, brother. I'll drop it. For now."

He had to leave it alone altogether. Though, I wondered if him asking me meant he'd accept my interest in her.

Wrong.

Wrong, wrong, wrong.

Surely, he wouldn't. He knew me. He, Country, and State *knew* me. Knew my past. Knew everything.

Turning, I jumped down the steps and landed on the ground.

"You gonna be warm enough?" Death called.

I stilled.

He wasn't going to tell me to fuck off.

He should have.

Why didn't he?

Didn't matter. It was too late now that he didn't stop me.

Grunting, I made my way to the fence and slipped over it. I went back into my hidey-hole and sat as I had been. Weariness tugged at me, but I wouldn't give in to it.

We'd figure this out. We'd keep Wrenley safe and make sure she had the chance to dream peacefully.

CHAPTER THREE

WRENLEY

I'd needed a break from my online digital marketing course and the house. Grocery shopping was a pain, but it was slightly better than sitting at home and having my sister, as well as her biker boyfriend, looking at me like they were trying to work out if I was an alien or not.

Seriously, since they'd walked in the door this morning, I caught them watching my every move. I was sick of the hairs on the back of my neck sticking up from their stares, creeping me out.

Raya even tried to stop me from going out alone, and I was so close to snapping at her until Death stepped in, ensuring her I would be fine.

I'd figured they'd seen my reaction last night when I'd looked at the unwanted text and were waiting me out, hoping I would open up to them. At the time, I thought I'd hidden it well, like I had that first time Raya questioned me about reacting badly to some other messages.

Obviously, I needed to become a better actress if I wanted to keep hiding this.

At least back then I'd told her the truth when I said it was a guy named Tony who I knew from college. That I'd gone on a couple of dates with him. I'd even explained how he'd been a little persistent when he wanted my attention.

She'd tried to intervene, but I'd yelled at her to let me handle him. Honestly, it surprised me when she gave in and backed off. However, since I'd promised her that Tony was nothing like Elio, who had beaten and sexually abused Death's sister and threatened Raya, she'd had no reason to stay on my case.

That part had been a lie.

The biggest lie I'd ever told my sister, and my guilt still lingered.

Tony and his friends were self-centered see-you-next-Tuesdays and as bad as Elio.

Just thinking of them had my skin crawling.

They thought they ruled the college, and in a way, it was true. They were the spoiled rich boys with enough money to throw around; they could bend anyone to their will. At the beginning, when I'd first been introduced to them by our common friend, Penny, they'd managed to charm me right away and made me feel like I was something special. Especially Tony.

It only took a few weeks to see the signs of their arrogance with how they treated outsiders to the group. Even professors were intimidated by them.

After a month in their company, I realized I needed to distance myself from them. They weren't my people. When I started declining their invitations to drink or darted in the other direction if I saw them around, they noticed my lack of fawning.

Tony had been the first to figure out my distaste. One night, while we'd been out in a group setting, I'd caught him watching me after I'd been looking at Penny with my upper lip raised in disgust while she gushed over the bracelet Mitch had given her. The same bracelet design I'd seen him gift to two other women in classes we'd shared. I suspected he'd bought them in bulk.

Penny had also witnessed at least one of the other exchanges, yet she'd acted like he'd hung the moon for picking her to be his next target.

When I'd looked away from them, my gaze had landed on Tony's cold stare, making me swallow thickly. His expression quickly softened when he smiled and tipped his drink my way. Despite fear settling in my stomach, I'd grinned back. I'd felt like something bad would happen if I didn't pretend everything was okay.

Since then, I'd done everything in my power to avoid him and his group. I'd even distanced myself from the friends who introduced me. I went to my classes, back to my room, and then to the cafeteria.

Tony had still tried—in his charming, flirty way—to get me to give in and hang out, though.

When he'd called or texted, I was respectful and nice in return, but I used the excuse that I wasn't feeling well, had to work, or had to study for an exam.

I should have kept avoiding him. I should have buckled down and ignored the constant contacting.

I hadn't. One afternoon, Tony had worn me down and guilted me into seeing him.

"Babe," Tony said into the phone. *"I can help you study and make you relax with a nice massage. I promise I'll keep my hands in the safe zones."*

Tony had tried a few times to become intimate with me, but I wouldn't go further than kissing. It wasn't that I was a virgin—I wasn't. There was just something putting me off the idea of going further with him.

"I appreciate the offer, Tony. But I concentrate better on my own."

"How about dinner then? You must eat. All I'm asking is for you to grace me with your presence while we both eat. I'll pick you up and drop you back at your dorm before 9:00 p.m. What do you say?"

"I don't—"

"Please, babe. We haven't seen each other in such a long time. I miss you, Wrenley."

Sighing, I pinched the bridge of my nose. I just wanted this conversation and begging to stop. "Fine," I whispered.

"Great, I'll see you at six," he said before he hung up.

By the time he arrived, pulling up to the curb where I waited, I was already regretting my decision. I opened the door and slid in, holding back a sigh.

"Hey, babe." He grinned, leaning over to kiss my cheek since I didn't give him my mouth.

I smiled. "Just in case I'm getting something."

His lips thinned as he nodded, but he replied lightly, "Thanks for thinking of me, darling."

More tension rolled through me as I clasped my hands together tightly on my lap.

Dinner. All I had to do was get through dinner.

Besides, while I'd been getting ready, I figured this dinner could give me the chance to call things off with Tony. Not that we were exclusively dating. We'd been on a handful of outings alone together and another handful in group settings. Still, it was time to tell him I wasn't ready for a relationship or even hooking up.

He'd understand. I was sure of it, and it wasn't like he didn't have other women interested in him. I'd seen them trying to get his attention.

"Um, how was your day?" I asked.

"Good. The guys and I took the yacht out for a while. They're heading to Monroe's later. I said we might catch them there if you're feeling up for it. But if you're not, that's okay. I'll drop you back at the dorm and head home." He didn't live in a dorm at the college. He and his friends had a house for their fraternity off campus.

"Please don't feel like you have to go home after you drop me off."

"So, you've already decided you won't go out?"

"Tony, I told you I wasn't feeling the best and I had to study. You were okay with just doing dinner earlier."

His laugh sounded strained.

"You're right. Of course, I'm okay with dinner if it means I get to spend time with you."

Had he always been this cringey in trying to be charming? Why hadn't I noticed it before?

"Thanks." I smiled at him when he glanced over.

He took me to the restaurant that he loved near his house.

It was after he tried to order for me, which I declined and got what I wanted, I excused myself to use the bathroom. But really, I just wanted a breather.

After washing my hands, I considered calling my sister to get me out of the dinner, but then I remembered I needed to tell him I wasn't looking to date anyone.

Sucking in a deep breath, I walked back out there with a fake smile.

"Sorry about that," I said as I sat.

"Everyone has to go." He laughed and then slid a glass of wine my way. "I took the opportunity to order us a drink."

"Oh, um, thank you. But I don't really want any alcohol tonight."

He pouted. Actually pouted. *"Come on, babe. One drink. Don't make me have one alone, and besides, this bottle cost me a small fortune."*

I ground my teeth together. He knew how I hated to waste money. The bastard.

"One," I said tightly.

He winked. "You got it." He raised his glass toward me. I picked up mine and clinked it against his. "To us."

Shit. *Guilt sank my heart. I couldn't tell him I wanted to be friends after he said that. Taking a gulp of courage from the wineglass, I shook my head and looked down at the table.*

I had to be strong. I couldn't go on like this either. I'd just do it later when he dropped me off.

I didn't get a chance, though.

The next thing I remembered was waking up naked, handcuffed to his bathroom sink.

As I woke, a scream built and burst out of me. I scrambled up from the floor to sitting beside the sink where one wrist was cuffed. I tugged on it while I used the other hand to reach for the bath rug on the tiles to cover myself. Tears welled and fell. My heart raced fast enough that I could hear it. Another horrified scream dropped from my lips when I felt the ache between my legs.

The door opened, and I broke off in a whimper.

A dressed Tony stood in it glaring.

"Shut up," he clipped low and harshly. "There are guests in the house."

"W-what did you do?"

He smirked, crossing his arms over his chest as he leaned against the doorframe. "What do you mean, babe?"

I gripped the rug to me. "What did you do?" I whispered and whimpered when I shifted a little. A painful throb started between my legs. "What did you do?" I asked again. "What did you do?" I yelled.

He stomped forward and kicked at my legs. I cried out, cowering in on myself.

A click had me looking up at him. I blinked the tears away to see him holding his phone. He crouched and turned the screen my way.

There were topless photos of me passed out on a bed. One after another.

I didn't care about that.

Shaking my head, I trembled against the cold wall. "What did you do to me?"

"What? You don't care about the photos?"

"Tony, please. What did you do?"

He sighed, sitting on the floor opposite me. "I get what I want, Wrenley. I wanted you. I drugged you, had you, and left you so my friends could take a turn."

My eyes widened just before I turned and vomited all over the floor.

They'd touched me, violated me, while I was unconscious.

My ears rang, and a sob got caught in my throat as I threw up again.

They'd touched me.

Raped me.

And I knew nothing about it.

Except the pain.

Heaving, I closed my eyes, praying that this was a nightmare and I'd soon wake from it.

He gripped my hair and tugged my head back. The stench of booze washed over my face. Tony spoke roughly when he said, "I know you're trying to get away from us. I saw your look that night. But no one leaves until we've had our fill."

I gagged.

He shook my head roughly. "Keep it in." When he released my hair, I dropped my head, crying. He wasn't finished, though. "You're a trailer-trash piece of shit who will do everything we say, or we release those photos to the student body, to the professors, and online. We can make your life a living hell if you don't do as we say."

Shivering, I gripped the rug. My stomach churned. I heaved, but nothing else came up.

"Do you understand me, Wrenley?"

They'd touched me, and I had no memory of it.

"Wrenley, do you understand?"

Someone screamed. Cried. Whimpered.... So many noises.

A kick landed to my legs, my side. "Shut up, shut up, shut up."

They were my sounds.

I had to get out of there. I had to leave. I had to act. I had to... wash.

I can't remember. I can't remember. Just pain now. Pain.

Sucking in an unsteady breath, I tried to focus. Breathing deeply through my nose, I thinned my lips to keep the gagging on the inside.

Nodding to myself, I glanced up at Tony and noticed for the first time that his pupils were blown wide. He was high. Would he even remember this?

I had to get on his good side. I had to get out.

Licking my dry lips, I nodded again. "I-I won't say anything, Tony."

"I don't believe you."

"I-I promise." My bottom lip trembled. "I'm a good girl, right? I always follow along. I do what you guys want."

He studied me in thought. "I suppose you do."

Smiling wobblily, I winced when I sat up. "Tony, come on. We've had fun. I won't hold out on you anymore. I was a fool to do so in the first place."

"You were."

Humming, I cleared my throat and added, "I wanted you when I first met you, but I didn't want to seem too eager."

"You're lying," he clipped.

"I'm not," I said quickly. "I promise I'm not. Come on, Tony. I'm a good girl."

My pleading went on for some time that night before I'd somehow convinced him I would do anything he said from then on. He really thought he had something on me with those photos, but at the time, and even now, I didn't care who saw my body.

After he'd got me out—thankfully without seeing

anyone else—and drove me to my dorm, I'd showered and gone straight to my parents' place.

Snorting to myself, I shook my head and gripped the steering wheel.

At the time, I hadn't been thinking. I hadn't been in my right mind.

If I had been, I wouldn't have gone home.

I wouldn't have walked in on my father killing my mother in a drugged-out rage.

That was nearly a year ago.

When my sister swept in to help me take care of things and life grew busy with her, the police, and reporters, Tony backed off.

Raya had thought I'd been distraught over what I'd witnessed, and I had been, but that wasn't all. I was going through a lot more, was traumatized. Not that she knew. And in my own way, I wanted to protect her from what I went through. Since our father had murdered our mother, the weight on our shoulders was insurmountable. Raya had already condemned herself for not being there for me, even when I'd told her she wasn't at fault for anything. Her hating on herself gave me another reason to bottle up what happened.

I also figured that if I kept my mouth shut, Tony and his friends would leave me alone. And they did. Then I was somehow blessed to have been able to move without their notice. They'd tried to contact me, but after a month of their calls and texts going unanswered or unread, they gave up. Their threats weren't working.

After everything, I thought that if I could leave them

behind in that old town, I would heal emotionally like I had physically.

I wasn't sure if not knowing everything that happened to me was better or worse.

What plagued me still and made it impossible to forget was the morning after... his words and the way my body felt. But also, the worry that ate at me until I could get away on my own again to go to the doctor for blood work. It'd been a sigh of relief when I received the all clear from the tests. Out of everything, that was the only good thing.

Closing my eyes, I shook my head and stopped the memory there. I had to. If I didn't, the fear building inside me would take over, and I wouldn't be able to move.

Keep going.

Just keep going.

Tears clouded my vision as I blinked and stared out the windshield. I wiped at my cheeks, but the tears didn't stop.

Since Jupiter's situation, Death's sister who'd been beaten and raped, I'd been even more of a mess. Yet, the turmoil that rose and twisted my insides was also from that... *monster* trying to get in contact with me again.

Every recent text or call he made was a slap in the face.

Luckily, Raya hadn't been around when I received the first text. I'd been a mess, body shaking, bile rising, and a coldness seeping in as I ran for the toilet to lose my lunch.

His threat was that if I didn't come back, he would release those photos.

When I didn't respond, he sent me a video of people looking at my photos and laughing.

After I still didn't respond, he switched it up and started

pleading with me to come home. Even went as far as trying to tell me that he couldn't live without me.

He was trying to get me to believe he'd changed so he could get me back there to ruin me once again.

They wanted someone weak to use.

It wouldn't be me.

I should have gotten rid of my phone. I should have changed my number. Yet, keeping the same cell and number was my small way of being strong. He saw I read the texts. He knew I answered the calls and quickly hung up.

It was my "fuck you" to him.

Silly perhaps, but despite that, I was in the car crying.

He still held a sickening control over me.

One I hadn't noticed until recently.

CHAPTER FOUR

I wasn't sleeping. I could barely concentrate, and I was becoming more snappish as time went on. I was tired of pretending. Tired of hiding. Tired of everything.

Worst of all, I was back to being scared.

I constantly told myself he wouldn't find me. He would give up on contacting me.

But what happened if he didn't?

What happened if he showed up in this town and dragged me back?

Fear raged in me when I woke screaming from nightmares of invisible, unwanted touches.

What he'd done to me shouldn't have been allowed to happen. I should have done more. I should have said something. How had Death's sister been so brave when she reached out to her family, and yet, there I was acting like a fearful little kitten cowering?

I'd been there for Jupiter. I'd told her everything would be okay and that she had done the right thing by saying something and making that man pay so he didn't hurt anyone else.

I was a fake.

I didn't even listen to my own advice.

Stupid, stupid, stupid.

I was safe now. I had people who cared about me. I had people who would protect me.

I could lean on them. I was allowed to.

They wouldn't push me away like our parents had all our lives. They'd open their arms and help me.

It was time to talk and stop being a secretive little twit.

So, screw it.

If Tony called or messaged again, I would tell Raya.

A simmer of courage rose. I roughly wiped at my face as the tears slowed, and I drew in a shaky breath.

I could do this. I had to. If not for me, then others.

He could be tormenting another woman right now, and it'd be all my fault.

Oh shit... it really *would* be my fault.

I didn't stand up to him. I didn't go to the police.

But at the time, I'd run from what happened with him straight to my parents' place to witness... all that blood.

Everything had changed. I'd gone from a trauma I didn't remember to one I'd witnessed. What I'd seen had altered me irrevocably. I'd forced my thoughts about the attack aside to deal with the horror thrown in my face.

I'd pushed and pushed and *pushed* it all down inside me.

I hadn't really dealt with anything to do with Tony until I received that first text.

Now I would.

I had to.

How many more days could I go on like this?

Screw waiting for another call.

I tightened my hands around the steering wheel, closed my eyes, and dropped my forehead to the top of it.

Be brave. You can do this. Think of Jupiter. Death will help. He'll be there for Raya. You can do this.

I can.

Clenching my teeth, I sniffed.

I had to do this.

Drawing in another deep yet still shaky breath, I straightened and wiped at my face once more. Clearing my throat, I took another long inhale through the nose and checked myself in the visor mirror.

Shaking my hands out, I bit my bottom lip.

Just keep moving and deal with it when it comes.

Rolling my shoulders, I climbed out of the car and made my way into the supermarket.

I probably looked a mess, but I held my head high and entered.

After grabbing a cart, I headed through the front entrance.

For the time being, I wanted to forget everything again and walk around the store without him on my mind, without fear in my belly, and without the stress that had built to bursting point.

As I shopped, I forced myself to think of something else.

The first thing I conjured was when I'd met the dog Harley and his owner, Torch.

Harley was just adorable. He'd been all gruff and mean to start with, but I knew I'd win him over. Smiling to myself, I grabbed some items off the shelf.

What surprised me the most when I met Torch that night was how he hadn't frightened me when he'd appeared out of nowhere.

Maybe it was because I knew Death and Raya were there, and that I was at a compound full of bikers I trusted.

Though, I was halfway certain the main cause of my fearlessness had been from Torch's soft gaze.

There'd been something about him that had calmed me. Maybe that sounded crazy, but I'd never had an instant feeling of safety around a person before.

His good looks didn't slip my notice either. A brief pang of sorrow had touched my heart when I'd noticed his scars. He had an old slash in his eyebrow and on both cheeks. Those marks must have been deep to heal that way.

Did he have them in other places?

I hoped not.

Silently, I cursed myself when a flush filled my cheeks at the thought of seeing his naked body. I shouldn't even be thinking about his body in a way that brought heat to my skin since I'd only met him briefly. I didn't know the man.

But there's nothing wrong with admiring, I tried to tell myself, only to shove those thoughts away while I put my attention back to shopping and grabbed some milk.

Torch did seem different, though.

And now I'm back to thinking about him.

But he wasn't like any guy I'd met before. He even stood

out from his brothers. Maybe it was the way he spoke or how he held himself. But he was unlike anyone I'd met at the compound so far. Though, I was sure I hadn't met everyone since there were a lot of bikers in the club.

Torch was also the first guy who had piqued my interest in a long time. Yes, the brothers I'd been introduced to at Death's house were handsome. But they hadn't made my stomach flutter like it did after I met Torch's gaze for the first time.

Even now, as I thought of him, there was a tingle once more.

"Wrenley."

I jolted, heart leaping, and spun to see Gun coming toward me from the end of the aisle. He was another member of the Diamond MC.

"Hey." I smiled, immediately calming. "What are you doing here?"

He stopped in front of me and bent to give me a quick hug. As he straightened, he nodded toward the next aisle. "Saint's got our cart in another aisle, but he's slow as fuck shoppin'. I came to grab things while he read all the damn labels."

Laughing, I said, "That something an old man would do?"

I expected a snort or a chuckle back, but I got nothing. I glanced from the refrigerator to Gun.

"What's wrong?" he asked.

"Huh?"

"Wren, you look like you've been crying," he said gently.

Damn it.

Saint and Gun were partners and brothers of the club,

but Gun was also the guy I'd been opening up to about what I'd seen at the house when our father killed our mother. He'd been in a similar situation and shared his story with me before I'd even said a word about mine. His sharing had been an effective way to get me to relax and tell him about my ordeal since I hadn't wanted to speak with a therapist.

I waved him off with a roll of my eyes. "It's nothing. A silly video I saw on TikTok."

"You don't have TikTok."

I shrugged and grabbed my cart, pushing it further along. "It must have been Facebook."

Gun followed. "You have no social accounts, Wren. I asked you when we first met." His hand landed on my shoulder, and he gently turned me. "What's going on?"

The worry in his gaze had me caving slightly. "It's going to be handled. I'll talk to Raya when I get home. I have to tell her first."

His brows pinched. "It's serious," he stated.

I shrugged again, glancing off to the side.

His hands cupped my cheeks as he brought my gaze up to his. "You know you have people at your back. No matter what it is, we'll help you."

Tears formed and my heart clenched.

I did have people who would help.

Sniffing, I whispered, "I don't want to cry in the supermarket, Gun. Stop being nice." He grinned. "But thank you."

"Hey, lover" was called from down the aisle. "If you're hittin' on a woman, then I'm not doin' my job in the bedroom. Still, back the fuck off."

Gun sighed and turned to face Saint, which left me in full sight.

Saint smirked. "Hey, Wrenley. How you doin'?"

Gun crossed his arms over his chest and made a noise in the back of his throat. "Are you serious right now? You can't shout shit like that out, Zion."

Zion was Saint's Christian name.

Saint hooked an arm around Gun's neck and dragged him in, planting a loud kiss on his cheek. "You like it when I show the world you're mine."

"Shut up," Gun clipped as his face heated.

Saint tipped his chin my way. "You good?"

"I will be."

Saint grinned. "Cool. You let us know if there's anythin' we can help with."

Another hit to the chest of those warm emotions that had me drawing in a deep breath through my nose as I nodded to him.

Gun nudged Saint in the ribs. "Don't be nice. She doesn't want to cry in the supermarket."

"Did you tell her people already know anyway because she looks like she's been bawlin' for a week?"

Laughing, I mock glared. "Thanks, Saint."

He winked. "Pleasure."

My sister and I were honestly blessed when we moved in next door to Death. Not only did Raya connect with a protective, kind man, but we both gained some wonderful friends. It didn't matter that we were still getting to know them since I already trusted them in ways I would my own sister.

My heart was slowly being filled with a lightness that left me warm.

I just had to get rid of the mold festering in it to move on without fear.

"You mind if we finish shoppin' with you?" Saint asked.

I grinned. "As long as you don't take forever reading all the labels like an old man."

His narrowed gaze swung to Gun, who raised his hands in front of him, chuckling. "I didn't call you an old man. That was Wrenley."

"Wren, my body is my temple. I gotta take care of it, or my younger lovebug will leave me for someone prettier."

Snorting, I took hold of my cart and moved along with them beside me. "Your body is your temple, and yet I saw all the booze you drank last night at the compound."

"A god has to have a time-out from all his—"

Gun covered his mouth before dragging him into a head-lock. "Jesus, will you quit it?"

The whole scene lifted my mood and had me smiling wider.

Humor shone in Saint's eyes as he pulled Gun's hand away and used it to spin Gun around, dragging him into his chest. "Babe, is this your way of tellin' me you'll accept me no matter how I look?"

Gun's face went red. "Fuck off."

Saint chuckled. "I'll take that as a yes. What do you think, Wrenley?"

"I think you two are sickly sweet and you're giving me a toothache. Tell me where I can find my other half like that?"

They shared a quick look before Gun reached out and

ruffled my hair. "One day the love of your life will come along to annoy you."

Saint let go of the cart and clutched his chest. "Aww, boo bear, havin' you call me the love of your life is like you exploded my heart with all those fluttery emotions."

While I covered my mouth and snickered behind my hand, Gun raised a brow. "I exploded your heart?"

He nodded.

"At least he said with fluttery emotions," I offered.

Gun hummed under his breath. "I suppose."

Laughing, I shook my head and went back to shopping while I listened to them bicker in their own sweet way. Seriously, they were completely in love with each other, and it was nice to see.

I really, *really* wished I could find that eventually.

Someone totally devoted to me.

CHAPTER FIVE

TORCH

In the morning, Death sent me to the compound before he went into Raya and Wrenley's house. I knew he'd watch out for her. If he couldn't, he'd find someone who could.

I didn't need much sleep, so after I woke from a few hours, I showered and ate something quick in the kitchen. I figured by the time I finished, Tech would have some answers.

Walking down the hallway to my brother's large computer room, I heard voices coming from inside. I slowed my approach and quieted my movement until I was just outside the slightly opened door.

"—his name is Tony Handler. He attends Brown Hilltop College and runs a fraternity called Sigma Chi Handler. His grandfather started it."

"Get to the point that has you lookin' like you want to kill this prick," Country demanded.

I tensed. Tech had called Country in. That meant it wasn't good.

My mind cleared to lock on one name.

Tony Handler.

He was the one texting Wrenley.

Tony was the one I was after. I just knew it.

"Prez, from what I've got, it ain't good."

"Tell me."

"I got into Wren's phone and found out he's been callin' and textin' her for a while. Started out with threats. Said if she didn't come back and do as she was told, he'd release some naked pictures of her. When she didn't reply, he sent her a video of people lookin' at these photos. Fuck, brother. I saw them." A foul taste entered my mouth as Tech went on. "I didn't linger, but I noticed she looked passed out in that photo. The threats kept up for a bit, but now he's switched it up by tryin' to charm her back. This fucker likes control. Doesn't like she got away from him."

"Anythin' else?"

"That's it for now. But I reckon I've only touched the surface, and I ain't gettin' a good feelin' about this, Country."

"Christ. Keep searchin'. I want all the information before we talk to Death and Torch. How long do you think until you'll have it?"

It didn't matter that all the information wasn't there.

It was enough.

He'd taken photos of her.

Threatened her.

Tried to control her.

Clenching my fists, I stalked down the hall and made my way outside, ignoring the brothers who called out to me.

Tony Handler.

Tony Handler.

I had his name. I had his college. I had his fraternity. It wouldn't take me long to find him.

I raced to my vehicle, and I got in. I already knew the town but had to quickly search where his college and place were before I took off. With a full tank of gas, I'd arrive and get to him before the brothers found out.

It wasn't like I'd kill the guy.

Chuckling to myself, I shook my head.

No. I won't kill him yet.

Tony Handler had one chance to live.

The only way he'd stay alive was if he listened to me when I told him to stay away from my sweet obsession. If he didn't contact her in any way, then I'd allow him to continue to breathe.

A smile tugged at my lips when I hoped he didn't listen. I'd gladly end his life and have his blood on my hands if it meant Wrenley would be safe and happy.

I wanted her to continue to keep smiling like I'd seen her do. Like she'd gifted me. And not have it dimmed.

Halfway there, my phone rang. Country's name flashed across the screen. After his call, Death tried to reach me, then State and Tech.

It was too late. I already had a head start. I'd be able to do what I wanted before a brother showed. It was still early enough that he'd likely be at the fraternity.

Stretching my neck from side to side, I drove down the

street where he lived. An eager thump to my heart pumped adrenaline into my system.

Stopping a couple houses away, I took off my cut before I got out of my car and quickly made my way toward the huge house. There were a few cars in the driveway. One a Dodge Viper. My gut told me it was his.

Another car pulled up at the curb, and two guys got out. They started for the house, eyeing me as I stopped by the Dodge.

"Hey," I called. "This Tony Handler's car?"

"What's it to you?" the blond asked cockily.

I rolled my head back and to the side, grinning.

He paled.

The other guy pulled blondie back and said, "Yeah, that's his."

"Good. Get him," I ordered.

They both nodded and nearly fell over their feet to get inside. While I waited, I sat on the hood. Letting one foot dangle, I brought the other up to plant it on the metal while I pulled my blade free.

Come on, come on, come on.

Finally, a tall, slim guy with brown hair appeared. He saw me and jumped down the stairs. Three other guys followed him.

This was Tony Handler.

Tony Handler.

Who'd taken photos of her.

Who'd threatened her.

Who'd tried to control her.

My addiction. My Wrenley.

"Get the fuck off my car," he yelled, turning a funny shade of red.

I tapped the knife against my temple. "You don't know me."

Tony laughed. "And I don't fucking want to. Get off my car or I'll make you."

I tsked. "Don't." I slammed the blade into the hood. He yelled in outrage, but I went on. "Interrupt." I pulled the blade free and slammed it into the windshield, shattering it. He squealed some more. "Me." I yanked the weapon up, holding it in the air, but aimed it at the car while eyeing him.

He quieted, holding a hand up to the guys with him. Not that they were even trying to move. Just watched me. Maybe they were smarter than Tony and knew I wasn't in the right frame of mind to be ignored.

"Are you listenin'?" I asked as I ran the tip of the knife along the paint, scratching it.

"Yes," he bit out.

I watched my handiwork as I carved out the word *wanker* while I spoke. I'd always liked that word from the first time I heard it on a television show.

"You won't contact her again—"

"Who?"

"You'll forget she ever existed. You'll delete any photos you have of her—"

He laughed abruptly. "This is about that whore Wrenley—"

Using my foot as leverage, I jumped off the car and strode toward him. "Don't say her name," I snarled, tapping the end of the blade against my thigh.

Kill him.

"Never say her name." I ran my closed fists over my face, dragging my skin down and stopping at my neck.

Kill him.

Scowling, I threatened, "If you don't listen, if you go near her, if you call her, I'll hunt you down, torture you, and kill you." I smiled. "Slowly."

I caught him gulp hard before he nodded.

Dropping my hands, I tapped them on my thighs. "No daddy can save you from me, Tony Handler. No friend." I glanced to the guys behind him. The color had fled their faces. "You'll listen?"

"Yeah, man."

I stepped forward. They all shuffled back. I smiled again at the fear. I could see it in their eyes, in the way they held their bodies, and I swore I could smell it.

I fucking loved it.

Chuckling low, I pointed the knife at him and then up to my eyes. "I'll be watchin' you, college boy."

With that, I turned and went back over to his car. I slashed all his tires before giving them one final stare and walking off down to the road.

What I didn't expect was to see Blaze standing out front of their neighbor's house with a phone to his ear. "Yeah, you heard me. No blood, just a warnin' and a damaged car." He stared at me, so I stopped at his side. "Yeah, got it. I'll follow him back to the compound." He hung up and pocketed the phone.

"Country?" I asked.

"Yep."

I cocked my head to the side before I tipped my chin back to the fraternity. "You think they'll listen?"

"Did they need the warnin'?"

He hadn't heard about it?

"Yep," I mimicked.

"I reckon they will. You're a crazy fucker."

I smiled.

He grunted. "Especially when you do that. You get this look in your eyes."

Shrugging, I started for my car. "Why'd you follow me?" If he didn't like my smile...?

"Saw that same look on you as you were leavin' and knew somethin' was up. Made sure you had someone at your back."

Halting, I turned and studied him.

He didn't trust me, but he still helped me.

I wasn't the crazy one between us.

"You're all right. But crazy too."

He snorted. "Thanks. I think."

Not knowing what to say to that, I said nothing and kept walking.

"You would've killed him if he hadn't agreed to back off, right?"

"Yes." I wouldn't have been able to stop myself.

"In front of everyone?"

My upper lip raised. "Yes."

"Why?"

Stopping, I looked up at the sky. "He upset Wrenley in bad ways."

"Okay."

He understood. He got me. He would have done the same if it'd been Henri.

Maybe I could get along with him after all.

ONCE IN THE COMMON ROOM, I saw Country leaning his back against the bar with his arms crossed and dark gaze pointed my way. "Office, now."

I headed down the hall before he did and waited by the door. He wasn't alone when he arrived. Death, Tech, and even Blaze was with him.

Country unlocked the door and pushed it open. I entered after him and Death. Blaze stayed by the door, which he'd closed, and Tech sat in the chair to my left, Death on my right.

"Talk, brother," Country ordered as he sat behind his desk.

I bounced my knee in agitation, not liking being ordered or cornered. But I trusted my brothers. I knew to listen and respect them.

Family.

Wrapping my arms around my waist, I clenched my fists and explained that I'd overheard them in Tech's workroom. That I couldn't stop myself from hunting and warning him.

"I didn't kill him."

Like I wanted to.

Not yet anyway.

"I know, Torch," Country said, tone gentler.

I scrubbed a hand over my shaved head, then did it again and again. "I had to tell him. I had to warn him off. He has to leave her alone now."

"Or else?" Tech asked.

"He'll kill him," Death stated.

He read me right.

I grazed my hand over my mouth to hide my smile and nodded, then looked down to my lap.

"Torch, I've spoken with Death, but I gotta know. Do you want to pursue Wrenley? Have her as your own?"

My own?

She already was.

But I couldn't actually have her in my life.

I was too fucked up for her.

She wouldn't want me if she really knew me.

"No," I said tightly.

"Brother, you sure?" Tech asked.

I ran my hands over my thighs. "Yes," I hissed.

"You know you can have a woman—"

"No, no, no, no," I chanted. They didn't get to go there. They'd never asked before. But I didn't want to talk about women. I got my dick wet with the bunnies. It wasn't often, though. They faced the other way so we didn't have to look at each other. No words were said because they didn't like me. They were scared of me. Only joined with me because I was in the brotherhood. I couldn't blame them. I spaced a little sometimes. I killed. I hurt people, but I was good a lot of the time.

Until someone fucked with my family.

"Leave it," Blaze clipped.

"Torch." Country's hard tone caught my attention. I stilled and looked at him. "We'll leave that alone. But you know if you need to talk about anythin', and I fuckin' mean *anythin'*, you can come to any of us. Any one of your brothers will help you out."

I nodded, rubbing at my eyes.

A knock sounded on the door.

"What?" Country barked.

It opened, and Quake stuck his head in. "Death, your woman and her sister are here. Sister looks pissed."

All eyes went to Death.

"Fuck. Raya was gonna talk to Wrenley. Seems like she might have mentioned Tech hackin' her phone."

Shit.

CHAPTER SIX

WRENLEY

*I*rritation choked me, and anger boiled through my veins. But it was the hurt and embarrassment that punched me hard enough that I had to press a hand to my twisting stomach. What had they seen? What did they know?

Earlier, when I arrived home after the supermarket and a lunch date with Saint and Gun, Raya was in the living room. I knew she'd been waiting for me. The sadness in her gaze had shot tension straight into my body. Saint and Gun, who had followed me home, took one look at my sister and told me they'd get the groceries in and put them away.

Raya stood. "Do you have something to tell me?"

Bile rose at the thought of what she'd found out. *How* she'd found out without me telling her.

My mind blanked in that moment.

"Wrenley?"

Hesitantly, I'd asked, "What do you mean?"

Then she'd told me.

They'd looked at my texts.

They'd hacked my phone.

My privacy.

I'd walked back out the front door to the car and driven to the compound. There was only one person who worked on computers for the Diamond MC, and I wanted a word with him. I wanted to know who he thought he was to look in my phone in the first place without asking *my* permission.

He had no right.

It was up to me to tell people.

It happened to me.

"Wren, calm down," Raya tried as I stalked to the front door at their club. She must have gotten a lift with Saint and Gun, who now stood with her.

"Calm down? If I'd have said that to you after finding out—" Loud footsteps approached. Country stepped from the hall first, then Death, Quake, Torch, Blaze, and the man I wanted to see. "You," I bit out as I pointed at Tech.

He thumbed his chest. "Me?"

"You have no right to hack my phone. No right to my information. My privacy. Why'd you do it? Who asked you? Or did you just do it on your own because I'm not Raya—"

"Wrenley, no—" Tech tried.

I waved a hand in front of me. "What information did you get?" I shouted, voice almost wavering from anger and sorrow swirling inside me. "What did you tell them? How far did you go back?"

"Quake, clear the room," I heard Country order, but I took no notice.

"Wren, come on, come here." Raya went to wrap her arm around me, but I moved out of reach.

My bottom lip trembled. "Did you see it all? Did you see what happened? The texts he sent after it?" I'd kept them for evidence in a folder I thought I'd hidden well on my phone. I'd kept them in case I was ever strong enough to go to the authorities. He'd texted me foul things not long after he'd dropped me off, and he wasn't the only one either. His friend Mitch had too. "The texts they all sent?"

Oh God. Had he seen everything?

My stomach lurched, and I swallowed hard.

Had he told my sister before I could?

Was that why she looked sad?

"Wrenley, how about we—" Death stepped toward me.

"No!" I cried, backing up. Tears welled. "I-I didn't say anything because I couldn't remember. I didn't say anything because not long after that happened, I walked in on my dad killing my mom."

"Wrenley, maybe we should go somewhere private?" Raya said softly.

I huffed, wiping at my tears.

Shaking my head, I looked to Tech. "Why did you do it? Why did you look?"

Movement near him caught my attention, and Torch stepped forward. "Tech was doin' what I asked him to."

A sharp pain punched me in the chest. I rubbed at the spot, throat thick. "You?"

He nodded.

More tears welled, and my bottom lip trembled. "Why?

You didn't like that I was around your dog? You didn't like me around the club?" I shook my head at my stupid questions. I wasn't thinking, only acting, rambling. "It was my privacy. My life. My secrets."

"He hurt you," Torch voiced in a rough yet quiet tone.

He hurt me.

He.

Tony.

They knew about him.

They *knew.*

"I told him to stay away, to leave you alone."

I blinked at him. "You *saw* him?" I took a step back. "*You* went there?" I yelled. "What did he say? What did he tell you? Is it everything that Tech already knows? It was my business! I was going to tell my sister in *my* time. I was going to get help. You had no right. You had no fucking right to look for or go see that man. Did he tell you? Did he laugh with his friends about drugging me, gang-raping me, and handcuffing me to the sink? Did they? Did...?"

The room went deathly silent.

The already-tense atmosphere suddenly turned volatile.

Raya sucked in a breath as Country roared, "Saint, Gun, get them the fuck out."

I was tucked into a chest, and they moved me toward the door, but I looked back, not understanding what was going on. I didn't understand the urgency or why things were changing.

I didn't understand until I heard an animalistic sound fly from Torch, right before Blaze tackled him to the ground. Death landed on top of them, then Country, and yet Torch was still trying to get up, to get them off. The sounds he made were like nothing I'd heard before from a man.

The last thing I saw before the door shut after us was Quake and Tech joining the other shouting men to hold Torch down.

"I'M SORRY," I whispered before pressing my fingers against my mouth as my bottom lip quivered.

"Shh, it's okay, sweetheart," Raya said softly as she ran her fingers through my hair. I rested my head on her lap while we were on the couch.

Tears leaked. "I'm so sorry."

"What for, Wrenny?" my sister asked, tucking some hair behind my ear. We were in our own living room with the help of Gun and Saint, who got us home. I'd broken down on the way back and didn't register anything around me until now. I could hear the men in the kitchen talking softly.

My chest ached. My heart had shattered. The pieces were rattling around in my body.

Back at the compound, the combination of my anger and fear had caused me to act irrationally.

At the reminder, I shivered. "I-I shouldn't have done that. I shouldn't have said it like that in front of everyone. I just couldn't stop."

And then Torch had... he'd... lost it... because of what I'd said.

I covered my face and cried again.

Raya had told me that no one knew the full details of what happened. They'd only grazed the surface of what Tony was doing. They'd looked into it because of my recent reaction to a text.

Raya gently tapped my head. "You were justified in doing and saying whatever you wanted. You're allowed to let it out, Wrenley. And keep letting the pain out. Tell me everything, my sweet sister. Tell me what happened, please, Wrenny. Let me help. Let me in."

Whimpering, I shook my head. "Raya, no—"

"Please. I can help carry this with you. I want to. Don't do it on your own. Please, Wren. Please. Let me in. Don't hold it back. Don't hold it in."

Moaning, I curled myself into a tighter ball and told her. *Everything.*

"Oh, honey," she said after I finished, her voice soft and clogged with emotions. "Why didn't you say anything back then?"

I wiped at my face and drew in a shuddering breath. "I walked in on Dad the same day that I woke up in the bathroom. It was all too much."

Closing my eyes, I dug my nails into my palms and pressed both fisted hands to my lips.

"You didn't want to burden me with more," she predicted. "We're the same in many ways, Wrenley. I know that's what you would've been thinking. I'd have done the same. But believe me when I tell you this, *please.* You are not, nor have you ever been, a burden. I'm always here for you."

"I know," I uttered. "At the time, I could only handle so much. Since I didn't *remember* what they did, I pushed it down. The... the pain in my body didn't want me to forget, but my mind kept replaying the scene from home over and over."

"Shit, Wrenley, you went through so much. In a way, I guess your mind was protecting you from one ordeal by throwing a constant loop of the other at you."

I shrugged. "Yeah."

"They're going to help."

I knew who she meant.

"H-how? I don't want them to get into trouble."

"They won't. The club is smart."

Licking my dry lips, I asked softly, "Is it bad that I want them to deal with him?"

Raya huffed. "If it's a mark against my moral code or something by thinking he should.... No, he deserves to be dealt with, so I'll take that mark with my head held high. He'll get what's coming to him, Wrenley, and it'll be justified." Anger sharpened her tone. "How fucking dare he walk around this world thinking that what he and his friends did will go unpunished. If Leland and his brothers didn't know about this, if you had told only me, then I would have done something myself to make them pay. It may not have been as good as whatever the men in our lives come up with, but they'd have suffered in some way."

My sister.

I should have told her.

But there was no use wishing I could change the past; it got me nowhere. I'd just have to learn to live with the regret of not speaking up for the rest of my life.

Especially if Tony and his friends had harmed someone else.

"Raya?"

"Yes, honey?"

"I'm glad you're my sister and that you've got Death."

She leaned down and kissed my cheek. "So am I, Wrenny. We'll get through this."

"Yeah," I whispered.

Maybe one day.

The image of Torch being taken to the ground swept into my mind. The sounds he'd made rang through me.

Why had he acted that way?

Why did he look crushed when I yelled at him?

But most of all, why did he seem so destroyed learning what happened to me?

CHAPTER SEVEN

TORCH

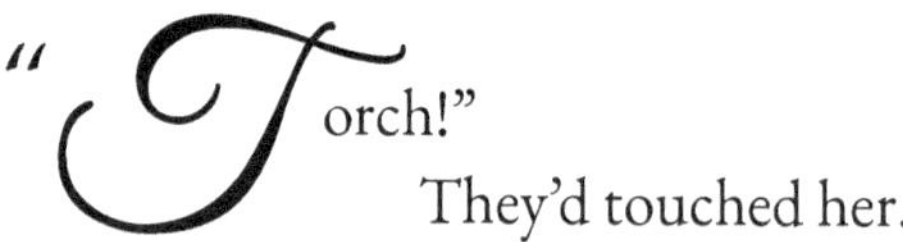"Torch!"

They'd touched her.

"Brother?"

They'd drugged her.

"Jesus, Torch?"

I'd make them pay.

"Brother, snap the fuck out of it!"

Their blood will pour by my hands.

"Torch, think. Think, brother."

They used her, drugged her, chained her, bruised her, hurt her.

"They will die," I snarled, focusing on the door that led out as I tried once again to lift off the ground.

I needed to get to them.

I needed to hunt.

To torture.

And kill.

"Torch. Brother, they'll suffer. They'll know what pain is, but we need to be smart about it."

No.

I clawed at the ground before I pushed up again.

"Let him up," someone said.

"*Mon amour*, no."

"Tech, get Henri out of here."

"Kind of busy."

"Do it. I'll help Torch. Country, I have this. Trust me."

Hunt.

Torture.

Kill.

"Fuck. Now," someone yelled.

The weight on me disappeared. I jumped up and started for the door until something solid knocked my head to the side, and I stumbled back.

Spitting blood out, I slowly moved my gaze to my target and grinned.

My smile disappeared when I remembered what I was meant to be doing.

I went to dodge Blaze, but he hooked his fucking beefy arm around my waist and threw me across the room, where I landed with a crash against a table and chairs.

Shaking my head, I stood and blinked at the guy.

"You with it now?" he asked.

"Sure." I smirked before I ran at him and threw my arm back to smash my fist into his gut.

He heaved out a breath, even as his punch connected with my ribs.

"You want blood? Take mine for now." His hand wrapped around my neck and squeezed.

Lifting my legs, I kicked out. Blaze flew one way, and I, the other, landing hard on my back.

My oxygen was gone.

I sucked on dryness, getting nothing in.

Blaze stood above me with blood trickling down from his hairline.

My lungs started working as he said, "We don't walk into their world without a fuckin' plan, Torch. You want Wrenley to suffer if you get her sister's man in trouble with the law? If any of the brothers get into trouble over her situation, it'd crush her. You don't want that, right?"

Closing my eyes, I clenched my teeth together.

Hunt.

Torture.

Kill.

Opening my eyes, I glared up at him as I knocked my knuckles into my temple.

Wrenley had been crushed enough.

I wouldn't put more on her.

"No."

Blaze grunted and held his hand out to me. "We'll get them for what they did."

I took his hand, and he pulled me to my feet. My body complained, but I ignored it. I pushed the pain down and focused on his words.

We'd get them.

They'd pay.

But we had to be smart so Wrenley didn't get crushed.

Nodding, I dropped his hand and my shoulders.

She was already crushed by me setting Tech onto her phone.

"Brother." I jolted slightly from the hand landing on my shoulder and looked up into Country's gaze. "You got it under control?"

"For now," I told him.

His grip tightened. "They will pay."

I nodded.

"What do you need to do?" he asked.

But I didn't understand the question.

Death stepped up. "He's comin' back to the house with me."

I shook my head. Wrenley wouldn't want to see me.

"Torch, Wrenley ain't angry at you."

"She is."

"She's not," Death said. "Obviously shit had already been on her mind. Then when Wren found out about her phone being hacked by us, it was the last straw that set her off. She might be a little annoyed still, but her anger wasn't toward you."

Clenching my jaw, I looked off to the side and knocked my fist against my thigh.

Didn't matter if she wasn't angry at me. I wouldn't put her through seeing me.

"I'll stay here."

Death's jaw clenched. "Brother—"

A little Frenchman saved me from hearing Death say more when Henri stalked out of the hallway spewing loud French words and pointing at Blaze.

Henri was beyond pissed, and all Blaze did was smirk at him, even when Henri smacked him in the chest.

Shock rocked through me when Blaze replied to him in French, since I didn't know he spoke that language as well. But whatever Blaze said caused Henri to huff, jut his hip to the side, and place his hand on it.

"Are you serious, *mon amour*?" He waved a hand toward the blood running down Blaze's temple. "You call this uninjured?"

"Henri" was all Blaze said.

Henri stuck his middle finger up in Blaze's face and turned to me. "Maybe you need to hit him harder to knock some sense into him, *oui*?"

Wee?

What did that mean again?

Henri waved a hand around. "Doesn't matter. Are you okay?"

"Yes?" My answer sounded like a question since I wasn't sure what answer would stop him from staring at me like a nice but impatient and intense parent who cared.

"Bien." He nodded.

I don't understand you, man.

He shot Blaze another glare before turning and strutting back down the hallway.

"Jesus Christ," Quake drew out. "How the fuck did we go from holdin' our brother down to two brothers fighting? And then that firecracker of a Frenchman defuses the situation more by swearin' and yellin' at Blaze."

The tension in the room lessened.

Death got close again.

Fuck.

"No doubt you're gonna go to her place anyway to watch over her from the outside while the other brothers figure out how we can take those bastards down in a way that won't come back to bite anyone on the ass?"

Goddammit

I nodded before stretching my neck and running a hand over the back of it.

He grunted. "Then I'll give you a lift."

Meaning, he didn't want to leave me alone in case I got any other ideas and went out on my own.

Which I could.

If things went down and the cops got involved after I took matters into my own hands, then them arresting me wouldn't be a problem. Not for me. Wrenley would be safe. I'd make sure those cunts were taken down in a way they wouldn't be breathing again.

I'd take the fall solely.

"Fuck that," Death snarled as he rested a hand at the side of my neck. "You're not goin' out on your own. You have people who goddamn care about you, Torch, so get that fuckin' idea outta your head."

Clenching my jaw, I thought, *How the fuck does he know?*

Country chuckled. "You should know by now, Death's a mind reader, but your thoughts were pretty fuckin' loud, brother." Country crossed his arms over his chest. "I'm orderin' you to leave them alone until *I* give the go-ahead, Torch. Hear me?"

Fucking hell.

"Yeah, Prez," I said tightly.

"Good." Country looked to Death. "Since Gun and Saint are already there, I won't send any more brothers as backup, but we'll all be on rotation as a just in case."

Death tipped his chin up. "Appreciate it."

Country waved him off, and the group went back to doing whatever they had been.

Warmth weaved into my chest.

This was my family.

Death tagged me by curling his arm around my neck. "Let's go. You're comin' in my truck."

I didn't bother fighting. They knew me and would now keep an eye on me more than usual until I could get my hands on those motherfuckers.

Death shook me a little. "We'll get them," he said, voice gruff and low.

The news of what happened to my Wrenley would be hitting him just as hard. She was his woman's sister, and he'd known her that little bit longer.

When I got into his car, I took note of how tense his body was.

Yeah, he was fighting the idea of going after those boys hard.

Hunt.

Torture.

Kill.

With my palm, I rubbed at my temple and reminded myself that we had to be careful. Wasn't for me. But for the women and club.

And I'd do anything in my power to protect my obsession and my family. Even if it meant I had to wait to have the blood of those fuckers running over my fingers while they writhed in pain by my hand.

"I should have done somethin' the first time I saw her reaction over a text," Death mentioned softly, yet there was a pissy edge to it.

"I ain't judging, but why didn't you?" I just wanted to understand.

"Raya said they'd spoken about it and Wrenley had asked Raya to let her deal with it. We were gonna step in if she needed help. She just didn't come to us, and fuck, brother, I was still new with Raya. I didn't want to push my boundaries. Raya will be kickin' herself for it enough. Christ." He slapped his hands against the wheel.

"Standin' back makes sense. Not like you could've done much back then when she wasn't ready." I ran a hand over my face. Hoped I was saying the right things. "She needs help now."

"And she'll get it. They'll fuckin' pay."

Teeth flashed. "They will."

Death pulled into his driveway. I got out and started for his side gate, which would lead me to the part of the fence I'd jump to be outside her window.

My pulse picked up, causing my heart to go crazy over knowing how close I'd be to her.

My obsession.

The one shining star in my dark mind.

"Torch, wait up," Death called, stopping beside the front fence where he jumped to get to his woman's. "Why don't you come in and check on her?"

Shaking my head, I took a step back. "No."

She wouldn't want to see me.

I was the one who got Tech onto her.

It was because of me her secrets were discovered.

Because of me she'd lost herself and screamed, cried, and was hurt.

I'd hurt her.

"Torch—"

"Leland, what are you doing?" Raya called.

Death watched as my eyes widened, and I took another step back.

"Nothin', darlin'. Just comin' over."

"Is Torch with you?"

I was going to choke on my heart as it crawled up my throat.

"Yeah," Death said, ratting me out.

Her footsteps approached the end of her porch. "Torch, can you come inside for a little bit, please? Wrenley wants to talk to you."

She wanted to talk to me.

Me?

Why?

Wasn't she scared by how I acted?

I'd lost myself to the darkness, and she'd seen it. She witnessed what I could become.

But I also didn't want to upset her again.

I couldn't stand to see her cry more. The tears she'd shed were already implanted under my skin.

"Torch?" Raya called.

Fuck.

Wrenley wanted to talk to me.

But if I made her upset again, I wouldn't be able to deal.

"Brother, it'll be fine," Death said.

I swung my wide gaze up from the ground to his.

"She doesn't need to see me," I told him and swallowed thickly. My gut twisted. Chest ached. Christ, even my hands shook.

"Torch, please," Raya said.

Fucking hell.

I should say no. I should hide.

Moving beside Death, I nodded up at a wrecked Raya with red-rimmed eyes as she smiled softly. I followed Death with my head down, body tense, and thoughts spinning.

And I promised myself that if she cried, I'd run. I wouldn't be the cause of her pain again.

CHAPTER EIGHT

When Raya and I heard Death's car pull in, we'd been sitting on the couch with a hot chocolate that Gun had made. I quickly placed the mug on the coffee table and kneeled on the furniture to look out the window. My pulse spiked when I saw Torch sitting in the passenger seat.

I twisted to Raya, grabbed her hand, and begged, "Can you get Torch in here? I want to apologize. *Please.*"

Her other hand lay over mine, and she squeezed. "Okay, honey. I'll go ask."

While waiting, I paced the living room.

Would he come in, or would he think I blamed him for everything and not want to see me?

I hoped he would come.

I needed to see him.

Now that I'd had more time to register his reaction, it gripped my heart in a way that I felt an urgent need to speak with him.

I wouldn't blame Torch if he didn't want to come in here.

Yet, if he didn't, I'd search him out to explain he wasn't at fault.

He tried to help me.

How he went about it perhaps wasn't ideal, but he'd gone out of his way to see if he could fix a problem of mine that he didn't even understand.

I pressed a hand to my fluttery stomach.

His fierce reaction showed me he cared.

The door opened, and I jolted as my heart skipped a beat. Turning, I watched Raya enter first, followed by Death. Licking my dry lips, I played with the hem of my tee and then let out a slow breath when Torch walked through with his gaze on the floor.

Death reached around him and closed the front door, and Raya shifted out of the way.

"Torch?" I called softly.

His head cocked slightly to the side, eyes up to my waist.

I swallowed thickly from nerves. "I'm sorry—"

"You have nothin' to apologize for," he told me before his gaze shifted toward the door. His hands tapped at the sides of his thighs.

"I do. I don't like that I yelled at you and blamed you. I know you were just looking out for me. And I'm sorry for... for saying what I did and how I said it."

His jaw clenched, and he finally looked at me.

I couldn't read what was in his eyes. They were hard yet soft.

His chin tipped up a little. "No need for sorry."

Did that mean he wouldn't accept it?

"Um, okay." I glanced at Raya, but all she did was shrug. Straightening, I said, "Thank you for looking out for me. That really means a lot." I took a couple of steps closer, hand reaching out—he shifted back quickly, upper lip lifting.

I stopped, dropped my hand, and tears welled.

He didn't want me to touch him.

Nodding, I looked away as the tears fell. I thinned my lips, but a whimper escaped.

Was he disgusted by me after finding out the truth?

No. He wouldn't have acted so distraught for me, right?

I sniffed and wiped at my eyes.

Torch made a noise in the back of his throat, which drew my attention to him in time to see him clutching his head.

"Brother?"

Torch hit his palms against his temples. "I made her cry," he bit out. He lunged toward the door and grabbed the handle.

"Wait," I cried.

He stilled.

"Death and Raya, can... um, please, give us a moment."

Death seemed uncertain, but Raya took his hand and walked them away.

I wiped at my face again. Torch didn't like seeing me upset. My chest swelled at the thought of his kindness.

"How's Harley?"

My question appeared to shock him; his hand dropped

from the handle, and he faced me. A small tilt to his head followed as he studied me.

"Good."

"Are the brothers still scared of him?" I asked, smiling slightly.

His lips twitched but straightened out quickly. "Yes."

Nodding, I glanced back to the couch. "Will you sit with me for a second?"

"Why?"

"So we can talk," I said.

"No, why would you want me in here?"

I drew my brows down in thought. "What do you mean?"

He shook his head. "Nothin'."

"So," I drew out, "will you sit down?"

He rubbed hard at his bottom lip as he glanced from the couch, to me, and back. Then he nodded. I sat down at one end, and he took the other. He hunched over to rest his forearms on his thighs and blinked down at the carpet.

"Torch, do you mind if I ask some questions?"

"No." He sat so still, I worried he'd turned into a statue, but his chest rose and fell too rapidly to be one.

I didn't want to just come out and ask him why he'd reacted so strongly at the compound or how he knew something was wrong in the first place. Instead, I jumped in with something easier.

"What's your favorite color?"

"Green."

"What music do you like?"

"Anythin'."

"What do you like to eat?"

"Meat."

Typical man, I thought to myself with an inner laugh.

"Do you work?"

"Escort agency and—"

A ripple of shock had me tensing. "As an escort?" I blurted. Not that there was anything wrong with that.

He snorted, glanced at me quickly, and then looked away. "Never. Security. At Death's workplace too."

"Oh, okay."

He snorted again, lips twitching before he thinned them.

"What's funny?"

His hands went together so he could pick at his thumbnail. "You. Thinkin' I could work there."

Why did he think he couldn't? "Why not? You're a good-looking guy."

His head jerked back to look at me. "Your cheeks are red again."

Puffing out a breath, I pressed my hands to them and admitted, "Because I told you you're good-looking."

He shook his head, fingers lifting to touch his scars. His hand dropped, and he rubbed both down his thighs. "Doesn't make sense."

"What?" I asked.

"This."

"I don't understand," I said.

He shook his head. "Doesn't matter."

Frustration gripped my throat. It *did* matter. I wanted to get to know him. I also wanted to figure myself out: how could I be distracted by a man when hours ago I was curled into a ball crying my eyes out?

Torch confused me but left me wanting to know more.

He took my mind off everything, and I didn't feel embarrassed about him knowing my history. I did get flustered, though, when I admitted he was handsome.

I liked being around him.

His company calmed and comforted me, both in a safe way.

I didn't understand how either was possible after only briefly meeting him, but I couldn't remember the last time I felt this protected.

"Torch, why did your brothers do that to you back at the compound?"

He tensed, not even blinking.

"Torch?"

When I tried to reach out again, he stood and shifted away.

My nose stung as tears threatened.

"Sorry, I-I won't touch you if you don't like it," I told him quickly. I would never want him to feel uncomfortable around me.

Another noise dropped from the back of his throat. He fell to his knees and slowly moved his hand my way, brushing his fingers against the top of my hand, which gripped my thigh.

"I'm different. Broken. Messed up." He pulled his hand away to tap his head. "My past.... Get Death to tell you. I can't talk about that. It fucks me up too much. I'll get lost to the thoughts. To the darkness. But never think that I don't want your touch. I just can't have it. It's not for me, and really, you'll see why when you hear how I am. What I've done. What I'll do to those...." His jaw clenched. "You need better in your life." He was on his feet and out the front door in seconds.

Before I could say anything.

Before his words really registered.

In his own way, he'd told me I wouldn't want him because of the way he was and what he'd done.

He didn't know me.

Death and Raya appeared and sat opposite me on their own couch.

"Gun and Saint have headed over to my place," Death said. "I'm sleepin' here, kid."

"Okay," I whispered.

"Wren, you okay? I know it's a stupid question, but I mean after havin' words with my brother?"

Shifting back on the couch, I brought my legs up and crossed them under me. "He told me he's broken and that I should ask you about his past because he can't talk about it."

Death's shock was easily read when his eyes widened and his body jerked. "He wants me to tell you about his past? How'd this come about?"

My face heated. "Well, I got a little upset when it seemed like he didn't want me to touch his hand. He told me it was the opposite, that I won't want him around me since he's messed up and has done bad things."

He thinned his lips and shook his head. "My brother's always harder on himself." He glanced at my sister, placing a hand on her thigh before looking back to me. "Country, State, and I are the only ones who know about Torch's past. The other brothers might have figured it out from comments he's made here or there, but they don't know his full story. Him askin' me to tell you is fuckin' huge, Wrenley."

I already guessed that. "I understand."

"But it is dark, kid, and I'm not sure now is a good time—"

"Death. No offense, but you're still getting to know me, and I might have broken down before, but it was more over the fact that I no longer have to pretend everything's okay. The secret was killing me the most. Yes, I'm scared of Tony and his friends still. And yes, what I saw our dad do still plays on my mind. But I'm dealing. I *will* heal. And I *can* take on more. I feel safe living here. Safer with you and your club in our lives. But the safest around Torch. I don't understand how or why, but I want to slowly get to know him more. So shouldn't I get a choice to know everything if he's given his permission already?"

"How about you sleep on it?" Raya suggested. Always the protector for me. My big sister. Death stared at her with such warmth and admiration, my heart clenched at the obvious love he held for Raya. "You've had one hell of a day, Wren. Just one sleep, and if you still want to know in the morning, then Leland will tell you."

Death curled his arm around Raya and kissed her temple.

"Okay," I said, more for her sake than my own. I'd still want to know. I'd already started to believe that something could grow between Torch and me.

CHAPTER NINE

awning, I made my way into the kitchen. I paused in the doorway when I saw Death already sitting at the counter with two mugs in front of him.

"Morning," I said, walking over to take the steaming coffee in front of my spot as I hopped up on the stool next to him. "I guess you do know me a little since you're here waiting for me."

"Kid, even a blind man could read that you need to know everythin'. Besides, spoke to Torch and he confirmed he wants you to know."

I thought he would check with Torch. Honestly, I was glad he did and pleased to know that Torch hadn't changed his mind. I took a sip of the coffee and hummed. Death had gotten the right amount of sugar and cream for me. Then again, I'd already figured out that the men of the motorcycle club took a lot more notice of things than other men I'd known.

"You all right after yesterday?" he asked.

It'd taken me a while to get to sleep last night as my thoughts had run rampant. Some of the weight I'd been carrying, though—from keeping this to myself—had lifted now that the people in my life knew the truth.

However, even though I felt a lot lighter, anxiety swirled through my bloodstream over the unknown that lay ahead.

Despite that, whatever happened to Tony and his friends would be well deserved. Plus, however the Diamond Motorcycle Club handled it would be the right way, and I suspected Tony wouldn't hurt a woman again.

All I needed to remember was that I wasn't alone in this any longer.

I *could* lean on people.

"Honestly, I'm doing a lot better than I was." Yesterday I'd been crying in my car and near drowning in worry. Now, I wasn't. My head was far above the water, and my life seemed clearer.

"Good to hear, kid." He took a sip of his coffee and then wrapped his hands around the mug as he placed it back on the counter. His jaw clenched.

"Death," I said softly. When his attention came to me, I added, "If you're not comfortable telling me, I can ask one of the others who know."

He shook his head and returned to staring down at his drink. "It ain't that, kid. It's just, hell... what Torch went through was fuckin' messed up. I worry about him. But— and I'm not sayin' you're this type of person—I can't help being afraid that after hearing it all, it'll change your thoughts about him in some way." He scrubbed at something on the counter with his thumb.

I shrugged and told him honestly, "I'd like to believe that what I hear won't change my mind. Yet, I won't know unless you tell me. I want to understand him. To get to know him. So, if he wants me to learn about his past so I can do that, then I need to."

He turned my way. "You got feelin's for him?"

"I don't know. I get butterflies when he's around, and I feel nothing but comfort and safety when he's close."

He grunted and nodded. After another sip of his drink, he started talking. "Country, State, and me had the club for a while before we found Torch."

I scrunched my brows together. "Found?"

He hummed with a nod. "Found him sittin' in an alley of a bar we frequented. He looked rough, skinny and dirty, with blood, bruises, and cuts all over him. He flinched away from us to start with, wouldn't talk. Just stared at the dirt as he sat on the ground, defeated. Eventually, when he realized we wouldn't hurt him, he talked." His jaw clenched again as his grip on the mug tightened. "He didn't know his parents. Didn't even know if they were dead or alive. All he had was a grandfather up until he was sixteen. But that man—" He snarled low and harshly, causing me to shiver. "—wasn't a good one."

My stomach churned.

"Our brother had put up with hell, livin' with the damn devil himself for those sixteen years."

"What happened?" I whispered when Death fell silent.

"Everything you could think of. He was starved, beaten,

shared among his grandfather's friends. Tortured in the worst ways."

I covered my mouth, but a whimper escaped as my tears welled and fell for Torch. For the boy he was. For the days he'd endured the pain and suffering by his own relative.

Oh God, Torch.

Death went on, "When they weren't using his body, they were trying different ways to torment him. Waterboarding, locking him in chains in a dark cupboard where he could hardly move. Electric shocks over and over—"

Reaching out, I gripped Death's wrist. "Tell me that... that *thing* is in jail. Tell me he's suffering."

"I wouldn't usually go into detail like that, Wrenley. But it helps you understand why his mind is wired a little differ-ent. Most of the time no one sees the difference in him since he's always been a quieter guy anyway. But when bad situa-tions, like your own, arise, a switch gets flipped inside him, and he hungers for violence, for revenge, and for justice." Death scrubbed a hand over his face. "That day when we found him, after he told us everything, he made us promise to never tell anyone or speak of it again. Until now. Until you. It's huge for you to know, Wrenley. Means something big." He shook his head and stared down at the counter. He wouldn't have seen how much those words meant to me. How I swallowed thickly and pressed a hand to my chest in case my heart flew out of it with the way it fluttered wildly.

Death went on, "Anyway, that same day back then, we asked him where his grandfather was. We were ready to deal with that motherfucker." His jaw clenched before he let out a long sigh. "We didn't get a chance to. Torch had already burned him and the house to the ground."

Closing my eyes, I nodded, pleased to know Torch's monster wasn't alive. Opening them, I asked, "Why did Torch trust you three to begin with?"

Death grinned. "He'd been followin' us for a while, and we didn't notice. He liked how, even when we weren't blood, we were a strong family. One he felt he needed to be a part of."

"And you took him in right then and there?"

"Sure did. Helped him come up with a story for the cops, and when the child protective services came and tried to take him away, he threw a fit. Thank fuck Boom was there. He'd already got custody of Gun, so they trusted him and Wendy to look after Torch. Though, Torch didn't want to go with Boom to his house. He wanted to stay at the compound with us. So, he did. He'd shared his darkest times with us. He'd trusted us right outta the gate. We wanted to show him that same trust."

Death's words kept playing in my mind.

It's huge for you to know, Wrenley. Means something big.

Why did Torch want me to know?

"Death, are you going to tell Raya this?"

"No. Torch said only for you to know. Unless Raya asks me, which I don't think she will because she respects people's privacy, I won't tell anyone else. It ain't mine to share, and I only do it now because he asked me to. I do this to protect him from relivin' those goddamn sickening memories. Ones he's locked away for a reason."

"Why me then?" I asked softly.

He turned to me with a smile that tugged up only one corner of his mouth. "I reckon it's because he wants to be your friend, but he wants you to know the baggage he holds in him. Why some things could set him off."

"I feel safe with him," I said again, looking away.

"Good. He'd *never* hurt you. Even when somethin' sets him off, know you'll always have his protection."

"I do." I believed that Torch would anguish over the thought of hurting me in any way. I could read it from his actions already. My tears tormented him. He suffered from *my* pain and hurt.

How could I not feel safe around someone who cared so deeply that he felt my pain?

I couldn't.

Knowing that he worried about me so strongly made me want to smile. Instead, I bit my bottom lip to contain it, hating that happiness pushed at me after hearing about Torch's tortured past.

Two sides warred.

"It's okay to feel good knowin' he cares about you, kid. His past is just that, a past. One he doesn't want to relive. One he longs to forget and has already locked away."

Raising my brows, I asked, "Are you sure you can't read minds?"

His chuckle was low. "Kid, I wish I could. I'm just good at readin' people. Besides, it was easy to see when you're tryin' not to smile."

Rolling my eyes, I smirked, but it quickly faded. "He's been through a lot, Death. Maybe Torch shouldn't be around me while all this is happening. It might not be good for him."

I wanted to protect him too.

"Sweet of you to want to help him, but being away from protectin' you will do him more harm."

Wings sprouted from my heart and fluttered.

"Okay," I said quickly—too quickly since it seemed Death smirked. "If you're sure."

Please be sure.

He nodded.

I wanted to see more of Torch. I liked being in his company. Even if we didn't talk, having him around was like a comforting caress.

Another question swept through my mind. "What did Torch mean when he said he'd done bad things?"

Death's lips thinned before he ran a tattooed hand over his neatly trimmed beard.

"You know the club now, kid. You know we protect our own. Some brothers more than others like to deal out punishments to those who wronged us. Torch is one. I'm another. Your sister knows this. She's accepted how the club is run. Now it's up to you to work out if you can or not."

I didn't have to work anything out.

The men in the Diamond MC had already shielded Raya and me in more ways than anyone else had in our whole lives.

Today, if knights in shining armor were real, they would wear leather vests and ride motorcycles while protecting the people around them.

Their way might not be morally correct, but I'd still stand by them.

"I've already accepted you and the club." I smiled softly and tapped my foot into his leg. "We'd never felt real safety until we moved into the house next to yours and you took us under your guard. Plus, I've never seen my sister as happy as she is when she's around you."

He reached out and bopped my nose like I was five. I swatted his hand away as he chuckled.

When he sobered, Death tipped his chin up at me. "Don't give up on Torch and growin' the friendship between you two."

My face flamed as I coyly asked without looking at him, "What happens if I want more than a friendship down the track?"

He snorted. "So, you do have feelin's for him?"

"I'm working it out."

"Ain't no rush. You're on his radar, Wrenley. He'd be anythin' you need. A protector from afar, a friend, and maybe even more. I'm not sure."

"Thanks, Death."

"Eases me, kid, knowin' that you're acceptin' all sides after learnin' everythin' about him."

I shrugged. "Really, there was never a choice. I was always going to." From the first night I met Torch, I'd somehow connected to him in a way I didn't understand but wanted to work out why.

He was worth knowing.

He was worth having in my life.

And I'd do anything to make sure he saw his worth eventually.

Death's lips thinned.

"What?" I asked.

He sighed. "There's one more thing you gotta know about Torch before you jump into growin' whatever this will be between you two."

A twist of unease threatened the coffee I'd drunk. "What is it?"

"Like most of the brothers, when we're in protective mode, we go beyond any means necessary."

"How?"

"Wrenley, my brother has been keepin' an eye on you since Raya and Jupiter had their shit to deal with from that motherfucker."

That's months ago.

Scrunching my brows, I shook my head. "But... I haven't seen him around, and why would he need to? I know you had the house watched around that time. Do you mean Torch was one of the men who guarded us here?"

Death pushed his mug away and faced me. "He was one who guarded through the night, and he heard you screaming from your nightmares. When the twenty-four-hour watch stopped, it didn't for him. He's been sittin' outside your room at night, wantin' to be there to protect you. Even from your dreams."

Even from my dreams.

Oh my God.

It felt like tiny mice were tap dancing on my heart.

Even from my dreams.

He'd been sitting outside my bedroom trying to protect me.

My bottom lip trembled at the thoughtfulness, and I bit down on it.

Maybe I should be scared or put off knowing a man had been right outside my bedroom window, waiting, watching.

Yet, I wasn't.

Did that make me more messed up than I thought?

Pressing a hand to my fluttering stomach, I gazed through wet eyes at the floor. Those dancing mice started to multiply, knowing Torch had wanted to be there for me even before knowing me.

He'd heard me cry and yell from my nightmares and had wanted to comfort me.

I wished I'd known.

But he hadn't wanted me to.

I liked that there was no ulterior motive to his actions. It was only a blind need to protect. He wasn't doing this to get in my good graces, to sleep with me, to use me, to pretend to care and then throw me away when he'd had enough.

He was a God's honest saint, showing a selflessness I'd never witnessed before.

Want bubbled to life in my stomach. I *wanted* him in my life.

Maybe even wanted to keep him.

If I could, nothing else would matter beyond keeping someone who was so supportive and sweet and harsh—when he had to be—in my world forever.

"Kid?"

Glancing up, I gave Death a watery smile. "He cares."

His gaze flared for a moment, and then he nodded. "He does. But I'm not sure he'll like that I've told you about how he spends his nights. And hell, I'm goin' against our code for even sayin' it. But I know he needs a happiness that's different than his family can give him, and I reckon you could give him that."

Nodding, I tapped my foot into his leg again. "I won't tell him you did. I'll stumble upon him somehow. But I won't let him stay out there again on another cold or rainy night."

"Glad, Wrenley. Still, not sure he'll want to come in or like you findin' him."

I smiled and shrugged. "He'll get used to it."

He would. If he was willing to go to the lengths he already had for me, then I would do nothing but the same back for him. Plus, I didn't like knowing he'd been sitting out there on his own at night.

"Shit," Death drew out as he studied me.

"What?"

"Know you will, but I still gotta say it. Take care, yeah? Don't push too hard."

"I won't. I promise."

I wouldn't. I'd never want to upset Torch or have him do things he didn't want to do. All I could do was try and hope he'd see that sitting outside every night wasn't good for him.

CHAPTER TEN

TORCH

Her curtains were open. Usually this late they weren't. Something happened. I just had no idea what. As I ducked down into my spot, I chanced a glance inside her room since the light still shone and found Wrenley sitting at her desk reading something.

I'd seen her reading many times before she got ready for sleep. I liked how sometimes she'd read a paragraph and then look off in the distance as if whatever she read took her mind to another place. Unless she'd thought that whatever she'd read was a crock of shit.

She hadn't reacted to the words since I sat down, though.

Some of her curls swung down over her face, which she tucked behind her ear as she used the other hand to turn a page.

My heart wanted to climb up in my throat at the thought of what happened in the living room yesterday.

Death would've spoken to her by now. I dodged him and her for the day. I didn't want to know about her reaction to my past.

Even though I felt jittery from not knowing.

If it was bad, I wasn't sure I could handle thinking she'd be disgusted by me.

Not when it was just yesterday that she'd willingly wanted to touch me, talk to me, get to know me.

I warned her, though.

I told her she shouldn't want that.

Now she'd know why.

Now she'd hold pity as she kept herself away from a man who liked to kill.

A man who was damaged.

I only stayed alive for my brothers. To help them. To keep them safe.

But for her now too.

As soon as I'd heard her screams that night, I knew she would go on my list of people to protect. But now her safe-keeping mattered to me more than my need to protect my brothers.

She was on my mind all the time.

Her lips, nose, hair, eyes... her body constantly rolled through my thoughts during the day and night.

My obsession.

My addiction.

And she was currently walking toward the window.

What the fuck?

I pushed back into the fence and froze. I didn't blink or breathe as she pulled her window open to stare out into the night sky with a sigh.

What was she thinking?

It was cold. Too cold for her.

Why did she sigh?

What was she doing up this late?

What troubled her and was keeping her awake?

She only stayed up late sometimes, and that was always in the living room to watch shows with her sister. She never used the television in her bedroom. She liked company to watch something.

Wrenley glanced around, leaning into the window frame.

My body begged for oxygen.

But I couldn't draw in a breath in case I made a noise and brought her attention to my creepy-ass self.

If she saw me lurking in the bushes, she'd know what a freak I was.

She'd run screaming and—

Fuck.

"Torch?" she whispered as her eyes landed on me somehow.

I let out a long, loud breath and filled my lungs again to accuse, "You can't see me."

Her cute lips twitched as she waved a hand around. "With the light on in here it shows a small part of you. Can I ask what you're doing out there?"

"Security detail," I said quickly. She didn't need to know I was here all night every night.

"So, the club is worried about those guys coming for me?"

The club? Probably.

Me? Definitely.

I grunted. "You don't need to worry." *I've got your back; no one will harm you again. Ever.*

"Am I allowed to ask a favor?" she questioned softly. Her tone was like a caress to my skin. I could easily close my eyes and listen to her voice for hours.

"What?" If I could, I would do anything she asked.

"I, um, can...." She blew out a breath as her cheeks pinked.

What was she thinking?

What would she ask that had her blushing?

"Anythin'," I told her.

Her teeth nipped at her bottom lip and scraped over it. "Am I allowed to request one guard for the night shift and only if he stays in my room because I don't like the thought of anyone staying outside all night on my behalf?"

Jealousy slammed into me, clawing at me.

My upper lip rose. Who would she want in her room? In her space? The thought of someone in her room while she slept, even if it was another brother, had me digging my nails into my palms.

"Wait," she said quickly. "I'm not talking about in my bed."

I fucking hadn't even thought of that.

Now I was. I got into a crouch, ready to grab any fucker who thought they could share her bed.

"I'll, um, get a mattress for the floor, and... I'd just prefer to not have so many people around me at night when I sleep. I-I have nightmares, and I, well, I wake up screaming sometimes. I don't like sharing that with everyone."

The fiery jealousy simmered.

How could I be angry when all she wanted was to feel reassured and safe?

I couldn't deny her this.

Slumping to my ass, I asked, "Who?"

She blinked slowly, and her lips parted for a beat before they turned up into a pretty smile. "You, of course."

Me?

Me.

No one else but me.

Christ. Why?

Why would she want me in her space?

She would have spoken to Death. She would know everything, and she....

I gripped at my chest as my heart quickened. It felt like the organ had grown under my ribs.

What was this?

I already knew I was addicted. Wrenley was my obsession. Now it felt like she'd grabbed every damn part of me and made them hers.

She was different to any other woman.

She was a shining light. A star. A fucking goddess.

Even after all she'd heard about me. All I'd been through. All I'd done and would still do, and I didn't see any pity or concern or disgust.

There was nothing coming from her but that sweet and pretty smile and kind eyes. I knew what she'd said was the truth. Wanting *me* in her room. She wouldn't lie. Not after hearing every fucking detail.

Shifting from my ass to my knees, I asked, "Are you sure?"

"Yes" was her instant reply, and she even tipped her chin up a little in determination.

I brushed the bush aside so she could see my whole face as I cocked my head to the side. "Just me, Wrenley. In your room, watching over you. Just *me*?"

The fucked-up one. The killer. The one who would slaughter again if it meant my family and friends were safe. If it meant she kept shining as she was now.

"Yes, Torch."

I told her I would give her anything.

I would.

And if that meant me keeping guard in the same room as her, I'd do it.

I get to watch her sleep.

I can wake her from her dreams.

I'll be the one she sees when she wakes up.

My gut flip-flopped. Nerves? Excitement? Maybe both.

"Okay," I told her, climbing out of my hidey-hole to stop in front of her window.

Her smile brightened my world some more when she moved back. I slipped inside her room and straightened. I rolled my shoulders and took everything in, even when I already knew what her room looked like, but this was at a closer and welcomed inspection.

The walls were a light gray, the flooring a wood panel with a big fluffy dark-gray rug that sat in the middle of the room and went under her bed. Her desk sat at the opposite wall to her double bed with a lamp and chair. The television sat above it with shelves at each side on the wall.

I liked it all.

She'd picked each item that was perfect for her.

Simple, sweet, and pretty.

"I'll, um, go see if we can pull the mattress from the spare room in here," she said. I turned, and her cheeks flamed to life as she waved an arm toward the window. "We can lay it in front of there, if that's okay?"

My chest expanded again at the thought of being able to stay in her room. To stay close to her. To drink in her scent as I was now.

Shaking my head, I studied the area instead of getting lost in the pleasant feelings flopping around in me.

The room was big enough, so it left me a heap of space to move quickly in if an attack came from the door.

"Yeah, it's a good spot," I told her.

"Are you sure you don't mind staying in here?"

Facing her again, I cocked my head, a little confused by her question. She wanted me in here. Didn't she know I'd do anything for her? I'd told her I would. Was she worried this was a chore for me? But this wasn't hard to do. Being around her was never hard. It made my gut flip-flop, my chest and body warm. I liked the way I felt around her. "You don't want me outside?" I was sure she'd said that.

"No. I don't like the thought of anyone sitting in the cold or heat for hours on end just because of me."

Sweet, soft, gentle.

And beautiful.

My addiction.

My obsession.

"I'll stay in here," I said and watched her nod while grinning at *me*.

How the fuck did I become so lucky to have her smiles aimed my way?

Glancing to the door, I said, "I'll get the mattress. What about your sister?"

Fuck me. I wished I could talk to her better, like I did with my brothers. Full conversations. None of this short sentences crap. But it seemed she activated my nerves, and I was still learning to relax around such a beautiful, caring soul.

Who wanted me in her room.

Shit.

"She's already in bed, but I'll text her and let her know you're staying in here."

Nodding, I silently made my way out and into the spare room. There were two single beds. I grabbed the mattress and blankets off the first one and carried it back into her room.

Wrenley was by her bed, out of the way, so I could drop it to the floor. She quickly rushed over to fix the blankets.

"If you want, I can sleep on this—"

"No." When she stilled and looked up at me, I realized my tone had been sharp. "Please," I added. People told me the word was good to use if I fucked up or wanted something really important. I would never take her bed from her. One she was comfortable in. One she was used to.

"Okay," she said in a hushed tone. She finished straightening the blanket, stood, and then went to her bed to grab a pillow.

When she stopped in front of me, she held the pillow out. "Take this one. I don't use it."

"I can get the other one from the spare—"

"Please."

My gaze dropped to her lips when she smiled.

Slowly, I reached out and took the pillow, hugging it to my chest.

"Thank you, Torch."

Brows bunched, I asked, "What for?"

"For being willing to stay in here."

I'd already told her anything.

Grunting, I tipped my chin up.

She clasped her hands in front of her chin and smiled again. "Well, I guess we should get some sleep. So, um, good night."

"Okay."

Okay? I should have said "good night." I should have said "sleep well." But I was suddenly tongue-tied, and my gut twisted.

Fuck. What was this? Was it from my obsession with her? Or could it just be nerves from her beauty and kindness that had my body reacting?

As she moved over to her bed, I dropped the pillow to the mattress and pulled off my jacket, boots, and jeans. I got into the bed, lying flat with my hands tucked under my head as I stared up at the ceiling.

I doubted I'd sleep since I was here to watch over her. But it would look better if I acted like it for her sake, so she didn't think I'd hover over her like a weirdo.

Though, the thought of watching her up close was appealing.

The light switched off, and I heard the rustle of her blankets, which ticked up my pulse.

"Torch?"

Christ. I would never get enough of hearing her voice like that. Sweet and tired and aimed at me.

"Hmm?"

"Um, if... well, please ignore me if I wake up screaming or make noises in my sleep."

"I have them too." My confession surprised me, but I couldn't stop from saying it.

She knew why. She knew everything.

Fuck.

I pressed a couple of knuckles into my temple while I used my other hand to dig my nails into my palm to try and calm.

I shouldn't have said that. I should have kept my mouth shut.

The urge to bolt rushed through me.

Until her gentle words stopped me.

"It sucks we have them. They make us feel like we'll never get over what happened. Well, that's what I feel. But... I also like to believe it's our minds showing us what we've overcome." She swallowed audibly. "It shows us the hell we've been through and that our days from now on can only get better. Even when we have setbacks." Her breaths deepened. "I'm sorry if I overstepped by saying anything. It's just—"

"You haven't," I told her quickly.

"Okay.... Night."

"Good night, Wrenley."

She was right. From now on, our days would be better.

Especially mine.

I had my Wrenley in my darkened life, lighting it. She'd already accepted me as I was. Even when she knew what I was capable of. She wasn't ever getting out of having me in her life.

She'd work that out eventually.

CHAPTER ELEVEN

TORCH

The beat to my heart was already erratic when my eyes sprung open, so I knew something had set it off. Straining, I listened as my hand wound around the hilt of the knife concealed under my leg in the bed and pulled it free.

Footsteps approached Wrenley's room.

How the fuck had I fallen asleep?

When did I go under?

Stupid, stupid, stupid.

Jumping up, I stalked toward the door as those heavy steps grew close.

Her door slowly opened.

A male hand reached in.

I grabbed it, spun them, and had the tip of my knife touching his throat in seconds.

A gun cocked.

"You wanna let my man go, brother? Then I won't have to shoot you."

Blinking, I dropped my hold on Gun and stepped back as Saint lowered his gun.

"What in the world?"

I shifted to see Wrenley sitting on her bed with a book in hand. She placed it on the covers as she said, "One second, you were asleep. The next, you were up and walking toward the door *silently*, then grabbing Gun and.... Sorry, but that was like it was out of a movie."

My lips twitched from the excitement in her voice. However, I turned back to Gun. "Sorry," I offered.

"Now that my heart isn't in my ass, it's fine, brother. We didn't know you were in here." Gun glanced from me to Wrenley over and over.

"Oh, I forgot to text Raya." She pushed the blankets off her bare legs to get out of bed.

My body heated.

Her legs were beautiful. Like all of her was. I wished I'd noticed them last night, but she had been in leggings and a sweater. Now she wore shorts and a tee that revealed her silky skin.

But... I wasn't the only one in the room seeing this.

Slowly, I moved my gaze to Gun and Saint.

Gun was talking to Wrenley about something until Saint grabbed the back of his neck and pulled him out the door.

"We'll see you both in the kitchen shortly," he called before shutting the door.

Wrenley snorted. "What was that about?"

Saint was protecting his man.

Not that I would have hurt them. At least, I didn't think I would. No, I wouldn't. I was sure. At least I think I was.

They were my brothers and Wrenley's friends. Plus, they dated each other. I didn't need to worry about them desiring what was mine. They wouldn't.

She wasn't mine, though.

I couldn't have her.

Realizing she waited for an answer while I stared at her, I rubbed the back of my neck and shrugged. "I'm not sure."

"Well, since you're awake, let's go get some breakfast."

There was a new spark to my Wrenley. Was it because she didn't have a nightmare? Other than a few little noises, she hadn't made a peep, and I would have woken if she had.

I still couldn't believe I fell asleep.

"Unless you're still tired... we could get back into bed."

My cock throbbed.

Shit.

"Breakfast." I went back over to my clothes and dressed quickly. I didn't want her to wait for me. When I turned back around, Wrenley had slipped on the sweater from the night before. However, her legs were still on display. But knowing she was comfortable around me to show them shot warmth to my heart, and so I ignored the unease in my gut over other people seeing them too.

She smiled, and my heart jumped.

So pretty.

"You slept well?" I asked.

Her gaze changed. It softened, as did her lips.

My chest expanded.

Christ, I was lucky to be in her presence.

"I did. Best night's sleep in a long time."

Her gaze widened a little when I grinned. "I'm glad." And I hoped it was because I was there. I'd fight her nightmares for her if I could.

Heat hit her cheeks, and it was on the tip of my tongue to ask why, until her stomach growled. She straightened out her sweater and cleared her throat. "Right, um, yeah. Let's go eat." As we made our way out, she asked, "What do you like for breakfast? We have cereal, toast, or I could cook some eggs and bacon. Coffee is a must, but we also have juice."

"I'll have whatever you are." I wasn't picky. I grabbed whatever I saw in the kitchen at the compound. Dusty, and now a couple of other old ladies, kept it well stocked with ready meals or they were in there most of the time cooking something fresh. On the nights I stayed there, I always liked the smell of the common room when I got down in the mornings because the smell from the kitchen had already filled it. Though, I always fed Harley first before myself. Tech was doing it for me while I wasn't around. Harley liked him, and Tech wasn't worried about Harley eating his face off. At least I didn't think he was. He never said.

"Okay, we'll figure it out together."

Together.

I liked that word.

Entering the kitchen, Wrenley called, "Morning," to Death, Raya, Gun, and Saint as I followed Wrenley around the counter to the pantry. "Okay, do any of these cereals tickle your fancy?" She pointed to the top shelf.

"Ah, Wren," Raya called.

Wrenley turned while I read all the boxes. I really would just have whatever she ate. I wasn't fussy about food.

"Sorry, I forgot to text you last night. I found Torch on

his nightly guard job and told him I'd prefer it if he stayed in the house."

"Oh, okay. That's fine."

"He's staying on a mattress in my room," she added.

"What about Harley, brother?" Death asked. His tone sounded lighter. *Why?*

Turning, I went to tell him about Tech, but Wrenley had taken hold of my wrist with a gasp. "We have to go get him. He can stay here. We have plenty of room in the backyard for him to play around in."

Her hand was warm on my skin. Gentle and soothing.

My gut flip-flopped pleasantly that she willingly touched my tainted flesh.

Someone cleared their throat.

Wrenley went to pull her hand away, but I quickly took it and placed it back around my wrist.

I met her gaze, saw her cheeks were flushed again, and told her, "We can bring Harley here."

We.

She would be with me on the trip to the compound and back again.

Then I'd be in her room again tonight.

Hell, I felt spoiled from having so much of her time.

"Okay," she replied.

"And that's totally fine with me," Raya added teasingly.

"Oops, sorry." Wrenley laughed. She glanced back to me and rolled her eyes. After a squeeze to my wrist, she let go, and the cold seeped in. "I think I'll have toast with jelly and a coffee. What about you?"

"Same."

"How do you have your coffee?"

She was going to make me a mug. I couldn't remember the last time someone had done that for me. "Cream and two sugars." I watched her move around the kitchen and strike up a conversation with Gun, who she'd become close friends with.

I could watch her all day. I already had.

Someone stepped up to my side.

"You good?" Death asked.

Nodding, I didn't look away as I said, "Yeah."

Saint got close too.

I turned to him. "Sorry again for putting my hands on Gun."

"I get why it happened. You didn't expect us to rock up. Gun wanted to see if Wrenley was free to hang at the compound for a while. Keep her busy."

And her mind off those.... *Don't go there*. I couldn't think of it. If I did, I'd want to walk out of the house to hunt them down.

Stretching out my neck, I placed my gaze back on Wrenley as she laughed at something Gun said.

"Brother, is Wren yours?" I heard Saint's low tone, but I couldn't answer him.

She was mine. She would always be mine.

But I couldn't claim her like he did Gun. Like Death did Raya. I wouldn't do that to her.

"I'm only askin', Torch, because I see the way she looks at you."

"Saint," Death warned.

But it was too late.

I'd heard and given Saint my full attention. "What way?"

I didn't see anything unusual. She looked at everyone with kind eyes and a sweet smile.

Saint glanced from Death to me. He shrugged. "I see she's interested in you, brother. But I wanted you to know about it so you can be careful with her heart if you're not gonna take her as yours."

Take her as mine.

She already was.

But could what he said be real?

Could she honestly want something with me?

Could she want my touch in those ways?

I rubbed at my chest as I went back to watching her. She caught me, and her head tipped to the side. Worry entered her eyes when she saw my hand pushing and pressing against the crazed organ that felt like it wanted to burst out of my chest.

No.

Fuck no.

Why would she want that? Want me? She shouldn't. She deserved better.

She didn't want me. Saint was wrong. She was being nice to me because I was a part of the club.

Tension tightened my shoulders.

A hand landed on one, and Death drew me into another room. He gently shook me before dropping his hand. "Don't brush away what Saint said and think he's wrong. He might not be. Wrenley knows everythin', Torch. Remember that. You might just have the chance for a damn good future if you open up to the possibility that someone can care for you as you are."

Slam, slam, slam went my heart.

"Wren," we heard Raya call before Wrenley appeared in the doorway.

"Is everything all right?" she asked, looking between us.

"Yeah, kid. Just talkin' club stuff."

"Oh," she said. Her concern shone on me. "Torch?"

I swallowed thickly, studying her.

Nodding, I said to reassure her, "Breakfast. Then we can get Harley."

"It's ready." But she didn't move.

Death did. He went back into the kitchen.

I started that way but stopped beside her when she called my name.

We were close. I dropped my gaze to her.

"Are you okay?"

She was worried about me.

Christ.

Sweet, soft, and gentle.

She was a damn treasure. I'd found the prefect treasure.

Could I honestly be that damn lucky to keep her? Hold her close, please her, pleasure her?

With a tight swallow, I slowly reached up and silently cursed my shaky hand, which only stopped trembling when I cupped the side of her neck.

She didn't pull away. She leaned into it.

Fuck me.

Fuck me.

Fuck me.

I brushed a thumb over her fast pulse.

"I'm okay."

Her hand wound around my wrist. "Good." She graced

me with another beautiful smile. "Then let's eat. I can't wait to see Harley again."

Nodding, I dropped my arm, and her hand fell away before she all but skipped back into the kitchen.

She was happy.

Happier than I'd seen her since I'd had my eyes on her.

It couldn't be because of me.

Could it?

My body warmed. I'd let that thought sink in. I'd allow myself to believe it was from me because it'd be a real honor that she acted in such ways over *my* presence.

CHAPTER TWELVE

WRENLEY

I stuffed my hands under my thighs as Torch drove us to the compound to pick up Harley. My body wouldn't stop reacting from being close to the man. I could still feel the imprint of his hand on my neck, and I was sure my blood had ignited the moment he'd brushed his thumb over my pulse.

I'd wanted to kiss him then.

Which told me just how strong my feelings had grown for the man who had become my own personal guard. He was the most selfless man I'd ever known.

"Won't know how long I'll be at your place."

Meaning he wasn't sure when they would be able to deal with Tony and his friends to make sure they were out of my life forever. Of course, the Diamond brothers had to be careful, considering who those men were in society, but more so with who their families were since some held high-ranking positions within the government.

"That's okay. It doesn't matter how long it takes. I know I'll always be protected with you around. As long as you're okay with the job."

His hands tightened around his steering wheel. "You want me to guard you day and night?"

Oh.... Well, that was embarrassing. I should've thought he'd want a break from me during the day. But it wasn't like he'd been ordered to guard me at night anyway. That had been his choice. Besides, he knew I had Death either next door or in our house every night. I hadn't needed anyone else, yet Torch had still wanted to be there for me.

Still, he probably had other commitments during daylight hours.

But he's not left your side yet.

Still, it was wrong of me to presume.

"Sorry, I... no. Not all the time." I forced a laugh. "You have other jobs to do. I don't want you to stop working for my sake."

Hands threatened the wheel again. He seemed nervous. Maybe he wasn't used to being around a woman all the time. He cleared his throat before saying, "If you're comfortable with it, I'll stay with you day and night."

A thrill rolled over me, and my heart fluttered under my ribs.

I'll stay with you day and night.

Yes, please.

"Only if you're sure."

Because I already knew I was completely safe with him

around, I wouldn't have to look over my shoulder or jump at every shadow.

Did it make me selfish? Probably. But if he was willing, I would accept his offer, especially as I wanted to get to know him.

"Yes," he replied as he glanced over at me to nod before looking back to the road just as we reached the entrance to the compound.

The brothers on duty saw Torch, and the gates opened quickly for us to drive in.

When he parked, I slipped from his car, met him at the front, and together we walked inside. Gun and Saint should be along shortly. They'd wanted to stay back to chat with Death about something. Earlier, when Torch had suggested for us to hang around for a little while before we grabbed Harley and took him home, I'd happily agreed. I loved the atmosphere in this building.

I peeked down at Torch's hand, wishing I could hold it, but we weren't there. Actually, I wasn't sure we ever would be. There was a possibility that Torch might not want to date at all. Had he even dated in the past, or had he just had casual flings with women?

"You okay?" Torch asked as he opened the door to the compound hallway.

"Yes, why?"

My stomach quivered when he briefly touched a finger to my lips. "They were pinched."

Smiling, I shook my head and stepped inside. "I'm fine. Promise."

I couldn't exactly say I was worried that he wouldn't want to date me. It was too soon. We were still getting to know each other, and I was letting the... connection I already felt toward him get me carried away.

Slow your roll, Wrenley.

"Okay," he said as he followed me down the hall.

We entered the common room that buzzed with members, family, and club women.

Stopping, I turned, and Torch nearly ran into me. His hands landed on my upper arms, and before I looked to the ground, I saw him scanning the room.

"What?"

"I-I just remembered the last time I was here and what I said." My stomach rolled. "They know everything, Torch, and... and I yelled at people. Tech probably hates me. I'm so embarrassed." I wanted to hide my face in his chest, but I didn't. Instead, I stood with my head hanging low while I prayed no one had noticed our entrance so I could sneak back out. Torch's grip loosened, I assumed since he knew there was no threat. I really shouldn't find his actions sweet, but I did.

However, I could admire and think about that at home, where I didn't have to face people.

"They won't care," he told me.

I shook my head. "Maybe we should just grab Harley and go?"

"Torch, you mind if I touch Wren?" I jolted at Gun's voice before he appeared at our sides with Saint at his back.

They'd arrived quickly.

And why would he ask Torch that?

I glanced up. Torch had his jaw clenched until he drew in a breath, nodded, and stepped back so his hands fell away from me.

Gun wrapped an arm around my shoulders and pulled me away from the others as he dipped his head to say, "We're friends, so you know I won't lie. You've got nothin' to worry about with how you acted in front of the brothers. It was called for, and hell, don't you think we've all had similar outbursts at some point in time? You know most of us have had some type of shit happen in our lives. It's why we joined the club, to find a family we can trust. A family that'll help us deal with our own hell in one way or another. Relax, Wren. No one here will judge you." His arm slid off my shoulders so he could grip the back of my neck and apply pressure. "Yeah?"

"Yes, Gun," I said. His words were an instant balm to my worry that had me dropping my shoulders. Everything he mentioned made sense. I was too quick to roll with my embarrassment and not consider anything else.

The club wouldn't care.

Gun grinned and winked; then, with his hand still on my neck, he led me back over to Torch.

"You good, Wrenley?" Torch asked.

"I am. Sorry for getting worked up."

He tipped his chin up at me. "Don't worry about it."

"Okay." I smiled.

"Who wants a game of pool?" Saint asked.

I glanced to the table and saw it was open. "I'm in. But be prepared to lose."

Saint snorted. "Ain't happenin', princess."

IN THE CORNER, Saint was pouting and talking to Gun after I defeated him for the second time. Though, after we'd had our first game, Gun had also won a round against his partner in between our two, while I'd sat with Torch, Quake, and Tech, who I had quietly apologized to, but he quickly brushed it off.

I held up the cue. "Does anyone want to take over kicking Saint's butt?"

"I'm not playin' anymore," Saint called.

Men around me chuckled.

"Sore loser" came a new voice, and I glanced over my shoulder to see Lucas, Saint's actual blood brother, approach with his husband, Wreck, who held their young daughter, Opal.

"Like you could win, brother," Saint teased.

"I could. But I don't have time."

Saint approached with his hands out. "Give me my niece. I need some extra lovin'."

Wreck's jaw clenched as he glowered down at his friend, but he finally relented and handed her over. Saint started cooing as he walked her over to Gun, and they both huddled around her. Maybe they were getting baby fever.

"A baby," Dusty cried. Okay, they weren't the only ones with baby fever, but at least Dusty, who was approaching fast, had one of her own coming soon. Saint dodged her grab for Opal and raced off with the little girl's laughter ringing out.

Smiling, I placed the end of the cue on the floor and held it between my hands while I watched them.

They truly were a family.

I sensed movement beside me before I felt warmth close to my side. Looking up, I found Torch's back brushing my arm, and I glanced around him to see he stared someone down.

"Don't even fuckin' think it," he snarled, hand coming back to move me gently behind him again.

Stilling, I waited for Torch to deal with whatever the issue was.

"Come on, brother. I was just gonna have a chat. Been watching her all day and—"

"Don't say another fuckin' word," Torch warned. "And I'm not your damn brother."

"Dagger, come get your friend before Torch cuts somethin' off," Quake called.

"Shit," another man said as he approached. "What the fuck you do, Sammy?"

"I was just gonna chat with one of the club's pieces—"

As Torch reached out, a voice boomed, "Stop."

Torch dropped his arm and shifted on his feet in front of me.

I got to my toes and peeked over his shoulder to see that people parted for Country as he approached. He took me in. "Wrenley?"

I shifted to the side of Torch but remained half behind him still. "I'm okay. Torch had it under control."

Country grunted, then stopped between the other guy and Torch. "What happened?"

A dark, low noise sounded from Torch, but it was Quake who explained while other people around us went back to what they were doing. I even saw that over near the bar, Saint had given up Opal to Dusty for some hugs while Opal's parents watched on with soft smiles.

Maybe I should have been concerned or scared by the guy who'd approached. Yet, I knew I didn't need to be with Torch around.

He honestly made me feel safe.

Like I was wrapped in a bubble, and no matter what went on near me, it couldn't harm me.

How he made me feel this, I wasn't sure, but I'd accept the warmth and reassurance.

Country's jaw clenched. "Dagger, who's this guy to you?"

"A friend who moved away and only recently came back."

"You didn't tell him the rules?"

"Didn't think he'd be stupid enough to approach a woman like that on our turf and say the things he did."

"Come on, she's just—"

"She's family," Country stated coldly as he took a step toward the guy. But my heart took a leap at his declaration. "Even if she wasn't and was one of our girls instead, you're not club. You don't get to talk to or touch any of them. Dagger should've fuckin' told you this. That'll be on him." He turned to Dagger. "Get him out and see Torch another time."

Dagger's mouth moved around a silent curse, but he

nodded before he grabbed his friend's arm and hauled him toward the door.

"This is bullshit," the friend tried.

Dagger smacked him in the back of the head. "Shut the fuck up, man."

I drew my gaze back to Country when he placed a hand on Torch's tense shoulder. "Draw blood if you must. But listen to your brother first."

Torch grunted.

Country turned to me. "How you doin', Wrenley?"

"I'm doing well, Country."

He winked. "Glad to hear it. Wanted you to know we're gettin' shit sorted."

Which told me they were still in the process of figuring out how to deal with Tony and his friends.

"I know," I said and smiled. "Besides, Torch said he was willing to be my personal guard. If that's all right with you?" Crap, I wasn't sure if Torch had run it by Country yet. I'd only just thrown this at Torch, so he probably hadn't said anything to his president.

Country's gaze moved to Torch, and I glanced to him also to see he had his head down. "He is, is he?" Country's brow quirked.

I winced. "Sorry, I only mentioned it to Torch last night, and then earlier, I practically begged him to take me on twenty-four seven. I mean, take on the security job."

Torch moved closer with his head held high. "I'll catch up on any jobs I miss, but Wrenley wants one person to take on the duty. She's asked me, and I'd like to do it."

My heart hammered in my chest and my stomach danced while I stared at Torch in awe. I'd heard he conversed easily when he wanted to and when he wasn't angered or nervous, but I hadn't really heard so many words come from him until now.

"You've got the job, Torch." Country grinned. "I'll talk to the other brothers and let them know you're out of action for a while within the businesses."

Torch dipped his head. "Prez."

Country waved him off. "No thanks needed, brother."

That was a thanks?

Why was I giddy over Torch thanking Country for allowing him to stay by my side? Actually, I suspected the swarming butterflies that tickled my rib cage were more about Torch getting permission to be my guard.

Twenty-four seven.

Country did look cheerful about the idea, though. I wasn't exactly sure why, but I wouldn't question it in case he changed his mind.

Turning to Torch, I asked, "Would it be okay if we got Harley and headed home?"

I watched his throat work over a swallow before he nodded once.

Country reached out and gripped Torch's upper arm. "We'll talk soon, brother."

Torch grunted and took a step back as he tipped his head toward the back door.

"Bye, guys," I called, and we got a chorus of farewells in return while we walked.

Another thrill went off inside me.

She's asked me, and I'd like to do it.

He told Country that.

Could I be hopeful that this guard duty could lead into

something personal between us, or was he just being thoughtful and doing his job?

I didn't dare ask.

Not yet. It was too soon.

I also wanted to see how Torch did being around me all the time. There could be things I did that drove him up the wall. I'd like to think there wouldn't be, but I didn't know if I ate in a way he hated or something.

The two of us being around each other constantly would be the best test.

And I already looked forward to seeing how it went.

CHAPTER THIRTEEN

TORCH

*H*ome.

Even a couple of weeks later, that one word still entered my mind from when Wrenley said it at the compound about me and her.

Like it was *our* home together.

Like *she* could see us in a home alone, together forever.

Unless I read into that word wrong.

I could have.

It wouldn't surprise me if I did.

But while I watched her during the time we shared, I kept thinking over what Saint said. That she was interested in me.

Interested in a way that got my chest warm, cock twitching, and gut rolling.

Our time together felt calm and natural, no matter what

we were doing. Like now, as we sat on the back deck watching Harley chase the ball.

It reminded me of seeing other brothers and their old ladies sitting peacefully in each other's company. And they were into each other. In a big way.

I also loved the times when Wrenley talked about anything on her mind. She didn't care if I joined in or not. She still smiled or laughed or kept chatting.

I liked this.

No. I fucking loved these days.

All my days with her.

Especially when I knew she was safe because she was at *my* side all the time.

The only times I didn't like were when she was in the bathroom. She was alone. I would offer to go in there with her, but I knew that wasn't the right thing to do.

My cock thickened at the thought of seeing Wrenley in the shower.

I clenched my jaw and scowled down at my dick.

I shouldn't be thinking of her like that.

Fucking moron.

I had no right to picture her without clothes or think about how I'd like to touch her soft skin. How I'd give anything to smell her up close instead of drawing it in when we were in the same room.

I wasn't completely certain she wanted me the way Saint thought. But if she did, it was new to me. No one had wanted anything from me. The club bunnies had been nice enough, but they never wanted to have me as an old man like they did with other brothers.

Wrenley was different from them, though.

She was so much more.

I had to be respectful.

Even with my own thoughts.

Until I knew we could be something more.

A deep warmth spread through me thinking about Wrenley being my true old lady. A woman who was just for me.

Someone who cared about *me*.

Someone who would welcome me inside them.

Someone who could love me as I was—screwed up and scarred.

And someone who would be my whole fucking universe, who I'd do anything for or burn *anyone* for.

The club was supposed to come first in life. The brothers.

They always had.

Until I'd heard her screams. Until I'd seen her beauty and learned her kindness.

Now, Wrenley was first in my darkened life. She brightened it, consumed it, and made my days better.

Everything she did fixed the lesions in my heart. Her actions, her words, all of her was a balm to the chaos in my head.

I wanted to do more for her. I wanted to help her with everything she did.

High on my list was to build up the courage to ask to brush her wavy hair. She liked to do it before bed and then in the morning. I always watched, transfixed on her hands, wishing they were my own. I'd give my left nut to have my fingers glide through her soft locks.

I knew they'd be soft. They looked it, and the bristles to the brush slid through easily.

She seemed peaceful when she did it with a slight smile on her perfect lips. It made me wonder what she was thinking.

Harley interrupted my thoughts when he dumped the ball in my lap. Smirking, I ran a hand over his head and picked up the slobbery thing, throwing it. He jumped the stairs and flew down the backyard to pick up his toy. But a scent distracted him, and he took off to sniff crazily. He liked it here. Not that he didn't like the compound. Dusty had done a damn good job on the yard. But this place was quieter.

And it had Wrenley here too.

Harley liked her a lot. When he'd first seen her that day a couple of weeks ago, I thought he'd turn himself inside out with all the wiggling and whimpering he did. The little shit had ignored me for a while because I'd left him with Tech for too long.

"Torch?"

I glanced from Harley and saw Wrenley looking at me. I tipped my chin up.

"Do you think Harley would be able to go to the dog park one day?"

He listened well to me. But I wasn't sure.

"Maybe. Haven't seen him around other animals, though."

She nodded. "Yeah, it's a risk. But he might have fun too."

Sweet Wrenley.

"We'll try it. One day."

Her smile thickened my throat.

Christ. I was damn fortunate to have her happiness aimed at me. My body and mind had never felt as settled as when I was around her. The only thing that annoyed me was my nerves had me fucking up when I talked to her. Not that she seemed to care. My beautiful obsession took me as I was.

So, I'd get there.

She was worth getting over my damn nerves to speak freely and naturally with.

"I'm sure he'll love it, and he listens well to you." She suddenly shivered.

"Cold?" I asked.

"Yeah, the afternoons seem to be cooling off quicker."

I stood, whistled for Harley, and he bounded our way. "We'll go inside."

Her laugh warmed me. "We don't have to go in yet. It's not too bad."

Shaking my head, I waved a hand toward the back door.

Wrenley rolled her eyes but did so with a grin as she stood and moved that way. Harley walked beside me as we followed her.

As soon as we were inside, I ordered, "Bed." Harley took off to the living room, where he had a bed set up. Though, some nights he liked to sleep outside and refused to come indoors, so he had a spot set up out there on the back deck too.

I turned to Wrenley in the kitchen and found her bent over, head in the refrigerator.

Her perky ass pointed my way. It wasn't wrong to look when it was right in front of me, right?

My cock thickened at the thought of my hands on her

round globes, which were hidden behind those formfitting jeans.

I ground my teeth together and forced my gaze away. I did it to test myself so I knew I could do it. But it was also out of respect. Even with what Saint said, I wasn't going to make her feel uncomfortable by drooling over her ass with a hard dick.

"Since Death and Raya aren't here for dinner, what about we make some pizzas?" She pulled out two ready-made dough bases.

Facing her again, I asked, "What can I do to help?"

She placed the bases on the counter and ducked back to grab some ingredients. "I'll get you to cut some things up, if that's okay?"

"Yeah." My skills with knives were outstanding—especially when using them on somebody who fucked over the club. Shaking those thoughts away, I washed my hands and dried them.

"If there's anything you don't like on yours, then don't cut it up."

Nodding, I picked up the knife she'd laid out and got to work while I also kept an eye on Wrenley as she moved around the kitchen doing her own jobs.

Home.

My heart grew heavy as it filled with soft and warm emotions.

This, us, right here, was the first time I truly felt like I was in a home with someone loving at my side.

Fuck me.

Fuck me.

Fuck me.

Home.

Wrenley was my home.

Closing my eyes, I clenched my jaw as the emotions shot higher.

I'd never felt like this.

What even was it?

Happiness?

Love?

Contentment?

Excitement?

What?

I opened my eyes when a hand slid onto my forearm, and I stared down at mesmerizing blue eyes. A wave of calm spread from her hand up and over my body, centering me.

"Are you okay?"

"I have a collection of knives."

What the fuck?

Why did I blurt that out?

Jesus. My gut hollowed out.

She's going to think I'm—

Her hand gently applied pressure. I moved my glaring gaze from behind her to meet hers.

"I know what you do for the club. I presumed you would have tools to take care of those... issues."

I searched her face. She really didn't care that I held weapons at the compound to deal out the punishment to those wrong types of people. Evil. The ones who had hurt us or the good people in society.

We righted the wrongs with our own rules.

And knowing my obsession accepted it, me... Christ, I was going to keep her forever. Even if she didn't want me in the end, I would always have her. If it had to be from a distance where I had to stay hidden, then so be it.

She graced me with another smile and ducked in to touch her forehead against my upper arm.

"You don't have to worry about what I think, Torch."

"I do," I told her.

I worried all the damn time. I never wanted to lose her light she shined on me or how she graced me with all that she was.

She was my obsession. My addiction.

Her head rose, and she looked right into my damn soul. Her smile softened, and her eyes warmed.

"Okay, Torch. But just know I have no problem with how you and your brothers run things."

I tipped my chin up slightly. She squeezed my arm and went back to what she had been doing. I picked up the knife, but I didn't start chopping yet. I used my free hand to touch a couple of fingers to my lips.

She'd got me grinning in a different way than I shared with my family.

My Wrenley was something very special.

I'd have to make sure, while she still wanted me around, to let her know she meant something to me.

CHAPTER FOURTEEN

*B*utterflies swarmed inside me when I entered my bedroom that night and found Torch sitting on the edge of my bed in jeans and a tee with bare feet. His club vest was on a hanger over the closet.

Slowly, I closed the door and watched him wipe his hands on his thighs as he stood. He seemed anxious about something, which had the butterflies dying inside.

"Everything okay?" I asked.

He nodded, then turned to the side and picked my hairbrush off the bedside table before staring, with a pinched brow, to the floor. "Can... would you let me brush your hair?" His jaw ticked as he ground his teeth together while red hit his cheeks.

Swoosh went my belly.

Meanwhile, my mind screamed, *Yes!* Instead of shouting, though, I calmly replied, "I'd like that."

His body relaxed, shoulders dropping as he breathed out deeply, and his hands loosened. He nodded once again.

"Um, how about you sit on the bed, and I can sit on the floor—"

"Beside me. On the bed. You don't sit on the floor."

My heart stumbled.

"Okay," I said and made my way over. "What about if you lean against the headboard and I, um, well, I sit between your legs? If that's okay with you? If not, you tell me where you want me, and I'll do it."

The temperature in the room shot up. I felt the need to fan my face, but I didn't since Torch watched me... until he moved onto the bed to sit where I'd suggested.

My pulse raced, and I worried my heart was about to thump its way up into my throat and choke me.

In a matter of seconds, I would be sitting close to Torch.

Stop thinking, stop thinking, stop thinking.

If I kept going along with those thoughts, I'd melt into a puddle of goo from swooning like a fangirl.

When Torch got situated with wide legs on the bed, I swallowed and crawled over the mattress to between his long limbs. I made sure I didn't touch him anywhere in case he didn't like it. He spread his legs more to accommodate my hips.

"Good?" he asked.

I tucked my hands on my lap and hummed under my breath. My eyes closed when I felt his hand slowly glide from the top of my scalp down to the ends before he gently started to pull the bristles of the brush through my strands.

When there was a knot, he'd curse quietly before he picked up my hair to hold it above the tangle while he worked out the matted part.

My sister used to brush my hair when we were younger. I'd always loved it. I even enjoyed brushing my own, but having Torch work on it felt different... intimate.

With my eyes still closed, I bit my bottom lip when his legs tightened at my sides. They rested along the outside of my thighs, warming me.

I would have given anything to rest against his chest. To have felt more of his body warming mine.

But I wouldn't risk scaring him away. Not when he'd been nervous about asking in the first place. An innocent act had his cheeks burning, which told me it meant a lot to him.

My stomach swooped low again and rolled pleasantly.

Had Torch been this sweet to his other women?

Opening my eyes, I scraped my top teeth over my bottom lip and scrunched up my nose at the horrible thought of Torch doing this for someone else. "Torch?"

He grunted and said no more as his hands worked on my waves.

I opened my mouth and closed it again, suddenly unsure about my question.

"Wrenley?"

"Um, have you done this for... say, um, any of the women at the club?"

"No."

A happy flush rose to my cheeks as I smiled.

No.

He hadn't ever asked another to brush their hair.

Dear God.

Knowing made me want to dance around the room, but I was enjoying my locks being brushed too much. I also didn't want to make a fool of myself in front of Torch. Even though it would show him how happy it had made me.

"Okay," I replied, since I felt like I needed to. "Torch?"

He paused, and his chest pressed into my back, causing me to shiver, before I felt his warm breath run over my ear. "Right here."

Goose bumps rose.

Laughing lightly, I nodded. "I know." He pulled away, which had me pouting, but it was washed away when he went back to brushing. "I was thinking that maybe one day we could go see that new action movie. But only if you like going to the movies."

His hands stalled for a beat before he continued. "We can do that."

"Great," I chirped. "Harley will be fine here in the house or the backyard. It'll only be for a few hours, so he shouldn't get too grumpy with us gone that long. Not like he did with you for being away for so long." Harley had ignored Torch for a while when we'd gotten to the backyard to pick him up from the compound a couple of weeks ago. He'd given me all the attention and turned his nose up at Torch. Though, it didn't last long. It was obvious Harley adored his owner.

Torch grunted. "He'll be fine."

He would. Harley had settled well here. When he first arrived, I'd wanted him in my room, but Torch had said he needed his space because he farted a lot. I'd lost it to laughter when he'd told me, and when I'd calmed down, it was to Torch watching me with a slight smile.

I jolted when Torch's phone rang. His hand settled on

my shoulder while he placed the brush on the bed and reached for his phone that had been sitting on my bedside table.

"What?" he answered. "Damn.... That sucks, but I get it.... Can I bring her with me? ... Yeah. Thanks, brother." He hung up and ran his hand down my arm as he explained, "Gotta head to the security office and take a shift. The brothers Death would usually call in either have somethin' going on or are sick."

I scooted off the bed. "No problem." I stood and clasped my hands behind me. He did ask if I could go. I didn't make that up in my mind. But he hadn't told me I was going yet. "Are Death and Raya coming back here?" I asked.

"They've still got his family over. You and me will go into the office. There's a couch in the screen room you can sleep on. We'll take Harley."

"Got it." I went over to my closet and handed Torch his vest before I took out an oversized sweater to place it over my tank top. I quickly slipped out of my sleep pants and replaced them with tracksuit ones that were comfortable to rest in.

Turning, I froze when I saw Torch's widened gaze on me as his chest rose and fell.

Heat hit my cheeks. "Sorry, I-I didn't mean to make you uncomfortable. I would have changed in the bathroom, but I didn't think about anything other than hurrying for you to get there and—"

I slammed my lips closed when he shook his head once and then rolled his knuckles into his temple.

Had I screwed up?

Did seeing me in my underwear really make him uncomfortable?

He scrubbed a hand over his face and looked to the floor. His jaw clenched. "You don't care I'm in here?"

"In my room or in my room while I change?"

"The second one."

I smiled softly, not that he would have seen since he still studied the floor. "No, Torch, it doesn't bother me. I'm comfortable around you."

He grunted and lifted his gaze to mine. Searching.

One corner of his mouth tipped up slightly. "Okay." He lifted his chin at me and went to the door, opening it wide.

I had a feeling that what I said meant something to him, because as I walked by him, I let out a small, surprised sound when he gently tugged my hair.

"Can I brush it again some time?"

He could do anything he wanted to me.

I hadn't been with anyone since what happened, and I'd never felt the need or attraction.

Until him.

Until Torch woke up my body and mind, and now, all I wanted was his attention.

"I'd like that," I told him a little breathily.

We grabbed Harley from the living room on the way out to Torch's vehicle. The drive to the office was silent, besides Harley's loud breathing, but I liked our silent times. Not once did I feel awkward or uncomfortable in his presence.

As corny as it sounded, this was where I wanted to always be.

By his side.

I didn't care that some might consider it was too soon

for me to even think like that. This was my journey, my emotions, and my experience. And my intense attraction—one I felt toward the man in the driver's seat.

I just hoped Torch didn't think I was out of my mind for even considering wanting to stay by his side all the time.

At least I had an excuse to have him close by. I wasn't sure what I was going to do when my problem had been dealt with and Torch wouldn't stay at my place any longer.

Kidnapping was a bit too far.

Torch had the skills to escape anyway.

Though, maybe by the time this was all done with, Torch would be charmed by me and not want to leave. He'd stay with me in my room, but the only difference would be that he'd sleep in my bed and not on the mattress on the floor.

"Your cheeks are red," Torch pointed out.

How could he see in the darkened cab of the car?

Darn him and his good eyesight.

I couldn't exactly tell him they were that way because I'd been thinking of him sleeping in my bed with me.

I fanned my face. "It's a little warm in here."

"It's not."

Snorting, I nodded. "Okay, it's not." The night air had cooled things off. "But that's all I'm saying about my blush."

"You were thinkin' of somethin'?"

I bugged my eyes out and choked on a breath.

"What?" he pressed.

"Nothing." We pulled into the parking lot for the offices. "Look, we're here. Let's go." I undid my seat belt, grabbed Harley's leash, and opened my door. Thankfully I'd been saved by arriving at our destination. Until I saw Torch standing at the front of his vehicle with his arms crossed over his chest under the streetlight that lit up the space around us and his stubborn quirk to his brow.

Why did he want to know so badly?

I stepped close, tipped my head back, and asked, "Why do you want to know?"

"So I can understand what's on your mind when your cheeks go like that."

He wanted to understand me more.

Dammit.

My face warmed again as I blew out a breath. "You might not want to know," I warned softly.

"It was bad about me?"

"No! Never," I said quickly and then groaned. I ducked my head and confessed, "I was thinking that when you stop guarding me that maybe sometimes you could stay in my room still...." I rushed out the last part. "But in my bed."

A single finger touched under my chin, and I lifted my head to see his was cocked to the side as he studied me and my stupidly overheated self.

"You'd want me in your bed?"

Dammit.

"Yes," I admitted quietly.

Because over the last few weeks, I've been crushing on you badly, and I'd love to date you, kiss you, hug you.

He dropped his hand to tap his fist into his thigh once, twice before he said, "Okay."

A quiver raced over me.

Torch turned and started toward the back entrance.

Okay?

What did he mean by okay?

I would have asked, but I feared he'd have me confessing my feelings for him, so I shut my trap while Harley and I followed him.

Torch pressed in a code to the keypad that opened the door. He moved aside for Harley and me to enter first. We stepped into the hallway and waited for Torch to shut the door and arm the alarm again. There were lights on already, and I could hear a voice coming from one of the rooms as we approached.

Torch turned into the room on the left. "Chaos."

A brother I hadn't met yet stood from one of the chairs that was set up in front of many, many screens with live feeds playing on them.

"Thanks, brother," Chaos said as he held his gut and glanced at Harley apprehensively.

I wasn't sure why a lot of Torch's brothers feared him. Harley was a big softy who loved cuddles.

"You good to get home?" Torch asked.

"Yeah, no problem. My woman should be here shortly." He noticed me behind Torch. "Miss Wrenley, nice to officially meet'cha. Sorry to drag Torch in here, but I ain't much of a watcher when I'm spendin' a lot of the time in the bathroom."

I winced and waved him off. "It's okay. I hope you're feeling better soon."

He tried for a smile and then slapped a hand over his mouth as he dry-heaved. Torch shifted back, moving to stand in front of me before he shifted us, with a hand to my waist, out of the doorway and danger zone. I made sure to keep Harley close to my side.

"Brother, no offense, but get the fuck outta here. We

don't want your germs," Torch said, and it didn't sound jolted or short like he usually was with me.

What made him speak different around me?

I knew he was shorter when he was angry, but that again was even different to how he was around me. When he was in his hunting zone, he was snippier.

With me, he wasn't curt or sharp, just shorter, as if his nerves got the better of him, and he didn't know what to say or how to say it, or he worried what I would think when he said something. Like he had in the kitchen about his collection of knives.

Did that mean Torch felt shy around me?

If so, that meant I did mean something to him, right?

Thinning my lips, I bit the insides of them to keep my happiness contained, worrying I read it all wrong.

Still, everything pointed toward Torch liking me.

Oh wow.

He likes me.

He really does.

CHAPTER FIFTEEN

TORCH

She wants me in her bed.
She wants me in her bed.
She wants me in her bed.
Holy fuck. Holy fuck. Holy fuck.

I couldn't stop thinking about being beside her in her bed, surrounded in her scent, warmed by her blankets, and feeling her pressed up to my side.

"Brother?" Chaos called.

"Huh? You haven't hit the road?"

"You didn't hear me, then? Just wanted to tell you West was called in as well. He'll be here soon. Now, I'm outta here."

"Later," I said with a flick of my hand. I needed Chaos to leave and take his sickness with him. Did we have some Lysol around to spray for the germs? After he left, I faced Wrenley and stilled.

I'd never seen her face like it was.

As if she tried to bite her lips off and was concentrating hard on it since she was squinting her eyes and bunching her brows.

"You okay?" I asked.

She nodded, humming under her breath. The face scrunching eased, but the lip biting didn't.

Should I question her some more? She didn't like when I had outside, but if I hadn't, then I wouldn't have discovered she wanted me in her bed.

My gut flip-flopped.

I wanted to reach out and run my finger over her tightened lips so she'd stop in case they were ruined before I got a taste.

If only we were back home now. I'd slip under her covers because she wanted me there.

I wouldn't have figured that out if I hadn't been called in to do my job.

Right. My job.

I stepped to her side and tipped my chin to the screens. "I better get to work, but I'll quickly grab some blankets for you." I pointed to the couch that sat against the wall.

"I can get them. Where are they?" She went to move toward the door.

I grabbed her wrist. "Hard to explain." It really wasn't. I just wanted to get them for her. "Won't take me long." Which was true. "Wait here." I slipped into the hall and to the room next to us that held some fresh bedding. We didn't often need it but kept them as a "just in case," and this was one of those moments.

Back in the room, I noticed Wrenley had dropped Harley's leash and left him near the couch since he'd already curled up for sleep on the floor while she'd moved closer to the screens.

After I placed the items on the couch and patted Harley's head, who didn't even stir, I faced Wrenley just as she looked over her shoulder to me. "There are so many places on here."

I nodded. "Death keeps gettin' approached from more people interested in feelin' safe, knowin' they're being watched over."

My heart hammered with how much I was saying.

She nodded. "I can understand that."

"We did have the live feeds of Polished here, but it made more sense to have the screens in the actual place with a security team there."

Wrenley stared at me. I didn't look at her, but I could feel it.

I knew why.

And even though my gut acted up and my mind screamed at me, *Shut up, she doesn't need to hear all that. You're making a fool out of yourself,* I ignored it and used all the words that had been wanting to come out.

Still, there was more.

"I prefer workin' here than at Polished. It's quieter. Calmer. But I'd take any job Country, Death, or State gave me. I like keepin' busy."

Shut up, shut up, shut up.

I pressed my knuckles into my temple, but I couldn't stop the bad thoughts.

You fuckin' fool. She won't want you. Keep quiet.

I ground my teeth together and pressed harder into my temple.

A warm hand rested on my arm, and I snapped my gaze to her in front of me.

Soft smile.

Warm and kind eyes.

Sweet mouth.

"I like knowing about everything that goes on in your life, Torch."

Slowly, I lowered my arm, and her hand stayed around my wrist for a beat, until she slid her hand into mine.

Fingers locked between mine. My damn heart filled and pranced under my ribs.

She shrugged. "I always ramble about things in my life. You already know how I like my vegetables steamed until they're soft and falling apart. Except my potatoes, which must be crunchy. And I've told you that I'm bored with my online course and that I'm thinking about a full-time job instead." Her hand squeezed mine. "No matter what's on your mind, please feel free to share it. I feel like I can tell you anything, Torch, and I hope you'll want to be the same way with me one day."

I did.

I really did.

I wanted to tell her everything that was on my mind, but I still panicked that it'd scare her. That one day I would say something to put a look of disgust on her face, and I wouldn't be able to stand it.

With another gentle squeeze to my hand, I locked my gaze onto her pretty one.

"There'll be nothing you say that will make me run from you, Torch." Lips tipped cutely. "Well, maybe keep quiet about the punishments the club deals out. Is that okay?"

I already knew her soul wasn't made for any of that type of information.

I had my brothers for that.

But Wrenley... I could have her for everything else.

Anything that was on my mind I could tell her, and no matter how it came out, if it was heaps or a little, I believed she'd take anything as it was coming from me.

Saint was right.

My obsession was into me.

It might not go that far, but she liked me. A lot. Enough to want my attention, to be in her bed next to her, and to hear my words.

"I like that you're honest." Using my free hand, I brushed the backs of my fingers over her cheek. "Even when you don't like saying things and get embarrassed."

She swayed closer and pressed her cheek into my hand.

My eyes flared and my blood pumped fast knowing she enjoyed my touch. Didn't care my tainted skin was against hers.

Christ. Realization dawned on me that she wouldn't want me to *just* be beside her in her bed.

She wanted me *in* her.

The heat in her gaze told me that right then as she stared up at me.

Just the thought of having my dick encased in her heat had it fattening.

Fuck.

I couldn't let her see yet.

"Torch?"

I tipped my chin up slightly.

"Would the thought of kissing me put you off?"

My eyes lasered in on her wet lips, and my gut tingled.

She wanted a kiss.

Why would she think I'd be put off by that?

"No," I told her.

A frown, drawn brows, and my hand slipped from her cheek when she stepped back and nodded. "Okay then."

"Huh?"

"No, it's okay. I, um, shouldn't have mentioned it." Her other hand released mine.

Cold.

A shiver raked over me while confusion slapped me in the face.

Where had I gone wrong?

All I said was no.

Jesus.

"Wrenley." She looked up. But my gut still burned at the touch of sadness I'd seen there. *I'd* put there. I wanted to reach up and smash my fist into my face over and over until I fell unconscious. But... I could make that look go away. At least I hoped. If I was right, which wasn't always the case.

However, I was sure about this.

Her.

Which was why I unglued my lips and told her gently, "The 'no' sounded wrong. It meant I wouldn't be put off." I scrubbed a hand over my face.

She doesn't really want you. She's just pitying you. You'll never have what your brothers do.

Shaking my head, I grazed a hand over my buzz cut and then touched the scar at my eyebrow. I slid my fingers to the ones on my right cheek before I dropped my arm.

"You want me to kiss you?"

I needed to hear it from her. I wouldn't fuck this up. *Not for her. Not for my Wrenley.*

My obsession.

My addiction.

Mine.

She drew in a sharp breath as her gaze bounced to me, and she nodded slowly.

Fuck.

I hadn't kissed the women who'd given me their hole to use.

This would be my first.

And I liked the thought of my first kiss being with my pretty Wrenley. So much so, my body vibrated from the anticipation of it.

Taking a step forward, I cupped the back of her neck and drew her into me. "If I do anythin' you don't like, stop me."

A soft smile greeted me. "It's just a kiss, Torch."

I shook my head. "Not just a kiss. It's ours. My first. And somethin' fuckin' special." With that, I leaned in, and since her lips were already parted in shock from my words, I swiped the tip of my tongue slowly over her top one before doing the same to the bottom. A deep grumble rolled from my chest at how sweet her lips tasted. I pulled away to suck and roll my tongue around in my mouth, savoring her flavor.

"Torch," she whimpered, eyes shining for *me*.

Unable to resist, I closed my mouth over hers quickly but moved my lips against hers softly and slowly. Until she parted once more. I dove in to twist, lick, and play with her tongue. She made a noise, and for a beat, fear slapped at me, urging me to stop, until her hands clawed at my tee under my cut. She pulled me in before wrapping her arms around my neck.

If I wasn't busy tasting, teasing, and memorizing every part of her mouth and lips, I would have roared in damn gratification knowing she enjoyed this as much as I did.

Harley growled.

A throat cleared.

Quickly, I broke the kiss, planted Wrenley behind me with one arm, and used the other to point my knife toward the door.

Adrick, the ex-mafia Russian, raised a brow. "We did not want to interrupt, but my West is here to do a job."

West stepped to Adrick's side and waved. "Hey. Sorry to stop that smoking-hot kiss."

The Russian snorted.

"Heel," I ordered Harley, who was still rumbling low. He cut off to go back to sleep.

I only relaxed when I heard Wrenley's laughter and felt her forehead press between my shoulder blades. Pocketing my knife, I nodded and noted Adrick released his hold on West's waist behind him. He must have wanted to keep his husband covered until I wasn't armed.

He was very protective of West, like I was of Wrenley. I'd even go as far as he did and snap anyone's neck who harmed her. Adrick had done it to West's father for abusing him.

Though, I'd want to torture them first. A quick death

wouldn't be enough for the person who thought to touch her.

Wrenley's hands wrapped around my upper arm, calming me as she moved to my side.

She grinned over at West and Adrick. "I probably shouldn't be distracting Torch from his job anyway."

Fuck, she was beautiful.

I couldn't stop staring at her.

West replied something, but I wasn't listening.

My Wrenley had allowed me to kiss her.

No. She'd wanted it. Asked for it.

I could still feel the warmth of her lips on mine. I could *taste* her. If we were alone, I'd kiss her again.

"—Adrick can rest on the couch with you."

"No," I stated and turned to the men. "Wrenley needs to sleep. I'll get another chair for Adrick."

The thought of another man being close to her soured my gut.

"But there's plenty of room—"

"Nyet, moya lyubov." Adrick nodded at me. He probably understood and wouldn't want anyone sitting close to West either. No matter who they were. My skin would have felt just as prickly if it were Country or State. I wanted Wrenley to be able to lie down and sleep if she could.

Reaching up, I patted her hands, and she dropped them with a soft smile up to me. I exited the room and went to the one I knew had a good-sized armchair that looked semi comfortable. I picked it up and carried it in. The whispered voices cut off when I stomped closer. They'd cleared some room near where West sat in his chair at his side of the screens. I dropped it there with a grunt and went over to Wrenley as she straightened out the blankets.

I brushed my fingers to her lower back, and she stood, turning to me. "I'll get to work now."

She nodded, smiling. "Okay. I'll be here resting, and if you guys need anything to eat or drink, I'm sure Adrick and I can find the kitchen to grab it."

That she wanted to take care of me while I worked heated me from the inside.

"Da," Adrick added as he scrolled on his phone. "Though, I do know where it is already."

Wrenley brightened. "See, we've got you covered for pick-me-ups if needed."

I'd kissed her.

She was mine now.

I'd tasted her, held her, and she'd accepted me.

Therefore, I grazed my fingers along her cheek and jaw. "Try and get some sleep?"

Her body relaxed, and she pressed her cheek to my hand before she nodded. Her smile slipped into a sweet one.

For me.

Mine.

All mine.

"I'll try."

I grinned, tipped my chin up at her, and went to work.

I wouldn't tell the brothers that it was the first night I'd been distracted at work.

CHAPTER SIXTEEN

I'd expected Torch to fall into bed and sleep the day away when we got home from the security office. I was exhausted for him.

Instead, he said, "Want to see that movie?"

I closed my gaping mouth and asked, "Aren't you ready to fall asleep?"

Death scoffed from the living room since we'd only just entered. "The brother is like a vampire. He never sleeps."

With a glare at Death, Torch defended, "When I want to." His hand slid into mine, and my heart skipped a beat at his easy touch. He'd been doing it all night, and I loved how my body reacted to his skin against mine. When he tugged me closer, I looked up at him. But I didn't miss the wide eyes gazing from the living room.

"Breakfast, play with Harley, and movie?"

I squeezed his palm in mine. "I would love that."

Even with his stoic expression, as his eyes searched my face, I knew that hidden beneath was so much more. He cared for me deeply. So, I let him stare and think. I didn't mind it one bit. In fact, it made me want to hug him and hold on tight. It was as if he just wanted to watch me because he couldn't believe I stood in front of him.

I'd never felt special before. Not in the way Torch made me feel, and I knew my feelings would grow and grow for this man.

"Okay," he said after a while. He glanced to Death and Raya. "You want food?"

"Ah, nah, brother. We're good."

"Thanks anyway," Raya added with a smile.

Torch grunted and led me into the kitchen with Harley at my side, who had slept on the floor all night in front of the couch I'd been on at the offices. Torch let Harley out back to do his business, and since it was raining, I waited by the door to open it again for him. Harley went crazy when he trotted inside, like he hadn't been with us all night, by wiggling his butt side to side in excitement as he rubbed his head into our legs. Torch had taught him not to jump up on people, which was good because he was a big boy.

I could feel Torch's warm gaze, and I looked up from patting Harley to find him leaning against the counter watching me.

"I'll cook," he said.

Nodding, I stroked my hands over Harley some more and cooed at him while Torch started on breakfast. He was making it easy for me to fall for him. I couldn't believe I'd read his "no" wrong at the office or how hard the word had crushed me when I'd thought he didn't want to kiss me. It'd been like a vise had squeezed all the air out of my lungs.

But then he'd quickly straightened out my confusion.

Biting my bottom lip, I pressed my forehead into Harley as I remembered his words.

Not just a kiss. It's ours. My first. And somethin' fuckin' special.

The kiss had been his first.

And for a first kiss, it'd blown my mind and nearly my panties.

A tingle filled me. I already looked forward to kissing him again. As well as more. At his pace, though. I wouldn't rush this.

With a final pat to Harley's head, I stood and went to the sink to wash my hands. The scent of bacon nearly made me drool. "Need help with anything?" I asked.

He ordered Harley to his bed in the living room before answering me with a curt, "No." His jaw clenched. "Thanks." Maybe his nerves were eating at him again and he didn't know what to say or was just shy around me. Whatever it was, I didn't mind if I got long, short, or medium responses from him.

As long as I had him here, that was all that mattered.

We could sit in silence, and I'd still be happy because he wanted to be here with me.

I admired him as he moved around the kitchen and then stood at the stove. While Dusty did most of the cooking at the compound and the brothers were grateful for it, I wondered who did it before Dusty got there.

"Who cooked at the compound before Dusty?" I asked.

"We took turns."

That explained why he easily moved around a kitchen. Not that any man couldn't, but there were a lot of men and women who didn't even know how to boil an egg.

"What things did you make?"

His lips twitched. But he also reached up with his free hand and pressed a couple of fingers into his temple. He cleared his throat. "Easy things. A lot of pasta dishes. Brothers would eat anythin', though."

Laughing, I nodded. "I can believe that. It must be nice to have Dusty there now."

He shrugged. "She's good for Country. Doesn't matter if she cooked or not. We'd manage."

Gah, he's too darn sweet, and he doesn't even realize it.

"But," he added, "her fried chicken and potato salad is pretty good. I'd stab a brother if they got in my way of it." He froze for a moment, until I started laughing, and he looked my way before relaxing.

We were still getting to know each other. But he'd soon learn that I knew when he was messing around with things like that.

With a nervous flutter to my belly, I walked up behind him and rested my hand to his shoulder while leaning into him a little.

"Smells good."

He hummed, and I could feel his chest rising and falling faster than normal.

Did my touch unsettle him?

No, I wouldn't believe it did, not after that kiss and those touches.

He cleared his throat. "I...." His jaw clenched, and he tapped his knuckles against his temple again.

"What?" I asked softly, sliding my hand down to his waist.

His nostrils flared, and something flashed in his eyes. He shook his head and took a harsh breath before clearing his throat again. "I like doin' things for you." He went back to grinding his teeth together like he felt he was a fool for admitting that.

"Thank you for telling me. I like it when you do things for me. Like brushing my hair. You were gentle with it. Not like when Raya used to do it. She'd yank at the knots, and we'd end up in a yelling match."

His body had relaxed under my hand and words.

"I like doing things for you, too, Torch."

He nodded, and I thinned my lips to hide my big smile when I saw pink on his cheeks.

"Food's ready," he said.

I moved back to get the knives and forks since he'd already set up the plates. When he placed them on the table, I passed him his utensils while staring wide-eyed down at my portion. There was a lot of it. More than what was on Torch's plate.

"Um, I'm not sure I can eat all of it."

He shrugged, gently pushing my plate closer to me. "Eat what you can. I'll take the rest."

A soothing sensation swept through me.

Just another gesture that made me fall for him.

"Okay," I said, picking up my fork and starting on the meal with a smile.

Later, I'd have to thank Death for suggesting I saw the dog at the compound that night. If I hadn't, I wouldn't have gotten to meet Torch.

I was glad he'd been there that night too.

I COULDN'T STOP LOOKING at our joined hands as we walked into the movie theater. Sneakily, Torch had already bought the tickets online, and I would have paid for the food, but we'd agreed in the car on the way there that we were still full of breakfast.

I'd make it up to him somehow. Not that I felt I *had* to, but I wanted to.

Things were growing between us, and I couldn't wipe the smile off my face thinking about where we were going from here. We were stepping into couple territory—not that we'd put a label on it. Our relationship was evolving. I doubted Torch would just casually touch someone he didn't want to be with. He didn't seem the type to play around.

Not when I'd been his first kiss.

Had he had sex before?

Heat hit my cheeks, and he happened to glance over as we made our way down the aisle to find some seats.

My belly swooped when he stopped, turned to me, and swiped his fingers over my cheek.

"You don't want to know," I told him before he could press. I quickly added, "*Maybe* later, in private."

"You're blocking the way," some guy said from behind me.

Torch looked over my shoulder and stared.

It was cold. Maybe even cruel.

But it didn't affect me like it did the guy who said, "No problem. We'll wait."

Torch placed his attention back on me, and the corner of his mouth tipped up as his chin did. We took our seats and settled in to watch with our hands clasped together, resting on his thigh.

When the lights went down, though, he tensed. I released his hand and moved the armrest between us to hug his arm with both of mine as I rested my cheek against his shoulder.

Tension slowly left his body, and his hand slid onto my thigh to squeeze once before leaving it there.

I loved knowing I could help him. That I could sense his tension and calm it.

Rubbing my cheek to his shoulder, I relaxed, and we watched the movie quietly together.

When the credits started to roll, I straightened and stretched.

Facing Torch, I asked, "What did you think?"

He rolled his eyes. "Entertainin' enough."

I grinned. "A little over the top?"

He snorted. "Never known a human to knock a person's head clear off with a kick."

Laughing, I stood. "True. But does that mean you know of a nonhuman to knock someone's head off?" Reaching out, I wiggled my fingers.

He stared at them for a beat, then stood and took my hand. "No monsters." He frowned.

Was he thinking he was one because of what he did and had been through?

His jaw clenched, and he pressed a couple of knuckles into his temple.

I squished myself up against his chest and wound my arms around his waist. When I had his focus, I told him, "I don't know any monsters either."

His fingers grazed over my cheek. "Too sweet, soft, and gentle," he murmured, and I thought it was more to himself than me. He took my hand in his, and my heart skipped a beat when he lifted it to kiss my digits.

This man was going to cause me to be a wired mess of sickly sweet emotions. Like Saint and Gun were. Exactly what I'd wished for.

Torch led us out of the theater and into the bustling streets. I glanced down the road, thinking we could get something to eat, but froze as a flash of fear prickled my skin.

Is that...?

I blinked.

And who I thought I saw was gone.

Torch crowded me, glancing left and right while he backed me into a wall.

I was okay. Mitch wasn't there.

Torch was here. He'd take care of everything.

But I didn't see who I thought I had. Mitch wasn't there. He wasn't.

"What's wrong? What did you see?"

I shook my head, dragging my gaze from down the street to him. "No one."

"Wrenley—"

Placing my hands to his waist, I tried for a smile, but it wobbled. "I thought I saw one of *his* friends, but I was imagining it. They wouldn't be in this area. They have no reason to be, and when I looked again, no one was there."

I overreacted. Disappointment tightened my belly.

Torch's jaw clenched as he turned to stare the way I had. He didn't move until he'd scanned everyone. Not that he'd know who to look for, unless he was trying to spot anyone suspicious. My shoulders dropped. I hated that I'd put him on edge after such a great morning.

"We're going," he said, curling an arm around my shoulders and leading us toward his vehicle.

"I'm sorry to spoil the day."

He brushed his nose against my temple. "You didn't. I just don't want to risk anythin' when it comes to you."

It was official, and I didn't care if it was too soon.

I was in love with Torch.

Completely. Totally. Utterly.

He ushered me into the car, reached over me to click in my seat belt, and shut my door. Even went as far as to lock the car until he was at the driver's side door to unlock it and get in. All while his eyes flicked around us.

He started the car and pulled out with his hands strangling the wheel and his eyes darting everywhere.

Thinning my lips, I clasped my hands together tightly.

He was stressing because of me. Unease pressed at my chest, knowing I'd set him off. But a part of me was eased knowing that Torch had it all under control.

Except, he possibly wasn't that controlled on the inside.

His thoughts were probably wreaking havoc, and I'd caused that reaction.

Dammit.

Should I reach out like I had at the movies to take his

mind away from those thoughts, or would he not want me distracting him while he scanned around us, looking for a threat?

Biting my bottom lip, I ran my hands up and down my thighs with indecision as I kept my worried gaze on Torch.

As if feeling me watching him, he didn't look my way, but he picked up my hand and kissed my fingers once again before placing my hand to his thigh and patting it there.

"I'm okay," he said.

He knew I was worried about him.

He knew and made sure to tell me.

Even if his being okay was only partly true, I appreciated his attention and reassurance. I squeezed his thigh but kept quiet while he did what he had to.

We'd work each other out one day.

CHAPTER SEVENTEEN

TORCH

I just needed to get her home. I had to get her home. Had to. She'd be safer inside. I had more weapons there.

I hadn't lied when I said I was okay. I was doing a lot better than I thought I would when I'd seen the brief look of fear tightening her expression. At least I didn't pick her up over my shoulder and run for the car before locking her in while I hunted the fucker down.

From our surveillance, I knew all his friends' faces.

My brothers and I had memorized them.

They were on my phone in a private file, and I went over them each night while she slept, reminding myself who I had to protect her from.

She would stay safe.

Pulling into the drive, I parked, turned off the car, and jumped out. In a rush, I was at her side and helping her out.

Gentle. I had to be gentle.

I got her inside and shut the door, locking it.

"What's goin' on?" Death called, coming from the kitchen.

"Wrenley thought she saw one of them near the movies," I told him.

"I was probably mistaken. He was there one second and gone the next."

Death and I shared a look. We had to be sure none of them were in our territory. We already had most of their phones tapped, and nothing about Wrenley had come up so far. But now there could be.

"Who, kid?" Death asked.

"Mitch."

Death tipped his chin up at me. He'd go see Tech at the compound to check if anything popped up on their feed while I continued to watch over things here. We didn't like to share any names over our own phone lines in case the cop, Harred Plank, had somehow managed to get through Tech's safeguards and was listening in. Plank had been trying to find something on the club for a while now and was pissed that no matter how hard he dug, there was nothing. We did a good job at covering our tracks. The cop would keep trying, though, since he suspected us of taking out one of his people.

We had killed him, but the cunt deserved it for harming and tormenting Death's sister and touching Raya. He'd also dealt tainted drugs to kids on the streets.

Officer Jones, Plank's partner, was another story. He

supported our club and how we ran things. He'd even helped us out when he could. He didn't like or trust his partner and had told us that Plank wasn't the only dirty cop involved with the drug trade.

"Darlin'." Death turned to Raya, who was leaning against the doorframe. "I'm headin' out for a while. Be back soon. If it's longer than a couple of hours, I'll call you."

She walked to him. "No problem, Leland."

I glanced away and down to Wrenley. She stood quietly looking up at me. She was worried, and my gut twisted that I added to her concern. It was why I'd try to control the burning rage under my skin to hunt.

My obsession was my priority. Wrenley's safety overcame the hunger for their blood on my hands.

"Later," Death called before he walked out the front door.

My brother had also just put his woman's care in my hands. I needed to keep them in the same room until he returned.

"Leland and I were just about to eat a late lunch. You two hungry?"

Food was the last thing on my mind.

"Meet you in the kitchen," I told them and quickly grazed Wrenley's cheek with my fingers before I went out the front door for a perimeter check. I'd then go in and secure the house. Harley would let me know if anyone dared come close to the backyard.

Once I got inside, I locked the front door and checked all the windows before making my way into the kitchen. For now, I'd leave Harley out back so he could be my alarm.

Wrenley smiled and blushed at her sister until their attention moved to me as I entered.

I stopped and cocked my head. Her blush reminded me of the one at the movies.

Was now a good time for her to tell me?

"Why—"

"Nothing," she shouted, cutting me off.

My blood slowed, my shoulders relaxed a fraction, and my lips tugged up. Her embarrassment was cute and funny. It made me lighter. Like the stress wanted to melt away. I could stay focused on the task of protecting them while enjoying watching Wrenley.

"Is it worse than you wantin' me to sleep in your bed?" I asked.

The blush spread, and she groaned, burying her face in her hands while Raya threw her head back and laughed.

That told me it was.

Could she have been talking about sex with her sister?

Was she wanting to have it with me?

Fuck.

I shouldn't think about that.

My cock started to fatten from the thought of being inside—

The temperature in the room intensified.

"Checkin' on Harley," I said and quickly exited out the back door.

Harley and the cool breeze were a good distraction.

Fucking focus, you fool.

She was at risk.

No one would touch her.

"No one," I muttered to Harley as I crouched to pet him.

It was nearing ten when we entered Wrenley's bedroom. Death had come back earlier with no news. But we weren't letting our guard down. While Wrenley didn't want to admit she'd really seen someone, I believed she had. Knowing one of them got to see her made me want to find him and gouge the fucker's eyes out.

Until I could take care of the problem, I was happy to be Wrenley's constant protection.

Even after things were sorted, I wanted to be around her.

I wanted to keep staying here in her house, room, and— my heart thumped hard—bed.

I'd yet to sleep, but at least I was used to going without. Though with Death back, I'd grab an hour or two.

In her bed.

Where she wanted me.

My dick throbbed as my gut flip-flopped.

When we entered her bedroom, Wrenley blew out a breath and tucked some of her partly dry hair behind her ear.

"Well, I'm, um, just going to the bathroom." She nodded, turning back around. With her hand on the handle, she added, "Make yourself comfortable in the bed. Unless you need the bathroom, then I won't be long, and you can take a turn."

She was talking fast. Nervous? Sometimes it was hard to

tell, or it was more that I wasn't confident in reading the cues right. But I was learning quickly when it came to my obsession, which made me think I was correct.

I hummed under my breath, and she exited, closing the door after herself.

I glanced to my cut hanging over the closet door and then to the mattress on the floor before I wiped my palms down the tracksuit pants I wore. Did I remove all my clothes? Maybe I just needed to take off my bottoms, leaving me in a tee and boxers? I hated sleeping in clothes, but I could do a tee. I'd done it for the last few weeks and had handled it all right.

I scrubbed my hands at my hips.

Blood pumped fast in my veins, and it felt like it was all draining down to my dick.

Fuck.

What did I do?

This was Wrenley.

My Wrenley.

My obsession.

Addiction.

I had to get this right.

Should I go ask Death?

Grumbling under my breath, I rubbed the heel of my palm into my eye socket.

I wasn't asking Death.

This was Wrenley. She told me to get comfortable.

I slipped out of my tracksuit pants and the tee, and I got in under her covers in my boxers. The cool sheets felt fucking fantastic against my hot skin.

The door opened, and I looked over, my gut sparking at

the sight of Wrenley in a tank top and sleep shorts. Her cheeks were already shining red as she closed the door, turned out the light, and made a dash to the bed. Her side dipped slightly when she climbed in.

"I guess you didn't need to use the bathroom." She laughed. "Unless you do, and I just turned off the light on you."

"I'm good," I said, rolling to my side her way.

There was a gap in the blinds that let the moonlight spill in so I could make her out. It lit up her side of the bed and left me in the darkness. I couldn't help thinking how appropriate that was.

She wouldn't be able to see me.

But I got to watch when she turned her head my way, trying to see me.

She rolled to her side, blinking slowly and then squinting.

My lips twitched.

Christ, she was cute.

My ears all but rang with how fast and loud my heart raced as I lifted my hand to press a finger to her mouth. She jumped a little but smiled against my digit. Her hands reached up and wound around my wrist.

My beautiful Wrenley kissed against my finger.

Swallowing thickly, I asked, "Can I kiss you?"

"Anytime, Torch. Anywhere. I promise."

Dick jerked. Heart thumped.

Fuck me.

I threaded my fingers into her curls, cupped the back of her head, and dragged her close.

Our lips touched.

Once. Twice.

I flicked my tongue out against her top lip. She parted on a soft gasp, and I took the chance to tangle our tongues together.

If I weren't already addicted to all of her, I would be now for her kisses.

The sounds she made. The way she glided her palm up and down my arm. All of this shot my cock to hard and aching.

"Torch," she breathed against my lips and hiked her leg up over mine before she shifted closer.

I fought to not grind my cock into her.

My body had never been this needy for someone.

Wrenley rolled into me. I groaned into the wild kiss when she rocked against my hardness.

Shit.

Fuck.

The urge to come grew, and I wasn't about to lose myself in my boxers.

Trailing my lips down her neck, I sucked and nipped at her skin.

Fuck me, she tasted good.

She smelled even better.

"Torch," she whimpered. "Is-is this too much for you?"

"No. Never," I got out. Tone low, rough, filled with want for her.

She rocked into me.

I knew what she needed, and I needed to give her what she wanted.

"Can I touch you?"

She swallowed and pulled her head back, trying to see me. "Um, you already are?"

More. I had to give her more. I had to please her. I wanted to make her quiver for me.

I rolled to my back, taking her with me. She let out a quiet cry of surprise but then sat up over me. Smiling down at me, she pressed her hands to my chest.

When I ran my finger up over her shorts where her clit was, Wrenley bit down on her bottom lip.

"Wanna touch you here, Wrenley."

She nodded once, lifting off me enough for me to get my hand down the front of her shorts to her heat and wetness.

Christ. She was wet for me.

For me.

As I circled her nub with my thumb, I rubbed a couple of fingers up and down her hole.

I wanted to beat my damn chest when she moaned, whimpered, and panted.

"Torch, yes," she said, pressing her pussy down on my fingers.

I gave them to her, pushing them up through her juices and inside her. In and out, I fucked her with my fingers.

My mouth watered, wanting to lick and suck at her. One day, I'd get the chance to taste her there.

My obsession was letting me touch her.

She was stunning with her eyes closed. Her lips parted as she breathed heavier from the desire *I* gave her.

She whimpered and dropped her heated gaze to me.

"Torch," she whispered.

Yeah, it's me touching you, my pretty addiction.

My cock throbbed and leaked into my underwear, but I ignored it.

This was all about her.

Her pleasure was mine. She was taking it from me.

My gaze lowered to her breasts gently swaying under her top with her movements as she rode and rocked over my fingers. I took my free hand from her waist and swallowed the nerves as I cupped one. The perfect handful.

"Yes, Torch," she encouraged.

Fuck me.

I wanted to watch her, touch her, kiss her, fuck her, lick her, bite her all at the same time. But I also liked what we were doing.

Besides, I didn't want to consume her to a point I'd scare her off.

Somehow, a part of her, whether you'd call it her essence or soul or something, had crawled inside me that cold night when I'd heard her screams and stayed.

Was a part of me in her?

My hand gently squeezed and rolled her tit before I pinched at her nipple, drawing a sharp gasp that turned into a low moan.

I'd easily go up in flames for her.

Just like I'd burn the world to keep her safe.

She rocked her hips faster. I circled and pressed my thumb to her clit more firmly and shoved my fingers deep, moving them, rubbing them in her.

She shattered on a cry of my name, and Christ, I wanted to beat my fucking chest.

Instead, I waited until I'd drawn her climax out and

removed my hand. I shoved my fingers straight into my mouth and groaned around the taste of her release.

Her eyesight must have adjusted to the dark because her cheeks heated, and she bit her bottom lip while she watched me.

I licked them clean and pulled my digits free when Wrenley started to move down my body.

My cock jerked.

But this wasn't about me.

Reaching under her arms, I lifted and placed her on the bed before I rolled her so she faced away from me. There, I scooted in close and wrapped an arm around her waist, snuggling in.

I pressed my nose into her hair at the back of her head. "This good?"

"What about you? I'd like to—"

"Another time. I wanted this to be for you."

To show I cared. *To cherish your body like it deserves.*

"But...." She pushed her ass against my hard dick as she grabbed my hand, wrapping both of hers around it before she brought it up to hug to her chest.

My gut flip-flopped.

Sweet.

My sweet Wrenley.

After kissing her neck, I rested my head on the pillow and said, "Next time."

"Promise?" she asked, and her tone told me she seemed a little peeved she wasn't getting me off.

"Promise," I told her.

I couldn't deny anything she asked.

CHAPTER EIGHTEEN

"What are you daydreaming about?" Eve asked. Her, Courtney, Raya, and I were sitting at a table in the common room at the compound. Eve was the sister to Tech, and Courtney was married to State, who was the vice president of the club. They'd been around a while and were some of the nicest women Raya and I had met.

It was a few of the club bunnies we had to keep an eye on sometimes when they got too bitchy. Courtney had told me one time that since the bunnies lived in the compound, to be at the beck and call of the single brothers, they thought they had more rights than the old ladies, which wasn't true.

Had Torch had any of them?

Nope. I wouldn't go there.

The past was the past for both of us, and we were working on starting something for our future.

I definitely enjoyed how things got started last night.

Smiling, I rested my chin on my hand as I searched out Torch in the room.

"And she's still dreaming," Courtney commented with a laugh.

Rolling my eyes, I laughed softly just as I found Torch over on the other side of the room talking with some of his brothers. My heart skipped a beat when I spotted Dagger with two wrapped-up fingers. Country's words from that day ran through my mind, *"Draw blood if you must. But listen to your brother first."*

Now they were talking and laughing with others, as if Torch hadn't done anything to him.

Maybe one day I'd understand the dynamics of everything about the club, but if I never did, I'd be okay with that. Nothing would keep me from Torch.

Warmth rushed through me when I found him gazing back at me. He tipped his chin up, which I dorkily returned, causing his eyes to lighten.

"That explains who she's dreaming about," Eve teased.

"Please, I'm her sister, and I don't want to know why Torch has given her that look on her face."

Eve snorted. "I can understand that. I do not want to hear about Tech's sexual adventures."

"But, *chéri*, it would be hot to think of your brother in that way," Henri said as he arrived and sat beside Raya, opposite Eve, Courtney, and me, who were on the long bench. I loved his French accent. I swore I could listen to him read the label on a can of soup and enjoy it.

When Eve screwed up her nose, then faked gagging, we laughed.

"Henri, if you think my brother is good-looking, then you need to seek help. Besides, I'm sure Blaze wouldn't be happy hearing that you have the hots for Tech." She smirked, raising her brow.

"My amour has already agreed with me on your brother's hot status. It is fun to look but not touch. I do get very bored when I am waiting for my amour to do all his computer stuff."

Eve opened her mouth and closed it. "I don't know what to say."

"Sometimes it's best to say nothing at all," Dusty said when she joined us. "Henri, shouldn't you be at the florist?"

Henri owned and ran a flower shop where Dusty also worked. Well, managed really, because it seemed Henri grew bored easily.

"The team has it in hand. It is what we hired them for. And when you pop out your *bébé*, you will be back to take care of things."

Dusty rubbed her belly. "Why don't you sell it? You haven't been happy there for a long time, and I might not come back for a while. Things around here keep me busy too."

"But then what would I do with the time I was there?"

"Dom told me there was a receptionist job going at Polished P and P," Courtney announced.

Henri straightened, lighting up while Dusty's eyes shot wide and she shook her head.

Eve, reading her, said to Henri, "Maybe it's best to talk

to Blaze about working at a brothel and escort agency before you even think about the job."

"*Non*, he does not decide for me, and I am liking this receptionist idea. Imagine what I would see working there, how much fun I would have."

Courtney winced, no doubt regretting her suggestion. "But still, it would be good to talk to Blaze. The hours are at night, so it might not work with Blaze being here and busy all the time."

Henri scoffed. "Maybe it would be best for us to be separate for a while. Then he might remember what a good fuck I am and pay more attention to me instead of his computers." He crossed his arms and huffed.

Country stopped by the table at the wrong time.

Henri pointed at him. "You. I am told there is job of receptionist at Polished. I wish to be employed. You know I have skills. I run my own business." He waved a finger side to side at Dusty. "Not a word. I would be good for this position, boss man."

Country quirked a brow and rested his hands on Dusty's shoulders. "And who's gonna run your business? It ain't Dusty. She's about to have my kid and won't be working—"

Henri shook his head. "I am selling it."

Country paused for a moment. "What about Blaze?"

Henri cocked his head and gave him a look that held a lot of attitude. "What about him?"

"Shouldn't you get his permission—"

"Permission?" Henri snapped and stood. "*Pardon moi*, did you say permission? That *I* would need *permission* from a man to do what I want?"

"Dusty?" Country tried.

"Oh no, don't get me involved. I may regret putting this idea in his head to sell his business, but you've just stirred the beast. Now he's risen and is very stubborn."

"I will have this job," Henri said, nodding to himself. "If you do not do the hiring, who does?"

"State and Wreck," Country said quickly.

Dusty covered her mouth, but I heard her snickering. I was holding mine in, as were Raya and Eve. Courtney grinned like she was having the time of her life.

"I will speak to them. They will know I'm good for this job."

"What job?" Blaze asked as he walked up behind Henri.

Everyone froze.

Except Henri, who spun on Blaze. "You will have your fun with your computers and spend more time with a man who does not suck your cock, but I am selling the florist and acquiring the receptionist job at Polished."

Someone snorted, then coughed. "Just to say, I'll never suck his cock," Tech added from somewhere.

Henri glared at him. "You never know, *mon ami*, you might enjoy it."

Tech spluttered and shook his head. "I know what I like."

"And we don't need to hear about it," Eve put in.

Blaze ignored them and scowled at Country. "Did you give him this job?"

"No. He doesn't even have it. I told him to talk to State and Wreck."

A tick started in Blaze's cheek.

Warmth hit my back, and I glanced up to see Torch there, but he was watching Blaze closely.

"Wanna take a walk?" he asked Blaze.

"No," Blaze clipped. Then his attention went to Henri, and he fired off fluent French. Henri replied snarkily in the same language.

"Anyone know what they're sayin'?" Tech asked.

"Nope," Raya replied.

I glanced to Dusty, and her face was burning bright, so maybe she knew some of it.

Blaze eventually sighed long and loud. "Fine," he snarled. His attention went to Tech. "We're moving our setup to Polished."

His eyes widened comically. "Say what?"

"He hasn't even got the job," Eve commented.

Dusty snorted while Blaze and Tech bickered back and forth and said quietly, "Do you know of a time when Henri didn't get his way?"

Eve opened her mouth and promptly closed it.

Torch rested his hands on my shoulders and applied gentle pressure. I took it as him asking if I was okay. Glancing up, I smiled and nodded. He tucked some hair behind my ear.

When I glanced back to Blaze and Tech, I realized that the room had gone silent, and all eyes were on us.

A blush rose, but I was more worried about Torch feeling uncomfortable with the attention, which was why I asked, "So what's the verdict? Did Henri get the job? Are you guys moving to Polished?"

"We are," Blaze stated.

"We aren't," Tech bit out.

Henri waved a hand in the air. "It does not bother me if they move or not. I am going to find Wreck or State and come back with good news." He glanced to Courtney. "Where is your other half?"

"Ah...." Courtney hesitated, like I would, wanting to protect her man. That or she just didn't know.

Henri smiled. "It is okay, *mon chéri*. I will be gentle with him." He winked.

Blaze broke off his argument with Tech to clip, "Henri."

Henri rolled his eyes and waited on Courtney. He didn't have to wait long; State walked in from the kitchen area and paused when he noted a Frenchman running his way.

"Mr. State," he called loudly. "I have a question, and I do not think you'll be able to pass on this opportunity. I have my own business, *oui*? I know how to run things. I am excellent in taking calls, booking appointments, and greeting people. Plus, I am handsome, *oui*?"

State looked over Henri's head to a glaring Blaze before returning his attention to Henri. "Where is this goin'?"

"I would like the receptionist job at Polished."

State shrugged. "Fine. On a three-week trial run."

Henri clapped and jumped on the spot. "Merci, merci, merci," he cheered.

"Fuck," Tech shouted before he turned and stalked out of the room.

"Why does he sound pissed?" Courtney asked as her man and Henri walked over to the table.

Eve laughed. "Because he knows he's screwed, and that he'll be moving his setup to Polished."

Which was understandable. The men around us were some of the most possessive and protective men I'd ever met. I'd heard Blaze was worse than them all. I didn't think it was that Blaze didn't trust Henri, but I suspected he'd have a problem with the men who visited the brothel. Henri hadn't been lying when he said he was handsome. He really was and often got attention from all types.

"Dusty, we must plan to sell. Come, *mon chéri*." Country shot him a look, and Henri quickly added, "Please."

Dusty sighed. "You and your whims, Henri. Are you sure—"

"Oui, oui. I am completely sure."

Country helped Dusty up off the seat, and Henri curled an arm around her waist to lead her out. They both called a goodbye. Blaze followed them silently.

"Brother, I ain't sure I made the right choice," State said to Country.

Laughter sounded.

Country slapped him on the shoulder. "Too late now. At least you said it was a trial run."

Eve cackled. "Dusty told me Henri is a whiz when it comes to running things. As long as he doesn't grow bored, and I don't think he will at Polished."

"And none of you mind the computer room being moved to Polished?" Raya asked.

Country shook his head as he crossed his arms over his chest. "Tech and Blaze have nearly finished creatin' a device where none of our phone lines will be corrupted by an outside source, no matter what they try. Plus, there's always brothers at Polished. Won't change much."

"Then why was Tech so upset about the move?" I asked Eve since she knew him best.

She smiled. "Have you been in their room? It's so big

and full of shit that it'll take forever and a day to get all those computers set up like they are."

"Oh," I replied with a grin. That would be a shitty job.

A phone chimed. Country pulled his from his pocket, and his mouth tightened when he read what was on there.

"State, Torch, with me now." He started for the hallway. State quickly kissed his wife while Torch ran his fingers softly over my cheek before following their president.

Tension settled low in my stomach.

The kitchen door opened, and Death rushed through the common room with a chin lift to Raya.

"Should we be worried?" Raya asked.

Eve shook her head. "Whatever it is, they'll have it handled."

Courtney nodded. "And if it's necessary for us to know, they'll tell us. But, to change the topic because I'm a nosey wench—" She turned to me. "—can I just say that Torch looks completely smitten."

Eve nodded, leaning in. "I've never seen him with that tender look in his eyes. Tell me you two are a thing?"

I appreciated the distraction, and I believed the women were right—the men would have things handled.

Until they wanted to tell us, I knew I was safe, which meant I could enjoy my time with the women around me.

I brushed at invisible crumbs on the table and said, "We're working on getting to know each other."

"While he guards her twenty-four seven and sleeps in her bed," Raya teased.

Eve and Courtney grinned, but it was Eve who stated, "They're together."

Courtney gripped my hand. "I can already see something special between you two."

"Really?" I breathed as my chest warmed.

"*Really*. And I love that it's you for Torch. I've seen him around his brothers, smiling, laughing, and talking, but it's never reached his eyes before. Though, in the last couple of weeks I've noticed that's changed. He seems more... I don't know how to say it."

"Alive. Happy. Content," Eve suggested.

Courtney grinned. "All of it."

That warmth inside me spread.

It was wonderful that other people saw me as a good thing for Torch. I was doing something right. I was helping by caring for him in every way I could.

He meant so much to me.

I'd never loved a man before.

Crushes, yes, but I'd never felt consumed by so many emotions that my body reacted all the time when he was close or far and when I just thought about him. I loved every look he gave me, every touch, or even when he tipped his chin up at me when he couldn't find words.

"Is it too soon to feel strongly for someone?" I asked softly.

"No, not at all," Courtney said quickly and then chuckled with Eve while Raya smiled and shook her head.

"One date," Courtney said as she patted my hand and let go. "That was all it took to know Dom was going to be mine."

"Most of these biker men work differently than others. The ones who want to settle will find their partner and know instantly. Unless they have their thumb up their ass like Country did with Dusty when he thought she could do better than him since he's older," Eve said.

"Or the woman refuses to admit her feelings and is scared to commit." Courtney stared pointedly at Eve.

There was definitely some sexual tension between Eve and Quake, who was Tech's closest friend in the club. It could be a reason why Eve wouldn't accept anything serious with Quake.

"Leave it," Eve warned icily.

Courtney's hands shot up in front of her, pressing on the air. "Calm the she-beast. I'm backing off."

Eve sighed. "Sorry." She shrugged. "Besides, the problem with Tech and him being friends is that I am warming up to emotions that I'm not used to." She glanced at Raya and me. "Tech and I had a shit life growing up. Hell, you two know what that can be like. We didn't trust or like anyone, and I'm still...." She shrugged again as her jaw clenched.

I bumped my shoulder into hers. "We get it."

She nodded and huffed out a phony laugh to cover the sadness. "Yeah."

Raya pulled Courtney into a conversation to get the attention off Eve.

My sister and I did know where Eve was coming from when it came to shit parents and family life. Though, not everyone's situation was the same. All we could do was be there for one another, and I had a feeling Eve knew that, as she glanced at me and smiled softly before she bumped back into me.

CHAPTER NINETEEN

TORCH

$\mathcal{P}$anic clogged my throat and punched me in the gut when Country ordered me to follow him. I knew something had surfaced about Wrenley and those....

Fuck.

Fuck.

Fuck.

Breathe, motherfucker.

But you left her out there unprotected. They'll get her. They'll hurt her.

Reaching up, I roughly tapped at my temple.

Shut up, shut up, shut up.

I'll get them. I'll make them pay.

She's safe here.

There're brothers everywhere.

A hand clamped onto the back of my neck, and I went

to grab my knife until I heard, "Relax, brother. We'll handle whatever it is," from State.

Country glanced back but then kept heading toward Tech's room. He threw the door open and stepped in.

I nodded to State and unclenched my jaw. "I'm good."

He gave me a quick shake before he let go, and we entered the room.

I went over to a chair at the table where Country and Quake already sat. State pulled out a seat and joined us as Death and Blaze walked in.

Death closed the door after him, and they both stayed standing with their arms crossed over their chest.

"What we got, Tech?" Country asked, leaning back.

Tech pressed a button, and voices filled the room.

"Plank?"

"Harred, I need advice."

"What the fuck are you calling this cell for? You use the other—"

"My son could be in trouble! There's a girl we need to get rid of—"

"Shut the fuck up. I'll speak to you when I can."

The call ended.

A girl we need to get rid of.

A girl we need to get rid of.

I stretched my neck and scrubbed at my face.

They're going to get her because you're useless.

They'll touch her, hurt her, and there's nothing you can do about it, you worthless—

"Who called Plank and when?" Death asked as his hand slid onto my shoulder and squeezed.

Breathe, motherfucker, and find out the information.

"Torch?" Country called.

"I'm good," I got out through clenched teeth as I ran my hands up and down my thighs.

Tech cleared his throat. "Chester Handler, who is Tony's father and a real estate tycoon. The call happened just a few moments ago. Once I heard the conversation, I did some diggin'. Chester owns a few warehouses in the area where the main drug supply is comin' from."

State scoffed. "Which means, he's lookin' the other way while Plank and whoever the fuck else he's workin' with produces and ships the shit out from Chester's properties. How fuckin' uncanny that the prick after Wrenley has a connection with Plank."

"Damn weird. Though, it could be good for us since Chester's already fucked up and called Plank's work number. Clued us in that they're workin' together. But what's this about another cell Plank mentioned?" Quake asked.

Tech grunted. "He must always have it on him or hidden in a damn good place, or else Wreck would've found it when he searched the guy's place. From what I remember Wreck sayin', his work cell was just sittin' on the kitchen counter, which was how he tapped it."

"Now we also know that Mitch saw Wrenley with Torch. Brother, were you wearin' your cut?" Country asked.

I nodded.

"Means Chester will tell Plank about Wrenley and her association with the club. Plank knows who Wrenley is since he knows Raya," Death said.

The fucker had questioned Raya about the dead drug dealer and rapist Elio.

I bounced my leg up and down, fighting with myself to stay in the room and not go on the hunt.

"What's the plan? I need a plan." I cracked my knuckles. "Can I hunt yet?" I asked the carpeted floor.

"I wish you could, brother. But this is bigger than we thought if Plank's gonna get involved."

"He can disappear too," I suggested with a sneer.

I wanted their blood.

I needed their blood.

Now.

"He's been a problem for too long," Death said.

He agreed—Plank had to go.

"He'll get what's owed to him," Country stated. "We dig some more and wait a little longer. We're nearly there, brothers. We'll have them in ways they can't get out of. Tech and Blaze, make Plank a priority. Get Wreck back in if we have to. I want that cell. I'll talk with Jones about what's happenin'. For now, Torch, glue yourself to Wrenley. She's not out of your sight. Death, you're at Raya's full-time for now."

I thumped my palm to my forehead before I ran it roughly over my buzz cut.

Wait.

Wait.

Wait.

It was all I was doing.

But I could. I would. For her.

My obsession.

Addiction.

Wrenley.

So, while my brothers did the groundwork, I'd keep her safe.

Taking in a huge inhale, I pulled images of Wrenley to the forefront of my mind, calming myself enough to stop the other thoughts.

"We'll get them, brother," Country reassured again.

"And then we make sure they hurt," Blaze snarled.

Country nodded. "They will."

My sweet obsession and I sat in the living room on the couch while we watched some television show that I wasn't paying attention to. My focus was glued to Wrenley as she rubbed herself against me once more.

She'd been attentive since I walked out of Tech's room at the compound.

She knew something was up and had set out to help settle me.

It was working.

She had my full attention now.

Especially after we got here and she'd changed into her denim shorts that displayed her long legs nicely. They were now curled to the side of her on the couch while she rested against my side.

My fingers idly played with the hem of those shorts.

She was safe here. At least I hoped no one was foolish enough to come here. Not when there was Death, me, *and* Harley.

Are you sure no one will come here?

They'll get to her because you're a fool.

I blinked out of the haze and watched Wrenley's hand running up my chest.

She already knew my body.

Wrenley could tell that my mind had drifted into the darkness, and she wanted to drag me back out with her touch.

My obsession was perfect.

She eased the itch under my skin to hunt, hurt, and kill.

There'd come a time when I could, though, and I liked that she'd accepted that side of me too.

A knock sounded on the door.

I stood with my knife in hand but paused when I heard Death coming from the hall. He shot me a glance and tipped his chin up as he stopped at the door.

Tucking my knife away, I stayed standing even when Wrenley took my hand in hers.

Death looked through the peephole.

"Fuck," he clipped low. "Plank and Jones," he told us.

Tensing, I allowed Wrenley to pull me down to sit next to her.

I couldn't kill him.

I couldn't kill him.

Death unlocked and opened the door. "Yeah?"

"Leland Thomas—"

"Death," my brother said harshly. "Just Death."

"You can't tell me—"

"Plank," Jones said and sighed. "Death, we got a call saying there was some trouble down the street, and the description of the woman being harassed matches Miss

Wrenley Moore. Someone said she was being detained and then got dragged to a car. We're here to check if she's okay."

I ground my teeth together and lifted my upper lip in a silent snarl.

Bullshit.

All bullshit.

This was Plank's way to check Wrenley was here and who she was with.

Damn, they worked fast. How did Plank pull this off with Jones? Though, it wouldn't surprise me if Plank showed Jones a forged complaint.

Breathe. Breathe. Breathe.

"Wrenley's fine," Death told them.

"We'd like to see for ourselves," Plank responded.

Death glared but stepped back and waved them in. Jones entered first and then Plank.

My body damn near vibrated with the need to kill him for even looking at *my* obsession.

"Raya," Jones greeted her as she moved up beside Death.

"Hello." She curled into my brother as he placed an arm around her shoulders, and then she waved a hand toward the living room. We were in clear view of them standing near the door. "As you can see, my sister is okay. I don't know who called the station, but they lied."

"We'll be the judge of that," Plank snarked. I tensed when he took a step our way. His gaze flicked to me before he turned back to Raya. "You just had to get your sister involved with these bikers. You should be ashamed."

Raya's head reared back. "Excuse me?"

"Plank," Jones warned.

"Get the fuck out," Death snarled.

"Please excuse my partner. He doesn't mean any disrespect," Jones tried even when his jaw tightened from his partner's words.

Stab him.

Burn him.

Kill him.

He's staring at what's yours. He has no right.

I inched my hand around to my knife.

Wrenley stood and moved in front of me. "I don't like the way you spoke to my sister or how you're judging us. You came here to check on me. I'm fine. Now you can leave before I ring your captain and make a complaint of harassment against you." Her chest rose and fell rapidly.

Pride and elation swam through me.

But it was mixed with fear since I knew Plank wouldn't like her threat.

Christ, I breathed just as fast as she did.

My hand ached for the knife.

I wanted to plant it in his neck and watch him bleed out.

"Plank, let's go," Jones tried.

Smart.

I was two seconds away from doing something that could fuck things up and disgust Wrenley.

I rose behind her and rolled my head back and around before I thumped my knuckles into my temple, gaze locking onto Plank.

He's looking at her.

A knife to the eyes will fix that problem.

Plank snorted. "You're all the same."

I slowly pulled my upper lip off my teeth and glared.

"Fuckin' leave," Death ordered once he saw me.

"We're going," Jones said.

I drummed my fingers into my palms.

Not yet. Plank can't die yet.

But he would.

He shot me a wary glance before he stormed out.

Jones watched him leave and quietly said, "I know this visit was something Plank set up, but I don't know why."

"Country didn't call?" Death asked. Jones shook his head. Death nodded. "He probably thought Plank wouldn't move this fast. You'll be hearin' from him. I'd tell you now, but with him out there, I ain't riskin' him gettin' suspicious."

Jones hummed. "I'll wait to hear from Country. Look, I haven't seen Plank this worked up. You need to keep an eye out."

"We will."

Jones quickly left while I took some deep breaths, and Death shut the door, locking it.

Wrenley turned to face me.

Plank had looked at her.

He wants to get rid of her.

Reaching out, I dragged her into my arms and held her close, touching my forehead to her shoulder as I ground my teeth together.

No one will hurt her.

I'll stop them.

Wrenley wrapped her arms around my waist as Raya spoke. "Is there anything my sister and I need to know?"

"Same rules, darlin'. Stay away from Plank. Both of you. If, for some insane reason, we're not around and Plank is there alone, you run. He's into shady shit. Trust no one but each other and the club, yeah?"

"I hear you, honey," Raya replied softly.

"Wrenley?" I muttered.

Her arms squeezed me. "I heard. I'll be safe. You don't need to worry."

But I would until the threat was dealt with.

CHAPTER TWENTY

orch and I lay in bed facing each other. He used two fingers to trace over my face slowly: forehead, eyes, cheeks, chin, jaw, lips, over and over. Like he wanted to lock each part away to memory by touch.

He worried about the corrupt officer.

Worried something would happen to me.

And maybe I should've been concerned too, but I wasn't.

Torch would be there. He'd protect me while I did the same for him somehow.

I believed he loved me like I did him.

"What's your Christian name?" I asked in a whisper.

His fingers stilled. But then he blinked before continuing his exploration.

"I don't like my name," he told me.

My chest tightened.

His top lip flicked up, then lowered when he clenched his jaw. "It was used a lot in the past. I-I don't like it."

I took his hand in both of mine and pressed my lips to his fingers. "Then I don't want to know."

"You can."

"No. I—"

"Chase. And I only tell you because I know I won't be taken back to those times when *you* use it."

Tears welled. I shook my head and kissed his fingers again as he stared at my mouth. "I don't want to use it. I don't ever want to remind you of.... I like your club name. I like calling you Torch."

Regret for even bringing it up washed through me.

"Say it," Torch ordered. He pulled his hand free and got to his elbow, looking down at me.

I shook my head, rolling to my back.

He made a noise in the back of his throat. "Need you to." He leaned in and licked at the edge of my ear. "Please." There was another lick and nibble, and then he added, "Replace what I hear in my head with your sweet tone."

"Torch—"

His hand pressed down on my chest, between my breasts. "You're breathing heavy. I've never affected anyone like this."

Snorting, I shook my head. "I don't believe it."

"Believe it. Only you, my Wrenley. Only you have the heart and desire to want me close. To let me kiss them. To let me touch them. To get excited from my touch. Say my name. Make it better for me."

I shook my head, fighting the pull to give in, especially

with the way he spoke low and how his lips felt over my ear and his palm between my breasts. But I didn't want to bring his past in here. If he woke from nightmares because of me, I couldn't forgive myself.

"Please, *my* Wrenley. My sweet, beautiful, addictive girl." His hand slowly slid down and cupped me between my legs. When I opened them for him more, I felt his smirk against my neck.

Where had this teasing, string-pulling, full-of-confidence man come from? I wasn't sure where, but I liked that he was sharing this side with me.

Two of his fingers tapped over my entrance. I gripped his shoulder, holding him tightly to me. I wanted his digits in me.

"Torch, please."

"What do you want, my Wrenley?" His lips trailed from my neck back up to my ear, where he sucked. I closed my eyes and moaned when he pushed his fingers against my clit over my sleep shorts.

"You. I want you. Always want you."

"How?"

For a moment I didn't get it, but when I understood, I told him, "I need you inside me. F-fucking me."

A growl rumbled up from deep within his chest.

"You want my cock in your pussy?"

Oh God.

"Yes. Please, I want you so much."

"Give it to me, then," he demanded low.

Swallowing, I met his heat-filled eyes and said softly, "Fuck me, Chase." He would get what he wanted, me saying his name, but I wouldn't use it all the time. Just in the bedroom. In times like these.

His grin was almost a snarl as he got up and stripped. Scars marred his body, but they didn't take away from how good-looking he was. Nothing would. They were a part of him, and I loved all of him.

I sat up and pulled my tank top off, throwing it to the floor. I shoved my sleep shorts down with my underwear and kicked them off as Torch climbed back on the bed.

He sat with his back to the headboard before he picked me up, drawing out a squeal of surprise from me, and placed me on his lap. I expected him to drag me in close, but he didn't.

Instead, I watched as his hungry eyes mapped out every inch of me. I smiled when he lingered on my vagina and breasts.

"Pretty," he mumbled, more to himself than me. While I rested my hands on his shoulders, he used his to smooth over me, up from my waist to my stomach, my chest, neck, thighs. Everywhere he could touch, he did while talking to himself. "So lucky. Mine. All mine. Sweet, soft, and gentle. My Wrenley."

His cock stood to attention between us, pointing at me, leaking a little. Waiting for my hand, but I also wanted to give him my mouth.

I felt Torch had enough time exploring. I had my own hunger to subdue.

Lifting, I scooted down his body on my hands and knees.

"Wrenley, what—?"

I lowered my upper body and looked up at his wide, burning eyes. After sucking him down until he hit the back of my throat, I slowly slid my lips and tongue back up.

His groan was long and dirty.

I licked over the tip, savoring his precum, before I glided my wet lips back down to breathe him in. I swallowed around him and hummed.

"Fuck," he drew out roughly.

His size was made for me. *Perfect.* Enough I could choke on it. Saliva dribbled into his pubes as I listened to Torch pant and curse. I swallowed again before licking all the way back up to the tip.

He lifted a hand from fisting the sheets and pressed fingers under my chin so I had to sit back on my calves. His thumb rested on my bottom lip and swiped back and forth as he gazed at my mouth.

"Don't wanna lose myself in here."

I nodded, understanding that he wanted to come while we had sex.

Leaning over, I grabbed a condom out of the drawer and ripped it open to roll over him while he watched.

"Soon, we'll both get tested. I'd like to have you bare in me. Is that okay?" I looked up just as he cupped my cheeks and drew me close, where we were inches away.

"You want me bare?"

"Yes," I breathed. I loved the thought of his cum dripping out of me, and I had a feeling he liked the idea of it as well with how wild his eyes seemed.

He shifted his hands. One pressed gently around my throat so he could make sure he still had my eyes while he used the other to cup my pussy and press two fingers inside me, causing me to gasp in pleasure.

"Bare in you?"

"Yes, Chase. I want to have your cum warming me inside."

His upper lip rose as a deep sound rolled out of him before he pulled my mouth down to his. He picked me up and planted me on his lap again as our kiss carried on and on. It was all nips, tongue, licks that drove me into a lust-filled craze.

Sucking on his tongue, I licked around it and went to my knees and scooted closer. I moved my hand between us to grip his hard cock, holding it out for me.

One of his arms wrapped around my back while the other stayed at the front so he could push me back a little with his hand over my breast to break the kiss. He looked down between us as I slowly sank onto him.

He was big and opened me up just nicely.

"Wrenley. Fuck. *My* Wrenley." He lifted his head and stared at me, almost in awe.

He took my breath away.

When I bottomed out and rocked over him, he let out another dirty noise and drew my mouth to his once again. I moaned into it when he teased my clit as I lifted and sank back down. Over and over.

The noises we made, the slapping of my body down on his, filled the room and made this moment that much more indecent. I wanted to squeeze him to me, become one. My heart jackhammered under my ribs, and I was surprised they didn't rattle.

He gripped my ass, helping me ride him faster.

I tore my mouth away and moaned loudly. "Chase. God, yes."

He licked and sucked at my neck, my shoulder, and back up to my ear.

Hearing his heavy breaths and the little sounds of desire while he toyed with my clit was enough to force my orgasm out. My stomach tingled. My pussy pulsed.

"Torch," I whimpered, losing my rhythm, but he was there helping me.

"Wrenley. My Wrenley. *My* pretty addiction." He groaned low, and I ate it down with a kiss as I helped him ride out the last of it.

His arms curled around my waist to hold me to him. I wrapped him up with mine around his shoulders, kissing his neck and face, before I settled and rested my cheek down on him.

A small satisfied mewl left me when he twitched inside.

"Wrenley..." was all he said, and it sounded as if he wanted to say more but didn't know what.

"I liked that. A lot," I told him.

His quick burst of laughter surprised even him because he cut it off and rolled us so I lay on the bed with him hovering at my side.

I pouted at the loss of him, which his fingers traced. "Why?"

"I wanted to keep you in me longer."

His gaze flared before he closed his eyes and dropped his forehead to my shoulder.

"Torch?"

"You fill me up." He shook his head. "Never felt as good as I do when I'm with you."

Oh my God.

My insides danced at his words.

I rubbed my hand up and down his arm and admitted, "I feel the same with you, Torch."

He pulled back, nodded, and climbed out of bed. He slipped on some boxers and left the room. At least his quick departure gave me time to do a jig of happiness in bed that Torch shared his emotions with me.

This, being with the right person, made me feel like I was glowing.

He looked at me like I was a true treasure to him.

Smiling when I heard his footsteps, I glanced to the door.

When he entered, he stopped. "Do you need anything?"

I melted. "No, I'm okay."

His hands fisted. I quickly sat up, a brief flash of concern hitting me. Did he regret what we did? Had it been too soon for him? Was it too much? Did he worry about what he confessed?

"I need you to get dressed. In case...."

Oh. I'd started to panic for no reason. I took a deep breath and nodded.

He was worried if I went unclothed, we could get caught in a difficult situation while I was naked. I doubted anyone would try to come here, but I understood his concern.

"Okay. No problem." I smiled, and his shoulders relaxed. I got out of bed and found my sleep clothes again, slipping into them.

When I held out my hand, he walked to me and took it but then used it to pull me into him.

Once more, he searched my face, and a small lift to the corner of his lips graced me.

"Thank you."

I went to my toes, kissed him, and said, "Anything." I grinned, thinking back to when he'd said the same thing to me. I knew he meant it then, like I did now.

CHAPTER TWENTY-ONE

I wasn't sure what woke me. Squinting at the bedside lamp shining brightly, I noticed Torch sitting, dressed in jeans and a tee, with his elbows on his thighs at the edge of the bed, beside my hip.

Reaching over, I rested my hand on his lower back as I rubbed at my eyes. "Can't sleep?"

I hoped it wasn't because of what we'd shared or from me using his name.

He shook his head.

My stomach cramped with worry.

Sitting, I rested against the headboard. That was when I saw the knife he twirled in his left hand. "What's wrong?"

He glanced over his shoulder. "I don't know."

But something had him unsettled, and I wanted to help him relax in some way.

I kicked off the blankets, climbed around him, and got out of bed. Grabbing a sweater, I pulled it over my head and said, "We'll go see if Death and Raya are awake and check on Harley. Maybe once you see everything's okay, you can get some sleep." I picked up a hair tie and pulled my strands up into a messy bun.

He straightened his spine but stayed seated.

I held out my hand to him and smiled.

He glanced from my hand to me and then over to my window just as glass shattered. I screamed, and something heavy landed on the floor.

Torch grabbed me around the waist, lifted me off my feet, and started for the door. There was another sound in the air, and Torch stumbled. Smoke filled the room, but it didn't smell like fire.

I coughed and choked.

Torch reached the door and yanked it open. Some of the smoke blew away so I could see through watery eyes that needlelike things stuck out of Torch's shoulder.

Fear slammed into me.

Not for me but him.

"Torch," I cried.

"Death," he roared through the house.

"Get her out" was bellowed back.

I heard it then—*pop, pop, popping*, like something was going off.

My blood froze at the realization that it was a gun.

No, no, no. They're fine. We're all going to be fine.

Torch fell to his knees but drew me behind his body to sit me on the floor and lean against the wall. I struggled to keep my eyes open.

"Torch?" I muttered, blinking up at him.

His next roar hurt my chest. There was so much terror inside the sound.

My arms grew heavy, harder to move, but I tried to touch him as he crouched over me with knives in his hands.

He snarled at the movement around us.

"He's still awake?" someone said.

I blinked, but things started to blur.

"We need to go. The second team can't get to the other people in the house. They're staying back longer to distract them, giving us time to get away."

Raya and Death. They were safe at least.

Just take me. I tried to speak, but my mouth felt like it was full of cotton.

Leave him. Please. Just take me.

Torch moved in front of me, snarling and growling.

"Fuck, he nearly sliced me."

"How the fuck can he see and function? The girl only had the gas, and she's out of it."

"I don't know, but we've got to get gone with them right now."

There was another sound, a roar, and then a heated weight fell on me as I blacked out.

GROANING, I sluggishly ran a hand over my face and cringed at the sound around me. Someone was yelling, but I couldn't understand what they were saying. There was a hard throb at my temples. Bile rose, but I swallowed it down.

Torch.

I opened my eyes, ready to search for him, only to shield them with my hand from the bright light.

"She's awake," someone said.

A hand fisted my hair, and I cried out when I was pulled up to my knees. I gripped and clawed at the wrist holding me.

As my eyes adjusted, I saw everything.

Breathing heavily, I watched as six men held Torch to the ground on the other side of the warehouse.

"Don't fuckin' touch her. Don't. Touch. Her," Torch boomed.

His furious gaze had locked onto the hand holding my topknot.

"It didn't have to come to this."

That voice. That damn voice I knew too well.

Tony yanked my head back, so I had to look at him.

My stomach sank. I swallowed thickly as tears welled.

"Leave him out of it," I pleaded.

Torch grunted as he lifted off the floor a little but was forced back down.

Tony laughed. "Isn't that sweet of you. But he's staying right there. He's going to watch what we do to you, and then we'll kill you both." He shook me by my hair. Pain sliced at my skull, and I sucked in a sharp breath, but I wouldn't cry. Tony sneered and tsked at me. "I should have taken care of you a long time ago. But then you had to get *him* onto us. He scratched up my car. He threatened me. Made me look like a fool in front of my friends. But they now know the lengths I'll go to end my troubles. Don't you, boys?"

There were mumbled voices behind us. I couldn't see them with the hold Tony had on me. Not that I wanted to.

Tony laughed. "And soon, my father will see what I can do too. He didn't think I could manage getting to you, but I have. He'll see."

Tony cackled again as I met Torch's gaze and smiled softly at him.

It's going to be okay.

We'll be all right.

"The bitch isn't even listening to you." Mitch moved close to my other side. How many were behind me? And who was holding down Torch? I didn't know any of them.

Mitch pinched my cheeks and forced my head up. "Stupid little cunt thought you could run. Poor little Wrenley saw her daddy kill her mommy, and now she's just going to end up like her. Dead. But that's after we get to play again. This time you'll be awake for it all."

"Don't. Touch. Her," Torch snarled.

Mitch let go of me and faced Torch with a grin. "Don't touch her," he mimicked in a higher tone and then snorted. "What are you going to do about it?"

Tony tugged my hair hard to drag me up to stand between them. A whimper escaped, until I clamped my lips together.

"There's nothing he can do," Tony said. "So, I'll do anything I want."

His hand squeezed my breast. Mitch grabbed the other. I cursed and dug my nails into their hands as I pushed them away. Mitch laughed, jumping back when I tried to scratch him. Kicking out, I aimed and connected with Tony's shin before he shook me by my bun again. The sharp sting had the fight draining out of me.

A grunted growl started from Torch. It grew louder and louder, gaining everyone's attention. He forced his elbow back, managing to hit one of the people holding him in the throat. That man fell to his ass, coughing and spluttering. Torch took the advantage and rolled with a roar, punching, kicking, and pulling another man down on top of him, locking an arm around his neck, choking.

Screaming started, orders for him to stop, but I knew he wouldn't. He wanted to get to me. He wanted to help me.

Even when the others started punching and kicking Torch, he didn't let go of the man he held, whose face was now a bright red.

"Tony, we should leave. Take Wrenley and go," someone said from behind us.

"Yeah, man. That fucker is crazy," a new voice commented.

"He's going to kill him. Choke him out and come after us if they don't get a handle on him. We need to leave," another male voiced.

"Shut the fuck up, you pussies," Mitch ordered. "What, you're good enough to mess with an unconscious girl, but you can't handle the harder shit?"

"Tony—"

"Listen to Mitch," Tony snapped.

There were four others in Tony's group.

How were we going to get out of this?

No. I wouldn't go down that train of thought. We would

get away. I couldn't question how. I just had to believe we would. Somehow.

The man Torch held stopped struggling and slumped over him just as a gun fired.

A panicked cry left me when I thought they'd shot Torch. But it'd come from the man standing over their group, who had sent a shot into the roof. Bits of rubble drifted to the concrete floor.

"Get this fucker back over on his stomach and fucking hold him," the man ordered. "Who the hell is this guy?" he demanded from Tony but kept talking, "He didn't go down with two tranqs. He's awake earlier than anyone else would be, and now he's managed to kill one of my men."

"He's a nobody. Just someone this bitch dragged into her home."

Torch laughed then. Low and crazed.

He didn't have his club vest on, so the guy wouldn't know Torch was a part of the Diamond MC, and it was obvious Tony hadn't informed them either.

"You're a fool," I said.

Slap. Mitch cursed at me, stepping back as he dropped his arm.

I rightened my head and smiled through the burn to my cheek.

Tony glared. "I'm not the fool—"

Looking past him, I told the man, "He's not a nobody."

A ragged breath flew from my mouth when Mitch punched me in the stomach.

Noises broke from Torch. A keen, a growl—it was almost animalistic.

"Stop," the man bellowed, firing off another shot.

"When you hurt her, he goes ballistic. You've risked my men too much tonight."

"You're being paid handsomely for it," Tony grouched.

"Your money ain't shit when I lost a man. You said it'd be easy. You said it was a quick in, grab, and out. Who is this motherfucker?"

"You don't get the details—"

The man aimed the gun at Tony. "Listen, you little shit, you obviously lied when you said these two stole from you. That they were just college kids who you wanted to scare. It was fucking lucky I had the stuff to drug that damn dog and send in two groups instead of one. Tell me who this guy is."

"If you shoot me, you don't get the rest of the money. You're here just to hold him while we teach him who's in charge when it comes to this piece of ass."

"Holding him ain't fucking easy, dickhead. Who is he?"

"You don't need to—"

The roller door to the left swept up.

Torch stilled to take in whatever was about to happen when an older man walked in with two other middle-aged men who were dressed in suits.

"What is this? What's going on?" the older man asked as he slowly approached. The guys at his sides pulled their weapons free but held them down.

"Oh, Tony, what have you done?"

"Who're you?" the man with the gun asked, which he swung their way, causing the other two to aim at him in return.

"You told me I wouldn't be able to handle the situation." Tony waved his free arm around while shaking me a little with his other. "I've handled it."

"No, no, no, son. You don't know who she belongs to."

Tony scoffed. "Belongs to? That guy?" He nodded toward Torch, who was still being held down.

Tony's father cursed.

"I told you I could handle it. They don't scare me," Tony yelled. "No one knows it was me who took them. That's what I hired Bentley and his group for."

"Don't use my goddamn name," Bentley yelled, but he was ignored by father and son.

Tony's father pinched the bridge of his nose and shook his head before lifting and locking his gaze onto Tony. "You've made a big mistake, son."

Tony scowled. "I handled the situation. The one you didn't think I could."

"I told you to leave it for a reason, Tony," he snapped, then sighed and shook his head. "Why would you come here of all places? You know it's off-limits." He pulled a phone out of his pocket and started typing.

"Why are *you* here?" Tony countered, voice wavering a little.

"Hang the fuck on," Bentley said, waving his gun around, but was ignored again.

"I'm here for other reasons before I meet with someone. Now I have to get him to go elsewhere. You better hope he gets my message."

"Do your other reasons have anything to do with the meth lab in the back?" Tony asked.

His father scowled. "You know nothing, Tony. If you want to keep living the way you have, you'll keep your mouth shut and make sure your friends do too."

Two cars pulled close to the roller door.

"Fuck," the father clipped.

Tony's hand tightened in my hair, and I winced, meeting Torch's gaze.

"It's okay," I mouthed.

His jaw clenched, his nostrils flared, and he tried to get up again. I could read the fear in his eyes.

Fear for me.

Car doors opened.

Bentley yelled at Torch to keep still.

He didn't. Torch groaned, growled, and tried over and over to get out from under the other men.

"Stop moving," Bentley screamed. He kicked at Torch before he moved near his head and pressed the tip of the gun to Torch's temple.

"Don't," I screamed.

Torch stilled, falling back down to lie flat on the ground.

"What the hell is going on, Chester?"

Ice filled my veins as I slowly turned to see Officer Plank with ten other men standing inside the entrance.

CHAPTER TWENTY-TWO

TORCH

My blood boiled. I had to get to her. I had to protect her. I had to hunt, hurt, and kill all who touched her. All who thought they could look at her. All who wanted her harmed in any type of way.

Kill.

Kill.

Kill.

Even with a gun pressed to my head, I wanted to fight to get to her.

But then I heard her screamed word.

It broke through the fog, and I slumped to the ground. Stilling.

She was scared for me.

I didn't want to worry her. I didn't want her to live with the sight of me getting my brains splattered over the floor.

I would stay still and pretend to be calm until I could get the upper hand.

Until I could get free and burn them all.

"Plank, you didn't get my text?" Chester asked. He looked a little twitchy with fear by the cop and his friends arriving.

They're not your problem, Chester.

I would be.

When he'd arrived, he didn't tell his son to let my Wrenley go. He didn't stop anyone. He was going to comply with whatever they'd planned.

Plank snorted. "Looks like your son has bigger balls than you, Chester. You ran to me to fix your problem, and he took matters into his own hands. Too bad he's a damn idiot for bringing his trouble here and keeping this one alive." He threw an arm my way.

"Who is this guy?" Bentley demanded.

Plank sneered before he bit out, "Who are you first?"

"I hired him to grab them from the house." The stupid fucker Tony sounded proud. "And I'm not an idiot for planning all this in a warehouse that belongs to the family. Besides, Dad was shitting himself when he found out where she was and who she was hanging with. Like she couldn't be touched." Tony laughed. "Obviously she can."

He shouldn't be so cocky. He should be scared.

I'd make him fear for his life before I tortured him for touching her.

"I organized all this," Tony shouted.

Plank took a step closer. "Yeah? You want a medal or something? You don't even know you've gone and fucked up." He faced Bentley. "Were there more at the house? Did you get them as well?"

"We couldn't in the time we had to get these two away."

Plank shook his head, jaw grinding. "Fucking hell, they could already be here or on the way."

Chester took a step toward Plank. "Fix this, Plank. Get my son and his friends out of here and make sure no one knows."

Plank grinned. "Sign over your warehouses to me, and I'll see what I can do."

Chester looked like a gaping fish out of water. "No. I can't. I...."

Plank sighed, shaking his head. He turned back to the door and started walking. "Then you're on your own." He stopped and gave Bentley his attention. "My advice, kill that one quickly. He's a feral fucker with a hard-on for that girl. If he gets loose, you'll all die."

"No, please, leave him alone. Please," my Wrenley cried out.

"Plank, wait. You can't walk away from this. It's your business in the back. Your trade will suffer. I own all the warehouses you deal out of. If you don't help, I'll close them all down, and you'll have nowhere to go."

Chester was a weak man trying to protect his ungrateful idiot son. He trembled from his threat to Plank.

The cop stopped. His men watched him, waiting for a command.

He faced Chester. "I can get rid of you and your family myself and make sure you've signed over all properties to me before your last breath. But I doubt we have fucking time to hash this out. Your moron of a son kidnapped a man from the Diamond MC. They're a thorn in my goddamn side but smart motherfuckers. Means they'll probably be here any moment. We need to get the fuck out, and *then* we'll work out what type of threat you want to give me, Chester."

"The Diamond MC?" Bentley spluttered. He swung the gun at Tony. "You little fucking shit. You should have told me who he was."

Mitch took a step back while Tony forced Wrenley in front of him.

"I didn't know—"

"Bullshit," Plank said. "He would have known. His father would have told him."

"I didn't," Chester yelled, moving toward Tony.

"Stop," Bentley barked.

Plank hoped they killed one another, along with Wrenley and me. His smug smile was enough of a sign.

"We all need to get out," Plank said and then waved a hand my way. "Kill him first. The girl we can use to get the others off our—"

Fire licked at my skin from the inside.

It spun me into action.

A roar left my lips as I pushed up again. Muscles straining, body aching.

I would get to her. I would save her.

Something hit me in the side of the head. I shook it off.

Guns fired before pain slammed into my arm.

Screams.

Wrenley's.

I had to help her. I had to get to her.

Yelling.

There were too many voices.

I got to my knees. Felt wetness on my hand but ignored it.

Eyes trained on Wrenley, I focused on her moving lips. Terror was clear in her gaze.

For me.

Thump.

Thump.

Thump.

She'd gotten my heart beating again. For her. Only her.

She would be safe.

I'd kill them all for her.

Kill.

Kill.

Kill.

I grinned, dragging one man around and snapping his neck.

Another shot and more pain swept over my shoulder.

Laughing, I palmed another face and squeezed while I wrapped my other hand around his neck, taking his life from him.

All of them would die.

She would be safe.

And even if she didn't love me in the end, with all their blood on my hands, it didn't matter.

All that did was that she was safe.

"Torch, please. Torch." Her high-pitched voice drew my attention to her. She struggled against Tony, who said something to her, but she ignored it. Gaze fixed on me, she said pleadingly, "You're hurting. Please stop. I'll be okay."

Hurting?

Me?

I cocked my head but then felt something pressed to my temple.

Slowly, I twisted my head to Bentley and grinned.

CHAPTER TWENTY-THREE

WRENLEY

He was gone. Lost in his need to hurt everyone around us, bar me. All Torch wanted was to kill to protect me. I had to reach him. I had to help him.

"Move, bitch," Tony clipped and shoved me into Mitch, who roughly took hold of my upper arm. Tony ordered, "You take her. Wait for me to get my dad, and then we're getting out of here." He took off to where Plank and Chester took time to have words, knowing Torch, Bentley's guys, and Plank's men would keep one another busy and distracted.

I had to stall. I wouldn't leave without Torch.

What could I do?

I tugged my arm from Mitch's grip while he watched Torch lose it and laughed when Bentley pressed the gun to his head. But then Torch dropped, kicked out, and swept

Bentley off his feet before diving down on him. He whispered something in Bentley's ear that had the man frozen.

Torch would have all their lives.

And he deserved them too. They'd kidnapped us. They'd hurt him. They would have stood by and watched while Tony violated me.

Torch would have their blood.

Watching the man I loved, I realized Torch was on a different level than any other man here.

And he was all mine.

Slap.

Ignoring the sting, I blinked up at Mitch as he got in my face. "What're you smiling at?"

"That you all are nothing but boys trying to play in a real man's world."

His hands wound around my throat but didn't tighten, just held me close. He breathed heavily down on me while the other friends either encouraged him to hurt me or begged to leave. Their chances of escape would soon be gone once the other men turned their attention on everyone else in the room besides one another and Torch. Some finally knew it was a mistake to come here—to take on Torch—and they wanted to run with their tails tucked between their legs.

"You think that psycho is a real man?" His grip on my neck tightened. "I just wish we had time for him to watch us fuck you again, all take turns, because that'd send him over the edge. He'd probably kill himself knowing he couldn't help you. That'd be poetic."

I scratched and pulled at his hands, and when that didn't work, I went for his face. Red painted his cheeks after I'd clawed at his skin.

He hissed out an order, and hands grabbed my arms, stopping my fight by pinning them back. I tried to kick to wiggle free, but my legs were held down, feet to the floor, with hands around my ankles while Mitch applied pressure to my neck.

My lungs ached. I needed to breathe. I wouldn't die like this.

Not when I finally had happiness.

Rapid gunfire went up around the room.

"Don't fuckin' move" was boomed.

My heart leaped.

Help had arrived.

The hold on my arms and legs disappeared. Mitch let go and shoved me hard. I stumbled back and fell on my butt while trying to breathe as I searched for Torch. He stood on the other side with bodies all around him. Blood coated his skin, his clothes.

I gasped for air, had to get my lungs working, my voice, so I could call for him.

"You have just interrupted a police investigation," Plank called angrily.

"Don't fuckin' try and pull that shit," Country snarled. "We have video proof—"

Plank ran.

He turned around and bolted our way while his men lifted their guns and fired at Torch's brothers.

I went to get up and run for Torch, who had started my way, but I was suddenly grabbed around the waist and hurled up.

"They won't hurt me if I have you," Mitch said as Tony rushed over with his father.

"Give her to me," Tony ordered.

"No. Let's just fucking go," Mitch said, backing up.

With my heart in my throat, I tried to drop all my weight so he couldn't take me. Tony stepped up, punched me, and picked up my legs.

"No," I screamed, kicking at him when I got one free.

"Fucking stop." He dropped my legs and grabbed my neck, squeezing, while Mitch had my arms pinned back. "I'll kill you right here, right now. Just do as I fucking say for once."

I caught his father's wide gaze, but he did nothing, said nothing. Just looked away.

There was shouting, more gunfire, grunts, curses, but all I wanted was to see if Torch was okay.

I needed to get to him.

I wouldn't be taken away from him.

Fuck you, Tony. Fuck you all. I'll fight back and get to Torch.

Tony released my neck and bent to pick up my legs. I kicked out and got him in the face hard enough to knock him onto his ass. His father went to help his cursing son while Mitch pushed me to the ground and kicked me in the head, the stomach.

I tried to reach out, trip him up, push him down, but he dodged my hands and kept kicking.

There was a roar, and then Mitch was tackled to the ground. Torch sat on him, punching Mitch over and over until there was nothing but a bloody mess behind where his face had once been.

"Torch," I called.

He stilled for a beat, stood, walked over to a wall, and

picked up a canister. Gas in hand, he brought it back to a barely breathing Mitch and poured it over him.

"Stop it, you fucking freak," Tony yelled.

"Tony," Chester scolded. "Let's just go." His other friends had already bolted when Torch had taken Mitch to the ground.

"Torch?" I tried again, but he wasn't hearing me.

Mitch groaned, shaking his head as Torch pulled a lighter from his pocket, flicked the flame to life, and dropped it.

Whoosh.

Wide-eyed, my stomach churned at the sounds Mitch made. He rolled side to side, and the flames died to nothing, but I could smell the damage it'd done. It was like the room had filled with scents of raw, foul meat and burned plastic. His clothes were stuck to him now. His skin was red, oozing, and charred.

He lay still but breathing, staring up at the ceiling as tears mixed with blood on his barely distinguishable face.

He'd hurt people.

He'd raped women.

He deserved this pain.

Torch had been beaten and shot.

They had tried to kill us.

Which was why I had no pity or remorse over Torch's actions.

With a slight whimper, I gripped my aching stomach and sat up, leaning against a wall to see that Tony and Chester had started moving away slowly.

Torch turned to them, and they literally squawked.

Despite the pain in my face, throat, and stomach, I smiled at the fear in Tony's eyes.

"You looked at her. *You touched her.* You hurt her, was gonna kill her."

"Now, wait here," Chester started.

"No!" Torch roared. "You stood back and did nothing."

Saint was suddenly at Torch's back with Wreck and Quake. They didn't move to stop their brother. They knew, as I'd already guessed, that Torch needed to do what he had to so it didn't haunt him in the future.

Tony cried, "Please, I didn't want to, but Mitch forced my hand."

A sinister grin appeared on Torch before he snarled, "Coward." He gazed with a murderous gleam down at Tony. "I'll enjoy carvin' you up before I take your life."

Tony looked at me and yelled, "This is the type of man you want?"

"Yes," I answered straightaway, a little croaky from the soreness. There wasn't any doubt about who I wanted at my side for the rest of my life.

Tony sneered. "You deserve each other."

Chester and I saw the gun on the floor at the same time.

We both dove and struggled to get a hold of it. The men around us shouted, swore, and ordered him to stop, but he wouldn't, and in a flurry of panic, Chester gripped my finger and yanked it back. The pain had me releasing my hold for a second, but that was all he needed. He swung around and fired. It echoed through the room, and then someone grunted. Chester went to shoot again, but there was only a click.

"Fuck me," Saint barked. "Kylo's gonna kill me for

gettin' shot again. No one tell him. Quake, give me your pants."

"Saint," Wreck growled out.

"Shit. Okay." He stormed over to Chester, though he limped a little. The old man sniffled and waved his hands out in front of him. Saint slapped them away and picked Chester up by the front of his suit. "I'll take this trash to the car."

"Wait, no. Leave my dad alone."

"Tony, don't worry about me," he called before looking to Saint and begging, "Please, just leave my son alone."

"Didn't you hear what your son did? He's gonna get what's comin' to him, and you're gonna shut up about it, or you'll die too." Saint walked off with a squirming Chester, who still begged for his monster of a son.

"Let me take him to the compound, brother," Wreck said, laying a hand on Torch's shoulder. "We can finish things there."

"Harley?" Torch demanded.

"He's fine," Death reassured him when he approached. I let out a breath of relief.

"Plank?" Torch asked as he glared down at Tony, but with a slight smile that told me he was probably imagining all the ways he would deal with the demon of my past.

"A group of the brothers are after him. He got out through a passage that wasn't on the blueprints."

Torch's grin vanished as he clenched his jaw and grunted.

"We'll get him," Quake said. "But he knows he can't go to the police. He knows what we recorded here this night. He's screwed, brother, and he'll fuck up again. We'll nab him when he does."

They'd recorded something?

"Take him," Torch ordered, then placed all his attention on me.

Wreck and Quake didn't listen, though. They stayed where they were. I suspected they were worried about their brother.

"Brother, you need to see Lucas, get patched up."

"Later," he told Wreck.

"But—"

"Later," he clipped as he crouched in front of me. He was covered in blood from his wounds and the men he'd killed. Bruises, cuts, and marks marred his skin. He slowly reached out to me but saw the stains on his hands and pulled back.

Shaking my head, I got to my knees and ignored my aches and pains to curl into Torch, with my arms wrapping around his neck. "Torch," I mewled, a sob caught in my throat.

We were alive.

We could heal together from this.

It might not be over with Plank still out there, but Tony and the rest of them would be dealt with. They'd never harm me or anyone else again.

We were safe.

"My Wrenley," he uttered into my neck, following up with a press of his lips. His body shook, but he held on to me in a warm, comforting grip.

"I'm safe. I'm okay. You did it, Torch. You saved me. Nothing else matters. We're here, alive, and together."

I felt him nod against my shoulder as I ran my hands down his back. He shuddered.

Pulling away, I took his hands in mine. "Come on. Let's go to the compound and get you looked at."

His brows pinched, and he ordered, "You too."

I smiled and finally relaxed, knowing we really would be okay. "I will."

"Kid." Death stopped next to us, and I was on my feet, wincing from the aches but hugging him still. "Christ," he said into my hair. "Your sister's fine. She's good. Just wants you back."

"Okay," I said, sniffing, clearing my throat only to cringe again.

It would heal. We would all heal.

And at least we were safe.

Hands at my waist gently pulled me from Death and into a hard chest.

Death's jaw clenched from locking his emotions in, but then he grinned at the man behind me. "Fuck, brother. Thanks for protecting her."

"Always," Torch replied.

"Now, can we get this motherfucker locked up in the basement and patch our brother up?" Quake asked, kicking a muttering and crying Tony, who'd curled up into a ball as he stared at Mitch. "I suppose we'll have to take that one too."

"Get Chaos to have a good chat with him on the way to the hospital," Death ordered. Quake ducked off to speak to the other brother.

In the distance, we heard Gun yell, "You were fuckin' shot!"

"Lover, I'm all right. It's just a little scrape. Wait... what are you doin'?"

"Callin' your mother." Gun stalked out of the warehouse with his phone in hand.

Saint quickly limped after him, saying, "Boo bear, don't you fuckin' dare."

A laugh escaped me, and I turned into Torch, smiling. I hugged him close as Wreck walked a dazed Tony from the warehouse.

CHAPTER TWENTY-FOUR

TORCH

At the compound, I sat on the bed in Lucas's treatment room so he could patch me up. He'd started on the bump I had to the head, then the shot to the shoulder and arm. But all that was after I told him to check Wrenley over first while I'd stood close, watching everything in case she needed me. She had argued it was important I went first... until I refused to get treated before her. She'd eventually conceded with a sigh.

Now, while Lucas fixed me up, Wrenley snuggled into me on the other side Lucas worked on, content to just hold me.

She didn't care I had blood on me. She didn't care I'd killed, tortured, or that I would again.

All she worried about was me.

My gut flip-flopped, and my chest filled with the lightness only she could put there.

My obsession was pure sunshine, warming and lighting up my dark and cold days more than anyone had before. More than the days I'd shared with my brothers.

Wrenley's presence was enough to bring my focus out of the darkness anytime she was close or when I thought of her.

I love her, I thought as she pulled her head back and smiled up at me.

No. It was more than love. I'd never felt this before.

But she'd always been my obsession, my addiction. *Mine.*

A knock sounded, and Lucas called out, "Come in."

Country, Death, State, Wreck, and Tech entered.

"Lucas, can you take Wrenley down to see Raya? She's climbin' the walls, kid. Needs to have her eyes on you."

"Of course," Wrenley told him, straightening.

"I've just finished anyway," Lucas said. "You're lucky they were minor, Torch, or you would be in a sling and not just have patches over the stitches."

I nodded. "Thanks, Lucas." I was lucky, and not just for having my life, but for Wrenley being with me.

Being mine.

She gave me a quick, shy brush of her lips against mine before she went with Lucas, closing the door after her.

Coldness seeped in as soon as she was out of sight, making me clench my jaw.

She was safe here.

The threat was minimal now.

I'd gotten to them. I'd held their blood in my hands, and soon I would have more when I went to the basement.

Wrenley, my sweet, soft, and gentle obsession, had wanted me to get looked at first before I had fun torturing Tony.

I tipped my chin up at Country and waited.

"Mitch promised he'd keep his mouth shut about what happened while he's gettin' looked at in the hospital before being transferred to jail after admitting to the authorities he was involved in sick shit. As soon as we're done with Tony, he'll meet his father and Mitch behind bars. Then we'll hunt the other friends down. After we teach them a lesson and hear their involvement, we'll decide if they go to Jones or not. With the mic that was attached to Wrenley's sweater, we got enough to put them away for decades. Funny enough, the feed got cut off before we arrived, so when we hand it over to Jones, they won't hear us."

A while ago, I'd planted devices on Wrenley's coats, sweaters, and cardigans—things she would wear outside. I only activated it when I picked her up to carry her out of her room.

I put them on her items in case I failed protecting her.

She's safe. She's breathing, smiling, and happy.

It was lucky they'd been stupid enough to take me with her.

If it'd been just her.... No. We would have found her in time, even when the device we had on her, which also tracked, had dropped its signal for about an hour. It was what caused the delay in the brothers getting to us. Something that Tech promised to investigate and get fixed.

We'd informed Jones about everything. He was going to make sure nothing would blow back on me or Wrenley.

The official line was that Plank had gone rogue with Chester—his partner in his illegal activities—and Wrenley had accidently found out about them through Tony and Mitch, who were also involved. It was why they'd kidnapped her to shut her up. And of course, I got dragged into the situation since I'd been with my Wrenley when it happened.

"The father's willin' to give Jones all the information he has on Plank."

Unease slid into my system.

"For what?"

"We can't kill his son."

"No," I snarled, jumping down from the table. "His life is mine to take. He hurt her. He'll die for touchin' her. For lookin' at her. For violatin' her." I fisted my hands at my side.

Kill.

Kill.

Kill.

Country took a step forward. "You can still have your time with him, brother. I'd never take that away. He *will* feel pain. He'll know he did wrong. He'll suffer for a fuckin' long time with the torture you'll inflict. But Chester can give us the names of who Plank works with. If we have them, we know who to take down. Our lives will be a hell of a lot easier without these toxic motherfuckers breathin' down our necks and creatin' drugs for the public in *our* own damn town."

I used my palm to hit, then rub at my temple.

He'll live.

He uses her and now they want him to live his life like what he did doesn't matter.

It did, though.

"I can't," I bit out.

His blood would coat my hands like the others who'd hurt her, touched her.

"Brother, know this sucks. We fuckin' *hate* that we have to make this happen. I know the need for vengeance. I got it, and it ain't goddamn fair we're askin' this from you, but he'll pay for what he did. You'll have your time with him. You'll get to make him hurt, and we can make sure he suffers every damn day behind bars. But we need him still breathin'," Death said. "For our future. For our women and men. For the club. And hell, for the people on the streets buyin' their product. The more we can shut shit down, the more we make everyone safer."

My gaze locked onto him before I closed my eyes and rolled my head back, tapping my fists into my thighs.

Fuck.

Fuck.

Fuck.

For Wrenley.

For our future.

"Fine," I clipped and stormed from the room. Blaze stood down the hall, and when I got close, he gripped the back of my neck, stopping me.

In a low tone, he told me, "I don't agree with them, and I know you don't either. You have your fun with him, but if you want him gone, I can make it happen. I know people on the inside. We'll get the information from his father. Make them think everything is fine, and then I'll make the order. You just tell me when."

Slowly, a grin pulled at my lips. He understood. I knew my brothers did, too, but they were looking at the whole picture. They wanted to take care of everyone, where

Wrenley was my main priority. Blaze understood the hunger for that motherfucker's life. Yeah, the club had people on the inside, too, but no one who would take a man's life. That would add to their sentence.

"What's going on?" Country asked.

"Nothin'," Blaze said, releasing his hold on me.

"Torch?" Death called.

"Blaze was just tellin' me he got me a new canister for my blowtorch, and I'm ready to use it on that fucker." With that lie, I made my way down into the basement.

I wanted this cunt to suffer, but I also wanted to get this done so I could get back to Wrenley. We needed a shower and some damn peaceful sleep.

Opening the door, I snorted when I saw the puddle under Tony's chair as Saint and Gun moved away from him.

"And here is the man of the hour now, ready to play with his tools," Saint said with a chuckle.

Tony started screaming and pleading. This was going to be good.

WRENLEY

FILTH AND BLOOD still covered me as I made my way downstairs, except for my hands, which Torch and I washed in Lucas's treatment room. But Raya didn't care as she pulled me into a tight hug. My sore body complained a bit, but I wouldn't weaken my hold on her. It was good to know she was safe and uninjured.

"I was so scared," she confessed.

"Me too," I admitted, then added, "But I knew the men would have things sorted."

She pulled back, nodding as she wiped at the tears that escaped my eyes before starting on her own with a slight laugh. "Tell me what happened. When Leland and I got to your room...." Fresh tears filled her eyes.

I took her hand in both of mine. "I'm fine."

She rolled her eyes and brushed fingers over my neck.

I gave her a thin-lipped smile. "Okay, I'm sore, but on the inside, I'm fine. Torch was there."

A throat cleared, and we looked at Courtney, State's wife, who said, "I'm sorry, but can we get a hug, and then we'll sit and talk?"

Courtney wasn't alone. Henri, Eve, and a few other women who belonged to members of the club were waiting to support me. I bit down on my bottom lip as it trembled from the onslaught of affection I felt for these people.

Nodding, I sniffed and opened my arms.

By the time we went over to the table, Lucas, West, and his husband, Adrick, had come from the kitchen with trays of food and drinks. Some of the women had left, after telling me they were glad I was safe, to get to work or back to their children, since it was early morning.

West gave my shoulder a gentle squeeze as he set a coffee down in front of me. "I'm glad you're safe, Wrenley."

"*Da*, it is good, or else Torch would be still running rampant," Adrick said.

"Adrick," West scolded as he walked around the table to where he sat. Adrick pulled West down onto his lap.

"It's okay," I told West. I knew exactly what Adrick meant. Torch would still be hunting and killing if anything had happened to me. It was why I had to make sure I kept myself safe for his sake, too, while I also protected him as much as I could.

Raya gently bumped her shoulder into mine. "I know I asked you to tell me what happened, but if you don't want to talk about it, I understand."

Smiling tiredly, I said, "I'm okay. I'll tell you, but first, while I eat something, can you tell me how you and Death got out of trouble?"

She nodded, and as I picked at a blueberry muffin and drank some of my coffee, Raya explained, "Leland woke to a noise, and I was forced awake when he rolled us to the floor just as our door was smashed in and they started shooting. Leland pulled the mattress over us, grabbed his gun, and returned fire. He yelled to Torch to get you out, and then he told me to crawl toward the en suite, and as soon as we were in, we shut and locked it. We got into the bath, which was what protected us when they started shooting at the room. It seemed like it was going on forever. After a while, they tried to kick the door down. Then they just left."

Wiping at my mouth, I nodded. "They were on a timeline, but when the team on you and Death couldn't get to you, they switched to distracting to delay you so no one could follow us right away," I said before telling the table my side of the details.

"Um," West said, "are you sure you're okay?"

"Yes. Lucas checked me over. Other than a few cuts and

bruises, I'll be fine. It was Torch who got shot. But apparently, they were minor." I shrugged. "I don't know. It looked bad to me." My stomach churned.

"No, ah, that's not what I mean when I asked. Wrenley, what you saw is a lot to take in and deal with."

My mind flashed to all the killing and the scent of burning flesh.

"Maybe I'm still numb. Maybe it's after seeing our dad kill our mom, but as of right now, what I saw doesn't bother me. I wanted to be safe. I wanted Torch and the brothers to be safe. No one other than the men who hurt us were either killed or harmed. I can't see anything wrong with that." With another shrug, I added, "It might sound terrible to be so flippant about seeing what I did, but that's just where I'm at." I took a sip of the coffee. "I don't want any of you to worry about me. I promise I won't bottle anything up. I'll seek help if I need it. I'm not even sure I'll have nightmares over this because Torch has even protected me from my previous ones since he's been with me at night. He's protected me inside and out." I smiled softly, realizing that it was all true. He was my honest-to-God knight in leather.

"Well," Eve started, "I believe you're going to be just fine. You *and* Torch. But if there's a time that you're not fine, I'm sure you know that all of us are here for you. Even if you just want to share what size cock—"

"No!" I shouted, my face burning.

Some laughed around me. Raya groaned and scrubbed a hand over her face.

"I would also prefer if you kept that information to yourself," Adrick said.

"I want to know," Henri piped up. "He is hot like a lot of them in this club."

When I caught West nodding, I laughed as Adrick looked at him with a glare.

West patted Adrick's cheek. "None of them are as good-looking as you, though."

He huffed and wound a hand around West's throat to drag him down into a kiss, which I turned away from, unlike Henri, who openly gaped.

"You two could be porn stars," Henri announced.

Adrick glowered. "I am sure you have said this before, but still I will answer again—no one but me sees my West naked."

Henri gave him two thumbs-up. "*Oui*, you scary ex-mafia man."

"I am surprised you have lived this long, Frenchman."

Henri nodded. "I am also surprised by my supreme skills of living, Russian man."

I loved this. After everything that happened, this was what I needed. But I could also use a shower and some sleep.

"Is there somewhere I could take a shower and have a nap?"

"Torch's room," a prospect at the bar called. He was one of the younger guys who was trying to get patched in to the club.

"Sorry?" I asked.

"Torch'll want you in his room," he said, coming around the counter. "I can show you." He suddenly stopped. "Actually, Lucas can show you. I ain't walkin' alone with you in case Torch sees a problem with it."

"And I can?" Lucas asked.

"You got Wreck. Torch would prefer that, or I could get one of the club girls to show you. They're in their main room."

"And I suppose they'd know where his room is," I snapped, then slapped a hand over my mouth.

The guy blanched as he cursed.

"Sorry," I said quickly. "I'm tired and dirty and sore."

"*Chéri*, the possessiveness from you is cute. You show those women who Torch belongs to."

Groaning, I shook my head. "That's usually not me." I turned to the prospect again. "I'm really sorry."

He waved it off. "All good."

Lucas stood. "Come on, Wren. I can show you."

I gave Raya another quick hug and told the table, "I'll be back down later."

"Take your time," Courtney said.

With a smile, I nodded and walked with Lucas upstairs, already looking forward to the much-needed shower and rest since it seemed the pain medication Lucas gave me earlier had started working.

CHAPTER TWENTY-FIVE

TORCH

She was asleep in my bed. My body settled as soon as I saw her under my covers. It'd been another story when I hadn't found her downstairs. My damn heart had wanted to claw its way out to search for her. At first, people in the common room had been too shocked from the sight of me covered in blood to answer when I'd asked where she was. Finally, it was Adrick who'd told me.

Drawing her scent in around my space calmed me some more. I locked my door and went for a shower in the adjoining bathroom. I wouldn't climb into bed and hold her until I was clean.

It was fortunate Lucas had put waterproof patches over the gunshot wounds since I scrubbed myself before getting back out to dry. Walking naked into the room, I slipped under the blankets and pulled her bare body close with my good arm. I adjusted her limbs until she had her head on my chest, a leg over one of mine, and her arm across my stomach. A little sleepy sigh slipped from her sweet lips. After curling her as close as possible, I stared up at the ceiling.

My aching body screamed for sleep, but my mind was wired.

I'd dealt with Tony by burning the bottom of his feet, taking each tip of his fingers slowly, and ruining his sight for looking at her by dripping acid into his eyes that Death and Country held open. I then used my fists to get my message across.

He shouldn't have touched or tormented her.

Once I was done having my fun, Tech gave us all an update on how Plank had fucking escaped. That he'd somehow managed to dodge our attempts at getting to him since. He hadn't even been back to his house, but we had a lot of brothers out searching. Tech and Blaze were also doing their thing with their computers.

The prick was running scared, which was good, but I also wanted him caught so we could somehow end all this sooner.

However, we'd at least gained vital information from Tony's father.

Plank had two partners.

The chief of police, William Elsher, and a detective called Marco Brown. They were the higher-ups in their illegal trade, and then there were about ten little players who helped make and deal the drugs.

No doubt Plank would have called his partners and told them what happened. Told them that the Diamond MC was involved.

We still had a way to go, but Country believed that with Jones's help, we'd get them and soon.

Plank and his friends had better play it safe and stay away from our families. If they didn't, Country had given the go-ahead to end them.

Finally.

Plank, the chief, and Marco would soon see what the Diamond MC could do to their lives.

At least we had names and knew who to watch.

In a way, I hoped they decided to fuck with us so *I* could end them all.

Until they did, we'd gather more information to pass on to Jones so he could take them down in a legal way, and they'd be locked away for a long time. But Country swore we'd get our justice with Plank before that happened.

Like I had with Tony.

Like I would with his fucking friends as soon as we brought them in. For now, they could go about their days like nothing happened, but I knew that on the inside, they'd be pissing themselves just thinking about me hunting them down.

All that mattered was that my obsession was safe.

And as long as I was alive, I would continue to do everything in my power to make sure she stayed that way.

Looking down, I watched my fingers as I ran them over her bare arm.

My gut tightened from the bruises marring her beautiful skin.

The worst of them were around her neck.

Tony and Mitch had put their hands there.

Fury swept through me again.

They'd gotten off easy. They should have suffered some more.

A soft mewl-like sound slipped from Wrenley's lips, distracting me as she rubbed her warm, soft body into me.

My Wrenley.

She was beautiful.

I didn't know if she'd guessed already, but she wasn't getting rid of me.

She'd let me in her body—her heart and pussy. She cared for me. She wasn't ever getting rid of me now.

I also wanted to keep sleeping beside her, wherever that would be while their house got fixed.

This relationship might not have been like a regular one. It was fast by most standards. But I wouldn't change it for anything.

She'd captured me wholly the night I'd heard her screams, and I knew right then I was a goner for her.

Picking up a strand of her curly blonde hair, I held it between my fingers and marveled at the silkiness.

She was mine.

Forever.

I had to tell her.

Soon.

I WOKE to a soft hand wandering up from my stomach to my chest. For a split second, I'd tensed, but as soon as I knew whose hand it was, I relaxed again and placed mine on Wrenley's over my heart.

Turning my head, I opened my eyes to see she already had her pretty blues on me. Chin tipped up with a cute, sleepy, soft look on her face that had my cock waking up.

She was safe and here with me.

My gaze caught on the bruises around her neck.

I ground my teeth together, upper lip flicking up over their marks on *my* property.

Her hand slipped out from under mine and cupped my cheek. "I'm okay," she whispered. "You saved me."

"They touched you. Marked you."

"And you've made sure they know how wrong they were to do that."

I did. I still would with his other friends.

Her fingers gently brushed over the bump on my head. "I don't like that you got shot and beaten because of me, Chase."

"It's nothin'," I told her. And it wasn't. I'd had worse. Those spots on me pulled and pinched, but it wouldn't stop me from doing anything. My tolerance to pain had been set high after that shit in the past.

Don't think about it. Don't let it in.

"It's a lot to me," she said, eyes misty.

I swallowed my heart and shook my head before I rested half of my body gently against her and placed my forehead to hers. "Please don't cry. Don't be upset for me."

She released a watery laugh. "How can I not be? I care about you a lot, Torch."

I groaned, a part of me warmed by her words, another part pained that she was upset.

My cock jerked and fattened. I wanted in her. To connect like we had before all the shit happened.

"Wrenley. *My* Wrenley." I kissed her nose, then her closed eyes and tasted the salt of her tears. Dipping, I pecked at her lips, and she shivered, dropping a soft noise.

"Torch," she breathed.

Carefully, I pressed another kiss to her lips, drinking down her sigh before deepening it.

I liked I could do this. Take her mouth and know she wanted it from me.

Know she enjoyed my time. My body. My kisses.

She was mine.

Mine.

Mine.

Mine.

A growl rumbled from within as I rolled her onto her back and slipped between her legs.

"Torch, your arm and shoulder."

Her worry quieted when I kissed her again.

"I'm good," I told her, hooking her leg up over my hip and brushing my cock over her pussy.

I would've questioned if I was being too much, too forward with her, but she already had a hungry gaze for me as she ran her hands up and down my sides.

Reaching over, I yanked the drawer open and managed to grab a condom before it fell to the floor. Wrenley let out a sweet laugh and lifted to kiss my chest.

My gaze latched on to her bruises, and I hesitated.

She's sore, you fucking idiot.

"Don't," Wrenley said. "I want you, Chase. Please. But as long as you don't hurt yourself."

I kissed her and rolled on the rubber.

Her legs widened as I trailed my lips and tongue down her body to drink down her taste.

Fuck.

Perfect, pretty pussy that tastes like heaven.

I could spend hours playing with her, but it'd have to be next time. I ached to be inside her. My damn body vibrated with need.

After I had her squirming on my tongue and fingers, I licked all the way up but stopped to nip and suck at her nipples.

"Chase," she moaned.

The only time I liked hearing my name was from her mouth.

I gently kissed her neck, over the marks. "My pretty Wrenley." I sucked on her ear as she gripped my ass, trying to pull me down. I grinned into her shoulder, liking she was eager to have me inside.

My arm and shoulder burned in pain, but it was easy to ignore when I had such a stunning sight under me.

"Please, Torch," she begged. I lowered my hips and brushed the tip of my cock over her wet hole before pulling back. She opened her eyes to glare up at me, which had me grinning.

She ached for me too.

So, I gave it to her, entering in one quick thrust that had her arching and moaning as her nails dug into my hips. Her pussy clamped down around my cock snugly. My body hummed from the sensation of being in her. Even when there was a barrier between us, her heat and the tightness drove me fucking crazy.

She was mine. I pulled out.

Mine. I pushed back in.

All fucking mine. Over and over, I drove in and out with a snap of my hips, with a flurry of emotions and sensations. My heart wanted out and inside with hers. My pulse sped through me, pumping hard.

"Yes, Chase. Yes," she cried, fingers sliding between us to tickle her clit. It only took a few swipes of her digit, and she whimpered, calling my name as she grew even more soaked around me, tightening.

Groaning, I fucked her through it, chasing my own release yet not wanting to come so I could stay buried in her.

Same as she wanted to keep me in her tightness and warmth.

We have many more times.

I got to keep her.

She was mine until I died. I'd make sure of it.

My release slammed into me. I bucked unsteadily into her as her hands traced over my body.

Exhaustion slapped me in the damn face, and I managed to slump down on the bed, rolling to the side to dump the condom.

She rubbed into me, almost like a cat would, and kissed my shoulder and neck.

"Gonna shut my eyes for a little while," I told her after I rested on my back and pulled her close to lie on me.

There was a kiss to my chest and some soft words, but I'd already headed under.

CHAPTER TWENTY-SIX

*L*ucas sighed as he applied a new patch to Torch's shoulder and arm wound. "I know this might embarrass all of us, but as the doctor for the club, I have to say it. Please abstain from strenuous intercourse and stick to easier... um, positions?" His face was probably about as red as mine.

Torch straightened and actually seemed smug or proud with the way his chest puffed out.

Lucas rolled his eyes while I thinned my lips so I wouldn't laugh.

"Now that's out of the way and I'm all done here, it should be almost dinnertime downstairs."

As if on cue, my stomach growled, and I pressed a hand to the borrowed tee I wore. Eve had been sweet to lend me clothes while Courtney had brought some things in for Raya.

Torch suddenly jumped off the table, took my hand, and walked us toward the door.

"You need to eat. Thanks, Lucas," Torch called.

Lucas laughed. "Anytime, but not again so soon."

I pulled Torch to a stop and glanced back. "Are you coming?"

"I'll just tidy up and come down."

A throat cleared, and I saw Wreck now stood outside the room waiting to get in to his husband. Torch and I moved to the side, after Wreck gripped Torch's shoulder briefly, to let him in.

Lucas's brows bunched together. "Where's Opal?"

Wreck's gaze narrowed. "Your brother stole her so she can protect him from Gun's wrath over gettin' shot."

Lucas snorted. "It won't only be Kylo's wrath he needs to worry about. Mom and Dad should be here soon."

Oh, this is going to be entertaining, I thought as I waved to them. "See you down there."

Wreck grunted while Lucas waved back.

I smiled up at Torch and squeezed his hand before he started leading us to the common room. It was busy with brothers, some old ladies who belonged to the brothers, and bunnies. It was hard to believe Dusty had started out as one of the bunnies before Country claimed her as his woman.

We hadn't confirmed our relationship yet, but I presumed I was classed as Torch's woman.

Thinking as much had my smile growing as people greeted us when we walked by.

Torch picked a table that held Country, Dusty, Saint, who held a gibbering Opal, Gun, West, Adrick, Henri, and Blaze. Torch sat beside Blaze and pulled me down onto his lap. My face ignited, but I curled an arm around his shoulders.

"It is good to see you are well rested, *chéri*," Henri teased from where he leaned around Blaze.

"Henri," Blaze warned.

Laughing lightly, I rolled my eyes. I didn't want Blaze to think we were offended by Henri's words, so I quickly replied, "It's amazing what a few hours of sleep can do to a person."

Henri snorted. He opened his mouth to say something, but Blaze shoved a buttered roll into it. Henri glared at his man while those who'd seen it laughed. Henri bit off a piece, chewed, and continued to scowl at Blaze, who looked at Henri adoringly while he waited for Henri's tantrum.

Henri started firing off rapid French while the loving gaze didn't leave Blaze's face. His lips did twitch, though.

Torch brushed his nose against my forehead before he said, "I'll grab us some food."

Meeting his gaze, I nodded and pressed a quick kiss to his lips before I stood. When Torch left to go into the kitchen through the swinging doors, I took his seat.

Blaze grunted.

When I stared up at him, I found his attention already on me. He asked, "Good?"

I nodded, almost laughing with how he reminded me of Torch. "I am."

He tipped his chin up at me.

"Wrenley," Country called from where he sat opposite us. I turned to him while Henri pulled others into a conversation. Country grinned at me, hugging Dusty close. "There ain't enough thanks when I see my brother relaxed and happy like he is when he's at your side."

Dusty gave me a warm smile with a nod.

"I don't need thanks," I told them.

"Know you don't. But I wanted to give it anyway because it means a fuckload to me knowin' he's settled."

My heart stumbled into my ribs. I shrugged, emotions clogging my throat. I loved knowing that Torch's brothers saw a change in him when he was with me. A happy change.

Licking my suddenly dry lips, I glanced to my sister, who was down the other end of the long table, before I met Country's gaze and said, "Raya and I were each other's family when our own parents didn't care. But it's nice to have more people in our family now."

He winked and kissed Dusty's temple when she sniffed. "Sorry, pregnancy emotions."

Henri scoffed. "*Chéri*, you are emotional all the time. Do not blame my niece or nephew. By the way, I would like to remind you both that the name Henri is good, *oui*?"

"No," Country said.

"But—"

"No," Country stated with a raised brow, as if daring him to ask again.

He opened his mouth but didn't get anything out since someone else had yelled, "Zion Storey, you were shot *again*?"

Saint spun his gaze to Gun. "I thought you didn't call her?"

Gun grinned. "*I* didn't."

"That little fucker," Saint snarled low.

Loud footsteps pounded the floor, and Lucas yelled, "Wait, wait." When he appeared, he breathed heavily and nodded. "Okay. I'm here." He rolled a hand around. "Continue."

Wreck walked in a lot slower and stood at his husband's back.

Gerry and Lucy, their parents, glanced back from Lucas to Saint and glowered. "You get shot and you don't call? Next time one of us are in the hospital, we're not calling you," Lucy stated.

"Yeah," Gerry added.

Saint stood, holding out the baby. "Look, Mom, it's your granddaughter."

I hid my laugh behind my hand.

Lucy started forward. "Don't just think you can distract me from yelling at you— Oh, my little beautiful butterfly. Look at you today. You look adorable in that little outfit." She pulled Opal from Saint's arms and hugged her close while her granddaughter grinned up at her.

Saint smirked over at Lucas and scratched his forehead with his middle finger.

"Mom, focus," Lucas called, coming over with Wreck following.

Gerry clapped his hands. "Lucy, give me toots while you deal with our son."

I was a little surprised Country allowed this to go on— or Saint, who didn't seem to care he was getting scolded like a little boy in front of his brothers. Though, a lot of the brothers were trying to hold in their own mirth.

Lucy handed Opal over to Gerry and faced her son again.

"Mom, I'm okay," he told her, bringing her in for a hug.

Lucy slapped his arm but then wrapped him up in a tight hug, and we all heard her choked cry.

"Goddammit, kid. You gotta be more careful. You can't make your mom cry," Gerry barked, but I saw his own eyes had welled.

"I'll be careful," Saint told them. "Besides, if I don't, Kylo will end up killin' me anyway."

Lucy sniffed, pulled away, and smacked his arm again. "And he'd have every right to." She turned her attention to Gun. "How are you, my dear boy? I'm sorry you have to put up with our son."

Gun nodded and gave her a hug. "It's hard sometimes, Lucy."

Gerry snorted. "No take backs. He's all yours now."

I loved all this interaction. I used to wish Raya and I had it with our parents. But I hadn't wished that for a while now. If things hadn't happened as they did, I wouldn't be here. I wouldn't have found Torch, and I wouldn't give him up for anything.

A plate appeared in front of me, piled high with all sorts of food.

I quickly shifted over a little to make room for Torch. He put his plate down and sat.

Bumping my shoulder gently into him, I gave him a grin. "Thank you."

He kissed my forehead and tipped his chin up, but his gaze lingered on my neck. I knew he'd be peeved at my bruises until they faded. I couldn't change his anger over it. But I could show him I was okay. I placed my hand on his thigh, picked up a fork from the container in the middle, and dug in.

I'd made a good dint in the food when Blaze asked Torch, "You stayin' at the compound?"

Torch glanced at me.

That was when I realized the damages to the house hadn't even crossed my mind. No doubt Raya would stay at Death's. "I-I hadn't even thought about the house," I admitted aloud. "It'll need fixing."

"Brothers are there doin' it and bringin' Harley here until we figure out where we're stayin' for a few days."

Where we're *staying.*

He wanted to continue living with me.

My heart galloped.

Smiling, I shrugged. "I'm okay wherever we stay."

"Wrenley," Raya called. "There's room at Leland's."

"We could go to mine."

I turned to Torch. "You have a place?"

He nodded. "Up the road."

"A house?"

I'd thought he lived in the compound. Why hadn't I even considered Torch had his own home? And since I hadn't, I felt horrible. Maybe it was because we just hadn't spoken about it. We still had a long way to go to get to know each other.

Although, I believed we knew the important parts.

He looked unsure at my question, brows furrowing. "Yeah."

"Sorry, I... I thought you lived here."

He shook his head. "Here most of the time. That's why I bring Harley. But slept most nights in my own place."

"But you've been staying at mine. I took you away from your home to stay in mine. Why didn't you say anything sooner? Harley's probably used to his own yard, and you, your own bed. I feel terrible that you've been away from your own home for so long."

He cocked his head to the side briefly. "Harley will stay anywhere I am."

"I think what Wrenley is trying to say is that she feels guilty for keeping you at her place when you could have told her about your house, and she would have stayed there for you."

Nodding, I pointed at Dusty, who'd explained it perfectly, while I'd been too busy working through my thoughts that I'd made him confused.

"But that's Wrenley's home. Her sister is there. Her things are there."

Country chuckled. "What Torch is sayin', Wrenley, is that he didn't care where he stayed. He just wanted you comfortable with him around in your space."

I'd already gathered what he meant. He always thought of my comfort over his. Then again, maybe he really didn't care where he was.

"Okay." Turning to Torch, I added, "I'd love to stay at your place, please."

"We'll finish eating first. Then go check the house and get some of your things."

"Deal." I smiled.

He leaned in a little. "You sure you want to come to my place?"

Why wouldn't I?

It was my turn to be confused. Unless he was concerned

that I didn't want to be in a house on my own with him. If that was the case, he needn't worry about that at all.

It seemed I still had a long way to go to prove to him that I completely trusted him. That I enjoyed his one-on-one company.

"I'm looking forward to the peace," I told him, lifting to kiss his jaw.

I jolted when it sounded like something smashed into a wall.

Torch's hand rested gently on the back of my neck as a voice boomed, "Look out."

A pitter-patter of claws hitting the floor sounded right before Harley entered the room at a full speed.

Torch whistled, and Harley aimed for us. We managed to get off the seat so he wouldn't knock any of the food or a person to the ground; instead, he jumped at Torch first, then me. Whimpering, crying, and wiggling.

"Down," Torch ordered when he went to jump at me again. Harley dropped to his bottom, and I crouched to wrap my arms around his quivering body as he sniffed, chuffed, and whimpered some more.

Torch dropped to his other side, and we both covered him in hugs and pets.

The poor boy had been beside himself.

"You're such a good boy, Harley. We're okay. We're right here," I cooed.

"Sorry," Quake called. "I think he could scent you two and pulled the leash right out of my hand."

"All good, brother," Torch told him, picking up the leash. "How's the house?"

"Gettin' there with repairs." He glanced to me and then

Raya. "Doesn't smell bad or anythin', so I doubt the gas ruined stuff."

At least there was that.

"Thank you," Raya called from where she rested against Death.

"No thanks needed," he said. "A few brothers are still there, but I wanted to bring him here since he was scaring some of them."

Torch snorted. "Nothin' to be scared about."

"No, there isn't," I agreed in a sugary-sweet voice to Harley as I petted his face.

I was beyond grateful he was unharmed. I wouldn't have been able to live with myself if something had happened to him because of me and my mess. The only thing that had me twisted up inside was knowing Torch had been injured. Not that anyone could tell from the way he held himself, as if pain didn't bother him. But I'd seen his injuries, and they were a reminder that my situation had gotten him hurt.

Still, I couldn't bring myself to be the hero and walk away so nothing else in my life harmed him.

Instead, I wanted to glue myself to him.

"Can we make a move to leave soon?" I asked him quietly, wanting to be alone with him.

He lifted his gaze, studying me. "I want that."

Smiling, I felt heat blooming over my face. "Okay."

He reached out and ran a finger over one cheek. "You like the idea of being alone with me?"

He'd guessed my intentions in one. "Shush, you," I told him, and he chuckled.

"Come see the pretty puppy," I heard Lucy say.

"Lucy, do not take my daughter to that dog," Wreck warned.

"Oh poo, your dadda is such a drag."

"Poo," Opal copied.

Lucas gasped. "Was that her first word? Oh my God, my baby girl. Say Daddy and Dadda."

Torch stood, holding his hand out to me. I took it, and he pulled me close, cupping the side of my face, and while the others went on about Opal, I got lost in Torch's warm gaze.

TORCH'S PLACE was a cute two-bedroom cottage-style home that really wasn't far from the compound. We could have walked, but it had been late and dark by the time we left. Plus, we'd stopped by my house first to grab clothes and toiletries. We didn't linger there, though. A part of me hadn't wanted to fixate on the bad things I'd seen in the house since I'd be living in it again.

Torch dumped my bags in his room, which held a beautifully carved, dark wood, queen-sized bed. A big, plush dog bed sat in the corner.

"Oh, Harley's allowed to sleep in *your* room," I teased. He leaned against the doorframe, watching me.

His lips twitched. "He would have taken your attention."

My belly swooped.

"Do you mean away from you?"

He nodded.

Oh God.

That was sweet to hear and had me swooning.

I winked. "Don't worry, you have most of my attention even when he's in the room."

Speaking of the monster, Harley strutted in after being outside and trotted over to his bed, lying down with a moan. He was glad to be home.

"I like this," Torch said.

I turned back to him. "What?"

"You in my room. My home. My space."

I melted once more.

"I like being where you are," I told him.

The corner of his mouth tipped up. "Crazy."

Rolling my eyes, I shook my head. "It's not. You're an amazing man, Torch."

Color hit his cheeks, and it was his turn to shake his head.

As I walked up to him, he tipped his chin down to keep my gaze. I rested my hands on his chest and said, "You are, and I won't have you think otherwise."

"Yes, ma'am."

Widening my eyes, I laughed. "Are you sassing me?"

"Never."

I hummed. "I think you are. But that's okay. I'll allow it." He snorted, and I grinned. "Let's go brush our teeth before we climb into that amazing bed."

His eyes darkened.

"Oh no, mister. The doctor's orders were nothing too strenuous."

"You could do all the work," he suggested.

I threw my head back as an abrupt laugh left me.

His arms wrapped around me, pulling me in as he ducked his head to kiss my shoulder.

"Glad you like the bed. I made it."

I stilled, and he lifted his head.

"Made it?" I asked. "As in put the sheets and blankets on?"

"No."

"You *made* that bed? With the wood and the carvings and the pieces?"

Amusement crossed his features, a lightness settling there.

Awed, I stared at the bed, then back at him. "Torch, that's a masterpiece."

"Took me five years between work and other things."

Turning, I walked over to it and brushed a hand over the fancy engravings in the wood. "It's amazing. You should make them for others."

"Not a job for me. Just wanted this for my place. To share with someone special."

Oh my God, this man.

I went back to hug him. My throat thickened with emotions.

I love him. So much.

His hand slid up my spine to hold the back of my neck. "Shared this with no other. No one else was allowed in my space. A place I wanted to keep for myself. Until you."

"Torch," I whispered, tears dampening his tee since I had my face smooshed into his chest.

It's too soon.

I can't tell him yet.

But I wanted to.

He had to know how he made me feel.

His hand slid around to the front so he could touch some fingers under my chin and tap. He wanted me to look at him. When I lifted my gaze, his lips tightened at my tears.

"They're not bad ones," I told him.

"How?"

"They're happy ones," I said, his brows furrowed. "I sometimes cry when I'm feeling so much. Like I am now with you."

He cocked his head to the side. "What are you feelin'?"

"I worry you won't want to hear it yet."

His gaze flickered over my face. "Don't worry."

I gave him another watery laugh. "Okay."

"Wrenley." He cupped my cheeks. "My pretty obsession. You have my heart. If I could carve it out of my chest and give it to you, I would, because you *own* it."

Sniffing, I took a shaky breath and blurted, "I love you, Chase. You're the man of my dreams, and I'm addicted to you in a way that should concern you, because I'll never allow you to get rid of me."

He groaned, crushing his lips to mine in a hot, deep, and wet kiss. Against them, he confessed, "You have all of me. My heart, my love, my soul. Love you."

I rocked up to my toes to have his mouth again as my body buzzed happily.

He loves me.

He said it.

I had all of him.

All mine.

CHAPTER TWENTY-SEVEN

TORCH

There weren't enough words to describe how much I liked having Wrenley in my space. How I enjoyed hearing her as she talked to me and Harley or when I listened to her laugh or watched her as she sought my attention.

Her scent clung to the couch, the bedroom, the bathroom, everywhere.

She'd been here for two weeks. Fourteen days, and yet it felt longer. Like I'd been lucky enough to have had her for years in the house. We spent most of our time inside doing nothing much but sharing time and thoughts with each other. And Harley... he loved her as much as I did.

Actually, no. I loved her the most, over anyone, and she loved me back.

Love.

It'd been a strange word to me until I knew how it felt. I cared about my family, maybe even loved them, but it was nowhere near as much as what I felt for Wrenley.

She was my world.

It was never just the physical attraction, but something more. Something deeper.

She didn't know that her confession of addiction for me was the best gift of all time. It meant she craved and needed me as much as I did her.

She was mine. All mine.

I hadn't been back inside her yet. She'd wanted me to heal more. I could wait. She already knew I would do anything for her.

What I didn't want to do was leave her alone, though, which was why I had Gun and Saint drop in after Country had called to tell me they had one of Tony's friends in the basement and other information about Plank.

Walking from the hallway, I glanced to Wrenley sitting on the couch with them. It was weird seeing my brothers in my space but necessary since I didn't want to have to drag Wrenley to the compound so late. The brothers were going to hang until I got back. If she decided to go to bed, she'd feel safer with them there.

"What was picked?" I asked, tipping my chin to the DVDs scattered over the coffee table. Gun had asked what apps I had. When I told him none, his eyebrows had almost touched his hairline as he muttered something about bringing some movies.

When Wrenley smiled as she was, with pure happiness, it always thickened my throat.

I'm gonna do anything to protect it.

She lifted a cover to show me. "*Nobody.*"

One I'd seen. I walked to her, and as I bent, I said, "Good choice."

Her head tipped back, and she took my kiss, reaching out and slipping a hand behind my neck so I wouldn't back away until she had her fill.

I'd give her my mouth and body any time she wanted.

Any damn time.

"See you when I can," I said.

She nodded. "I know. Be safe."

Harley jumped onto the couch between us.

"Down," I ordered, and he climbed off with a huff. He knew better than getting between us, but he liked to try anyway. He wasn't too pissed as he immediately got pats from Wrenley since he sat at, and nearly on, her feet. I tipped my chin up as I straightened. "Later, brothers."

Gun flicked his hand up while Saint called, "Don't stress. We'll take good care of your woman. Might even play a bit of strip poker."

I paused on the way to the door and turned back slowly.

Saint laughed, even when Gun slapped his stomach.

"I won't let him corrupt her," Gun reassured.

Saint shifted closer to him. "Just you, my boo."

Gun's face heated while Wrenley laughed. Sighing, I shook my head and walked out of the house to my ride. I could have walked, but I wanted to be able to get back to my addiction as soon as I could.

The compound was busy when I arrived. Dagger unlocked the gates for me to pull in. I parked near the back so it was easy to get out and headed inside.

When I stepped into the common area, Boom, an older

brother, yelled, "Church room." I shot a salute to Boom, letting him know I heard, and went down the hall that'd lead me to the large room.

When I entered, I took in who already sat around the long table. Country at the head like always. Death and State on either side of him. Wreck, Blaze, Quake, and Tech. I pulled out a chair next to Quake.

"Tell me we've found Plank's whereabouts." That fucker hadn't shown at his work, his house, or anywhere that he usually frequented. Wreck had managed to tap the phone of William, the chief of police, but he hadn't gotten to the detective's phones. Marco was smart enough to practically glue one of his cells to him. From what we'd heard on William's calls, Plank wasn't answerin' his calls or contacting the chief, either, which could mean Plank's only in contact with Marco.

Country snarled, "The fucker got on a plane."

"When?" I clipped.

Tech cleared his throat. "Cameras picked him up at the airport an hour ago. He got on a flight to Melbourne, Australia."

"At least he's runnin' scared," Quake offered.

"How the fuck are we gonna get to him now?" I demanded, running my hands up and down my thighs to try and control the urge to punch something.

Country nodded to the left. "State got in contact with his old lawyer friend. He has a son in the Hawks Motorcycle Club in Melbourne, Australia. We're gonna call in a favor from them."

"I'll take the debt alone. Not our club," I said.

"No," Country stated. "The club takes it on, brother.

We ain't just doing this for you. Plank's been gunnin' for all of us. We protect all who are a part of Diamond."

I nodded once, clogged with emotions.

Damn honored to be a part of this brotherhood.

"The chapter president is waitin' on a call from us."

"Let's do it."

Tech leaned in and connected his new device to the phone, which made sure no one else could listen in. He then pressed a few buttons, and it rang.

"Talon Marcus," a deep voice said.

"Talon, this is Country, president to the Diamond MC. Did Muff explain things to you?"

"He did. I also have Dodge on the line. He's the president to the Caroline Springs chapter, and he'll be the one to deal with this corrupt officer. But what are your terms first?"

"Our club will be in debt to yours if you're willin' to take him as soon as he steps off the plane. Hold him in a secure place, and if it'd be possible, teach him a lesson, but we'll want to see it via video chat before you hand him over to an Officer Jones, who will be gettin' on a flight tomorrow."

"How can we be certain none of this shit will stick to us?" another voice asked.

"Dodge, I presume?" Country asked.

"Yeah."

"We'll make sure you're all covered and protected from any of this. We now have enough evidence to control his moves. He just managed to get by our guys at the airport."

"Talon?" Dodge asked.

"We need to protect our families, Country."

Shit, shit, shit. He didn't sound like he was going to help.

The only people we had to use in Australia were about to slip through our fingers.

"I understand that, and we can make sure nothin' blows back on you and your club."

Leaning in, I said, "He's a cop who stood by while my woman's rapists held her from me and threatened to do it again in front of me. He was gonna walk away and let that shit happen. He produces drugs that are killin' people. We need the help to stop him."

"Even if you can only nab him and hold him until Jones gets there," Death suggested.

"Didn't we hear that the chief of police is involved? This cop could get let off once he's back in your territory." Talon asked.

"He won't. Not with the evidence we have," Country told him. "By now, Plank's associates know we're watchin' them. Know what we have on Plank, and they won't risk being taken down with him. For now, until we have Plank sorted, we'll let them think they're safe, and then we'll be turning all our attention to taking them out. We know what we're doin'."

"Wait a second," Talon ordered through the line. Voices in the background were muffled as he held a hand over the receiver. Even Dodge had covered his end and was replying through another phone.

"Country?" a new voice said down the line.

"Yeah?"

"This is Lan Davies. I'm a detective with the Caroline Springs station." We all tensed. "I'm also associated with the Hawks MC. My partner, Parker Wilding, and I are willing to pick up Harred Plank from the airport and take him to a holding room."

Detectives worked with the Hawks MC.

Looked like Jones wasn't the only one going rogue within law enforcement.

Country glanced to us.

State mouthed, "Yeah?"

Death tipped his chin up, and when Country looked to me, I nodded with the others.

"That works for us. We appreciate the help, and our club owes the Hawks MC a favor."

"Noted," Talon called, then added, "Dodge."

"Just thought I'd let you know that Lan and Parker can't always be around when they're holdin' someone. It could give some people an opening to get in and teach this fuckin' prick a lesson."

We all shared a grin, but it was Country who answered him gleefully, "How unfortunate that could happen."

There was some deep laughter from the other end.

"We'll be in touch," Talon said, and he ended the call, as did Dodge.

I sat back with a sigh. This was good. They were willing to help us.

"This could lead to a nice relationship with another club, even if they're overseas," Country said.

I relaxed at the thought of how much I would enjoy seeing Plank getting what was owed to him. It sucked we wouldn't be the ones to show him that it was a mistake to fuck with us, but at least he'd be hurting before Jones took him in.

"Torch," Country called.

I tipped my chin up.

He watched me closely. "Got a call from a guy I know at the prison."

I locked my body down so I didn't look at Blaze. It'd been a couple of days ago when I went to him and asked if he could make sure Tony wasn't breathing the same air as my obsession.

Sounded like I was about to hear that had happened.

"And?" I asked.

"Tony got knifed in the back in the showers. He's dead."

"I ain't sorry hearing it. Hell, I'd even send whoever did it flowers. Who was he? Did he say why he did it?"

"Tony stole from him."

While Country told me about the guy, someone on death row, I nodded along, acting like I didn't know any of it and hoped I pulled it off. But on the inside, I fucking cheered.

Now it was time to move on to the next situation.

"Sounds like Tony shouldn't have fucked with him." I needed to change the subject. I wouldn't waste any more time on that cunt. I asked, "Who we got downstairs?"

Country stared at me and briefly glanced at Blaze before sighing and scrubbing a hand over his face while he waved the other to Death.

"Jarred Kalb. But there's somethin' you gotta know," Death said.

"What?"

"Since we nabbed him, he's been cryin' that he didn't do anything to Wrenley." Blaze's jaw clenched. He didn't believe the kid's words.

I stood. "I'll find out exactly what happened."

When I reached the basement, I opened the thick door and stepped in.

As soon as Jarred saw me, he shook his head, yelling, "Please no. No, no. I didn't do that to her. I didn't—"

"Shut the fuck up," I ordered, moving closer. Chaos stepped away from him, until Jarred tried to stand from the chair. Then Chaos was there, gripping his shoulder. He slammed Jarred back down onto it again. The kid whimpered, and I watched impassively as his tears fell. Blaze and Death stepped into the room a moment later. Still sobbing, Jarred took them in and tried to tuck his head into his shoulders.

"You know who I am?" I asked.

He nodded.

"Who?"

"You're dating Wrenley—"

I gripped his hair and ripped his head back to get in his face and warn, "Don't. Say. Her. Name."

Another sob tore from him, and he squeezed his eyes closed.

"Shut up," I ordered.

He simmered to a whimpering mess.

"Tell me exactly your part in what happened." When he didn't begin, I asked, "Unless you talk, I'll get my blowtorch and start on the soles of your feet like I did Tony."

He drew in a shuddering breath. "It was Tony and Mitch's idea. The rest of us only went along with it because we're scared of them. They don't like losing, and they felt they had when Wre—when she didn't fall to her knees for them like all the other women. They felt they deserved to-to, ah, play with her." He winced when I clenched my jaw.

"What was your part in it?" Death demanded.

He shook his head. "I didn't want to be there, but... they made us watch. It was only Tony and Mitch that-that hurt her."

"Bullshit," Blaze snarled.

I released his hair and stepped back, crossing my arms over my chest.

"I promise. I swear. Ask any of the others. We all stood around while they... you know, hurt her."

"Stood around and did what?" Death questioned.

"Nothing." He shook his head again and dropped his gaze.

When I went to the counter where the good tools lay and picked up the blowtorch, he screamed and begged.

Then finally, he cried, "Okay, okay, I'll tell you. Just remember they made us be there. We're in debt in some way to Tony and Mitch. They made us do it. I swear. We have... fuck. We have proof to show you what they did and made us do."

If I saw any type of proof, I wouldn't be able to hold back. I'd kill them all, no matter what they did or didn't do.

I unlocked my jaw to ask, "What?"

"The video will show we didn't hurt her. We didn't have sex with her. That was all Tony and Mitch. But... while they had her unconscious, we may have touched her tits and jerked off on her."

They had a video.

Fire licked at my skin.

I dropped the blowtorch and rolled my head around.

They'd touched her. Tormented her.

Turning, I lunged and grabbed his arm. He screamed

when I gripped above and below his elbow, bending it back until....

Snap.

His shriek made me smile.

I dropped his broken arm and pulled his head back. Another whine left him as he clutched at his upper arm to hold it in place.

"That's for touching her. Think yourself lucky I don't cut off your hands." I got close. "I want to."

"Please, no. *Please*. I'll do anything. Please, no more. *Please.*"

"Tell the rest that we're coming for them."

"I will. I will." He nodded over and over.

"Tell them it's best they don't run. They need to take their punishment. To learn to never follow anyone like Tony or Mitch in the future. We'll always be watchin', Jarred Kalb."

"I'll tell them. I-I can get them to come here." He panted his words out, sniffing and whimpering from the pain he no doubt felt. "T-they will. They're scared. If-if I show them this is all you're going to do, they'll come here because we know we did wrong. We know we deserve this—"

"And more," I snarled.

He nodded, sniffing and wincing.

"You all deserve more." I stood, tapping at my temple.

Kill.

Kill.

Kill.

I wanted to. I really did, but they had to learn. They had to know never to torment again.

I needed to get back to Wrenley.

I needed her close to know she was okay.

Turning to Blaze and Death, I said, "I'm goin' home. Make sure he knows exactly what to do and they get rid of that video."

They grinned. Both wanted to make sure the message would be clear for him. Blaze cracked his knuckles as he stepped close to a begging Jarred.

"You got it, brother," Death said. "Get home to her."

Nodding, I walked from the room knowing Jarred would fear us for the rest of his miserable life while I got to go home to a woman who lightened my world for the rest of our days.

CHAPTER TWENTY-EIGHT

*A*fter I showered and changed clothes at the compound, getting rid of his sweat and tears, I made my way home.

I stopped outside my front door when the loud volume of the television suddenly switched off.

"You're falling asleep, Wren. You know you don't have to stay up," Gun said.

"I want to."

"Aww, she's totally in love," Saint teased.

I didn't want my brother to make her feel uncomfortable and was about to interrupt when she replied, "I *totally* am. I love him."

Unlocking the door, I threw it open.

Hearing those words again was like adrenaline shot straight to my dick. Selfishly, I didn't want her to give them attention anymore. I wanted it all to myself.

And Saint obviously read my intention. "Well, time for us to go." He took Gun's arm and dragged him to stand. "Wrenley, always a treat to have your company, but I feel your man wants your time to himself now."

"Later, Wrenley," Gun called.

"Bye." Wrenley waved to them on their way toward the door.

"Thanks," I said.

I didn't hear what they said. I'd locked onto Wrenley as she stood with her hands clasped in front of her and a blush on her cheeks.

She smiled shyly.

The door closed. I reached back and locked it.

"I'm sorry if you heard me telling your friends that I love you. I couldn't lie, though."

"I don't care."

"You don't?"

"No."

"Then why do you look, um... tense, maybe?"

"I'm locking down my body to stop from charging you and taking you to the bedroom to—"

"Yes!"

"You sure?" I asked, quirking a brow.

"Are you healed enough to enjoy—"

I stormed her way and picked her up. Instantly, she wrapped her legs around my waist and arms around my neck. With a laugh, she said, "I guess that's a yes."

I grunted. Licking, kissing, and sucking on her neck. The marks had dulled, but they were still present.

They'd pay.

"Are you sure you don't mind what I said to your brothers?"

I lifted my head as I lowered her to the floor in our bedroom. "I liked hearin' you tell them."

"Yeah?"

"Yeah, my Wrenley." Reaching out, I trailed my fingers over her cheek, chin, and down her neck.

She shivered for me, eyes getting lazy but heating at the same time.

I would never tire of seeing her desire for me.

She bit her bottom lip as I continued the trail down over her chest, breast, ribs, and stomach.

When I stopped at the bottom of her tee, I smirked when she lifted her arms so I could pull her top up and off her body, which was exactly what I did.

I drank in the sight of her perfect, pretty breasts encased in pink lace. I loved seeing her smooth, soft skin in any color, but most of all pink. Would she have matched her panties to her bra?

I liked when see-through lace covered her pussy.

It was like a treat just for me.

Her chest rose and fell rapidly as I popped the top button to her jeans. I slowly eased the zipper down and saw the flash of more pink.

"So pretty," I muttered, tracing my fingers over the V I'd exposed.

She smiled and hummed. "I noticed you like me in this color. Your eyes get that exact look."

Like I wanted to drop to my knees and sink my tongue into her sweet pussy.

"You did this for me?"

"When the girls, West, and Adrick went shopping yesterday, I stocked up on other pink items."

My cock throbbed. "There'll be more?"

She nodded, grinning. "Many more."

Cupping her breasts, I squeezed gently. "Fuck." I pinched at her nipples, causing her to suck in a breath only to let it back out on a moan.

Exposing one, I bent and licked around her hard bud as she arched up, offering me more. I took it between my teeth and lapped at the tip before swirling my tongue around it.

"Torch," she uttered, fisting my tee under my cut at my ribs.

Straightening, I removed my cut and placed it on the chair before turning back to her and drinking in her beauty. I tugged my T-shirt up and off, throwing it to the floor.

She smiled at me.

Pure sunshine.

Always my light to the darkness.

And all mine.

Cupping the back of her head, I fingered through her silky, curly strands and pulled her into me. She went willingly, hands sliding up my scarred chest as she tipped her head back, offering me her mouth.

I took it.

In a hungry kiss, we licked and sucked at each other's lips, twisting our tongues together.

Delicious.

That was what Wrenley was, and I loved when her taste lingered in my mouth.

Even more when it was her pussy's flavor.

I slid a hand down her spine and gripped her ass,

drawing her into me as I walked us backward toward the bed.

At the edge, I layered a few kisses on her before I helped her turn. I gripped the sides of her jeans and slowly revealed my treat. A low groan dropped from me when I saw her panties didn't cover her ass since it was a G-string.

My goddess let out a breathy laugh as I forgot about her jeans and palmed each globe. My beautiful obsession removed the rest and bent, placing her hands to the bed.

Fucking hell.

My cock ached from the sight before me.

Saliva pooled in my mouth from the thought of spreading her and tasting.

I dropped to my knees and went forward, running my hands over her.

I glided a finger down the pink lace that sat snuggly between her cheeks and felt her shiver.

"Pretty," I bit out, the hunger of desire riding my harder tone.

"Torch," she breathed.

Her reactions to my hands, my body, my words always made me want to throw my head back and crow to the sky in pride.

I slipped a finger between her legs.

Drenched.

I did that. I made her wet just from kissing and touching and talking.

Me.

She was my perfect, pretty addiction.

The woman who gave me a reason to exist without the darkness drowning me.

"Chase, please," she begged, jutting her ass back.

Anything.

But I did this with the greatest pleasure.

Hooking a finger under the string, I plucked it out and dove in. Wrenley dropped down to her elbows on the bed with a moan when I licked and kissed over her pussy. I drank and ate like a starved man.

A man who couldn't get enough.

"Yes, Chase," she cried when I inserted a finger inside, curling it and rubbing. Her legs shook as she panted and whimpered.

Christ. The noises she made were like my favorite song.

It was a tune made for me.

Only me.

She leaked over my fingers, and I lapped it up.

Kissing, tonguing at her drenched hole.

"Torch," she breathed and then moaned, clutching at the bed as her walls fluttered and pulsed around my fingers.

Drawing them out, I licked them clean and stood behind her.

"Can I fuck you like this?" I asked, rubbing a hand over her ass and lower back.

She hummed under her breath and nodded. "Please. And bare."

"Ah, fuck," I drew out, a thrill shooting up my spine. We'd had Lucas send away our blood, and we'd heard just yesterday that we could now go ungloved, and she was on the pill. My cock gave off a hard jerk under my boxers. "With pleasure, my beautiful Wrenley."

Kicking off my shoes, I shoved my jeans and boxers

down, tugging them and my socks off and throwing them to the side.

Dipping, I kissed her sweet ass, one for each cheek.

She sighed contentedly, but my obsession was impatient; she pushed back on me. "Need you in me."

"You got me, my pretty addiction." I stepped close, taking hold of my dick to swirl the tip around her hole. Both of us groaned.

Christ, this is gonna be heaven.

Mine.

Mine.

Mine.

Slowly, I pushed in, locking away the memory of the first feel of her silky walls squeezing my dick tightly, inch by inch.

She let out a panting moan when I thrust the last part in.

"You feel so good, Wrenley."

"Hmm, so do you, Chase, but I'm going to need you to fuck me now, babe."

She clenched around me, and my cock jerked inside her from that and the endearment.

More music to my ears.

Pulling out, I looked down at her wetness glistening over my cock before I rocked back in, which dragged out noises from both of us.

Never get enough.

Want to live inside her.

My Wrenley.

My pretty obsession.

Made for me. Just me.

Fuck.

Leaning over her, I rolled my hips, fucking in and out as I kissed and licked over her back.

"Oh God, Chase," she whispered, humming again in the back of her throat.

Loved her sounds. Her words. Her.

Pulling out, I picked her up to flip her over. She let out a laugh, but it faded to a moan when I thrust back into her.

She wrapped me up, arms and legs, then pulled me down for a kiss.

That was what I wanted. Needed. Her mouth touching mine, her teeth and mine nipping, our tongues tangling.

Tasting, claiming.

She tore her mouth from mine, arched, and clamped around my cock, crying out through her second climax.

Licking at her neck, I peppered it with kisses and scrapes of my teeth.

My release rolled over me, stuttering my rhythm, but I groaned into her shoulder as I filled her with my cum. Marking her deep inside, in a way I never had with anyone.

She kissed at my temple. "Love you, babe."

Lifting my head, I latched onto her bottom lip and sucked. She grinned around it, until I kissed softly there and said, "Love you, my sweet Wrenley."

EPILOGUE

"This is your first official day. Are you excited?" Raya asked as she walked beside me to the childcare room in the compound. I eagerly gave up on the marketing course when Dusty had hinted that she, Lucas, and some of the other mothers in the club really wanted to turn Tech's old computer room into a daycare, but they also wanted someone they trusted to run it. Stracey, a club woman, had said she had the qualifications to run it, but she wouldn't want to do it forever. Which was why I offered myself up without really thinking about it. But as soon as I had, I felt like it was the right move for me. I loved kids. Raya and I used to take care of a lot of the children in our old neighborhood when we were younger. So, I got my childcare license by doing some online courses while Stracey helped set things up for the room. Then, in between my shifts, I would continue my education to get my ECE degree. Eventually, I would take over running things.

"I'm excited and nervous. But as first days go, I have it pretty easy with it only being Opal, until Wreck finishes at Polished, and Seth while Dusty does a cooking spree. The rest are after-school care."

"You'll have more soon," Raya said.

I glanced at her. "Who?"

"Mine and Leland's."

I dragged her to a stop and squealed, "What?"

She nodded, smiling big as tears filled our eyes at the same time.

"Really?" I questioned again.

"You're going to be an aunty in six months' time."

"You're already three months?" I rested my hands to her belly and noticed she had a tiny baby bump under her blouse. "Oh my God, this is exciting!"

"And scary," Raya admitted softly.

I hugged her to me. "You're going to be the best mom."

"I hope so."

Pulling back, I shook my head. "I know so. Does anyone else know yet?"

She hooked her arm in mine as we started walking again. "No one. But I think Leland is telling his—" A loud, boisterous cheer went up from the common room we'd come from. "—brothers now," Raya finished with a laugh.

Grinning, I bumped her hip with mine. "I guess you caught the baby bug after Seth was born."

"It was actually more Leland. But when he mentioned how he'd like a baby, I was all on board."

"That's adorable. He got baby fever."

"It really was. But even though Leland has permanently moved into ours, and we now have a baby on the way, I don't want you to think we don't want you living with us. We're a family always, Wren."

I smiled. "I know. But I like where I am, and it's not like I've come back since being at Torch's."

She laughed. "True. You know I'm happy for you. We really won the lottery when it comes to our men."

"I couldn't agree more." We stopped outside the room, and I saw Dusty coming down the hall to drop off Seth. I looked at my sister, and my heart gave a squeeze. We really were lucky with where we landed. "I'm happy for you, too, Raya. Love you."

Tears formed. "Love you too."

"I just heard Death knocked you up. This is the best news," Dusty called, and we both laughed.

Our family had grown so much since we moved here. We had truly been blessed with the people in our lives, and I couldn't wait to see where my life would lead with Torch at my side. I just knew it would be amazing.

Torch

I PACED BACK and forth in the common room waiting for Wrenley to close the daycare and meet me out here before we headed back to our place.

Right then, I was more excited than I had been when, months ago in a video chat, I watched members of the Hawks MC beat on Plank, making his blood flow.

Yet, my nerves wreaked havoc on my gut.

I already knew she'd agree to my question. But there was always that doubtful voice in my head that told me otherwise.

Told me she was too good for me. That I should let her go for someone better. Told me I was a worthless piece of shit that didn't deserve her kindness, her love.

But lately, I told that voice to shut the fuck up.

And since I was also a selfish bastard who was obsessed with my Wrenley, I would make sure everyone knew she was taken by putting *my* mark on her.

"Torch, you good?" Country called from the table he sat at with his woman, their baby, and a few other brothers.

Nodding, I kept pacing and watching the doorway.

She'd be in here soon. I just had to wait to get her alone.

I wasn't sure why I picked today of all the days.

Maybe it was because she'd started her new job. A new beginning for her, and I felt it'd be better to have all the changes on the same day.

I didn't know.

My mind buzzed with too many thoughts.

I tapped and rubbed at my temple.

She'd want me.

She'd accept.

She was mine. I was hers.

I couldn't believe she hadn't mentioned going back to her house. She'd stayed with me and never brought up moving back home. In fact, she'd gone to get more of her things.

She would forever live in my space now.

She couldn't get out of it.

Not when I loved having her there. I loved waking and sleeping and drinking, eating, showering, fucking... everything with her in my home.

When I heard her sweet laughter coming from the hall, I stumbled to a halt while my heart crawled up my throat.

I just had to get her home, and then I'd ask her.

There she is.

She'd walked in with Stracey, one of the club girls, smiling.

She was happy.

Was always happy now.

When she spotted me, her head cocked to the side, and her words trailed off.

Fuck waiting.

I couldn't wait.

I had to do it. The need to mark her clawed at my chest.

She was mine.

I deserved her. I made her smile, laugh, and love me.

My treasure would have my ring.

Striding toward her, I swallowed thickly from nerves and stopped when I was right in front before I dropped to one knee.

Stracey drifted away while my Wrenley covered her gasp with a hand as tears filled her eyes.

I didn't like seeing them. But I guessed they were happy ones.

They'd better be happy ones.

"You're the reason I finally have light in my life. I'll always belong to you, heart and soul, my beautiful Wrenley, and I want to show the world you belong to me. Will you marry me?"

Pound.

Pound.

Pound.

My heart was about to burst.

There was nothing but silence behind me. Everyone watched.

I didn't care, but I hoped Wrenley didn't mind the audience. I hoped she didn't care that I couldn't wait. I pulled the ring from my pocket and held it up to her.

My hand shook.

I looked up and watched her tears tip over to her cheeks.

"I love you," she whispered, leaning down to cup my cheeks. She pressed a soft kiss to my lips, where she said, "I'd be honored to become your wife, Chase."

My chest filled with her light.

I slid the ring on her finger, stood, and picked her up to have her mouth, sealing the deal.

The room erupted in noise, but my focus stayed glued to the woman in my arms.

I placed her back on her feet, and she beamed up at me.

"Start organizing it," I told her, fingering the glittery ring on her hand. "Want the second band to join with this one and want one for myself. Need everyone to know we're each other's worlds."

Her smile turned wobbly as she nodded. "I love the sound of that."

Before we could get interrupted, I said, "Thank you for

lovin' me like no one else could. Love you, my perfect, pretty obsession."

"Love you, Chase." She jumped and I caught her.

I always would.

Read on for a look inside Fumbled Love,
a sports rom com with a guest appearance from State

CHAPTER ONE

REAGAN

The day was going to be a terrible one. I knew it the moment I woke up late, having slept through my alarm again. I really had to get one that sounded like a freight train going through my house because when I slept, I did so deeply.

To make matters worse, I raced from my room, skipped around the Pomeranian named Fozzie, and then slipped in still warm poop.

Gagging and cursing him black and blue, I quickly used some paper towels to wipe it off my foot and I let him out the dog door, which was already built in the door when I bought the house. Thankfully, Fozzie was my parents' dog, and it was my last night minding the little fella.

The cleanup took longer than I thought, which added extra time on my lateness. But I refused to leave my house stinking like dog doo-doo. It wasn't like I could go to work smelling like poop. I could already imagine the less-than-creative names my students would come up with.

Finally managing to get out the door without another incident, it was then I realized I'd put on the panties I should have thrown away a dress size ago. Yes, those deadly small panties. It meant the whole walk to work, they kept making friends with my butt crack. Mid-step, I glanced down and groaned; I'd also managed to pick out the worst outfit ever. A long red skirt, which had a tear in the middle, and a *rainbow*-colored tee. Not only did I look homeless, but it was like a Skittle had thrown up on me.

Of course, as I ran through the halls of Radley High School, where I taught English, the principal stepped out of nowhere, and I nearly collided with him.

With just one look at me, Tom Gallegan's eyes widened. "What happened, Reagan?"

"A rough morning." I hadn't even had the chance to inhale my much needed three morning coffees.

He cleared his throat, apparently not wanting to touch on the fact a unicorn farted rainbows all over me. His lips twitched. "Right, ah... I need your help. It's school assembly in a few minutes and Khloe is out sick. You'll need to fill in on stage."

And the morning just got worse.

Khloe was Tom's assistant; she regularly stood on the stage in assembly and, well, assisted with whatever she had to do. I didn't take much notice of what she actually did. I liked hiding in my corner with Brooke, my friend from college, who happened to get a job at the same school as me. We stood in the back and... to be honest, we bitched. Mainly about Elena, the witch I'd gone to high school with, and who'd made my experience hell. She also, unfortunately, worked at the same school as us as the family and consumer science teacher. I'd spent probably far too many hours considering other meanings for FACS, which seemed fitting for Elena. Though, my favorite was: Facts About Cockup Slags

"Erm, I can't."

Tom crossed his arms over his chest and rested them against his beer belly while he stared me down. We all liked Tom; he was a great guy to work for, like a father figure in a way, but there wasn't a chance I was getting up on that stage and pretending I wanted to be there. Tom tended to drone on and on and on. Once, Brooke had even elbowed me hard in the ribs because I'd dozed off standing up.

I could take him on in the stare down.

I really could.

With my hands on my hips, I leaned in a bit and stared right back.

Neither of us blinked, and my left eye started twitching seconds in.

The man was a master at the stare down. Damn him.

Sighing, I blinked a few times, and said, "Fine." I started stalking off, ignoring his grin of triumph.

"You're going the wrong way," he called.

"I need to see if Brooke has a spare top or I'll never live it down with the kids," I called over my shoulder.

I loved my students, and they loved me, but they could also be little shits. One time, I'd somehow managed to go to class with my slippers on, and a Twix chocolate bar stuck in my hair. I blamed the *Supernatural* marathon I'd had the previous night. However, I'd heard their murmurs of how they'd thought I'd been dumped and was wallowing in depression. Then there was also the day I'd got caught, after a quick visit to the restroom, with my skirt in my panties. They'd thought I'd ducked out for a romp with the phys ed teacher. After I'd swallowed the bile in my mouth—because no one would want to romp with stinky Steve, who I was sure didn't own deodorant, regardless of how many times Brooke and I chatted about how good deodorant was in front of him—I assured them it was an accident. I'd been rushing back so they wouldn't get into too much trouble. Or more specifically me, as I really should not be leaving the classroom unattended. But when I needed to pee, nothing was getting in my way.

I managed to catch Brooke as she was leaving her office. She was the school counselor.

My dear friend took one look at me and started laughing. "Oh God, Ree. Did you not look in the mirror this morning?"

"I was running late. Do you have a shirt I could borrow? I have to take Khloe's place on stage."

"Yeah, sure. It's in the locker." She stepped away from the door and started down the hall. "I'll see you on stage. Apparently, I have to help with something too," she yelled back.

Thank the high heavens I wouldn't be alone up there.

Quickly, I slipped into her office and took out a black shirt, then cursed. Damn Brooke was only a size smaller than my size fourteen, but I was larger in the chest area. My boobs looked like they wanted to burst free from the buttons. At least it was a bit better than my rainbow tee. I squished the girls down, so I didn't look like a tramp, and made my way into the gymnasium.

Bustling along with the other teachers and students, I managed to make it on stage just as the final bell rang. Tom ushered us to the left, near the opened curtain, and placed a huge-ass trophy in my hands. It also covered my chest nicely, thank God. Then he placed a small banner into Brooke's hands before he shuffled off. Brooke and I looked at each other. She then read what was on the banner before I could.

"Oh," she whispered.

"Oh? Oh, what?"

"We forgot."

"Forgot what?" I asked snappishly, because her concerned tone was freaking me out.

"That Carter Anthony was coming today." She winced at my face paling, and I knew it was because I suddenly felt sick.

Carter Anthony.

How could I have forgotten he was showing?

Maybe because I'd put it at the back of my mind, in the *very* back of my mind.

"It'll be okay. You don't even have to talk to him."

Nodding, I replied, "There is that. And anyway, it's not like he'll remember me. I was a nobody back then. We didn't even talk." He'd just been my high school crush, the popular football player, and I'd let my infatuation last for years. My love died once I heard him join in with his jock friends laughing at plus-size girls. It also happened to be just before he left town, accepting the big football scholarship with some college out of town. Apparently, he was still a star player and two years ago, he got transferred to one of our city's NFL teams, whatever they were called. Only he still opted to live away from his home stadium, picking to travel the few hours drive instead. Although, it could be possible he already had a place set up back where he was and didn't want to leave it. I'd also heard some talk he was thinking of moving back to settle down. While I knew next to nothing about the sport or even teams, I wasn't surprised by his success. He'd been a brilliant player even in high school. The most recent news I'd overheard was that Carter was finishing up his final year playing, and that he wanted to coach at a local college.

Not that I stalked him. I didn't. It really was the gossip around town.... Okay, so it was one night—two months ago when we found out he was going to do a talk at our school—Brooke and I were drunk and she'd googled him.

Shifting from one foot to another, since my tight panties had ridden up, again, I took the steps needed to move to the spot Tom gestured us to with an annoyed look on his face; we were off to the side, near the curtain.

"Stupid tight panties," I grumbled under my breath. I hadn't had a chance to pull them out discreetly. I scanned the audience and spotted Elena standing on the floor by the stage at the opposite end to us. She appeared eager, and I knew why. Carter had been her high school sweetheart for two years before he'd moved away.

Snorting, I took notice of her outfit, and I'd been worried about my top. Her breasts were close to popping out to say hello.

"What are we snorting about?" Brooke asked discreetly.

"*Her.*"

Brooke looked at Elena. "Oh, *her*," she snarled. Elena

was the worst. One of the coldest people I'd ever met. It was as if she was stuck back in high school and still thought she shit roses.

As Tom finally took to the microphone, I leaned into Brooke, and said, "Her boobs are so perky they're like a Disney Princess's on crack." Brooke coughed through her laugh. "Actually, I bet she'd want to be Dora the Explorer right about now."

She glanced at me, then back out to the audience of pubescent teens. "Why?"

"She'd want to be the first to explore Carter's whole body with her tongue."

She snorted. "Would she be the only one?"

"Yes." I nodded. I rolled my eyes as Tom went on and on about the great Carter Anthony. I was sure Tom had a guy-crush on him, like a lot of males all around the country. Even some of the male staff were salivating for a peek at Carter. Except for Larry, one of the math teachers, who I wasn't sure had moved out of his mom's yet, despite being thirty-seven.

"Why are you moving like that?" Brooke hissed at me. "Do you need to pee?"

"No, I have a wedgie," I whispered.

"What?"

"My panties are riding up my butt. You need to pull it out."

She swung her gaze my way and looked at me as if I'd lost my mind. "Come on," I pleaded. "I can't continue like this the whole time. It's so uncomfortable. My panties are up there making out with my butthole. This thing is too heavy to hold with just one hand while I fix the problem."

"I am not—"

"Remember the time you had me check your boob for a lump? I fondled it for a good while and only found a pimple under it."

"But—"

"Or the time you broke your arm and had trouble dressing, showering, and going to the toilet?" Looking over to Tom, I pretended to pay attention, and snapped in a low tone, "It's only a piece of fabric, but it's annoying the heck out of me. Can you please…?" I felt fingers on my bottom, and then sweet relief. My panties were adjusted. Only what was strange was when my friend patted my ass after it. Still, I said, "Thank you." Then I glanced back to Brooke who had wide eyes. I added, "See, it wasn't that hard."

"Reagan—" Brooke bit out. However, Tom then boomed through the room, "And here he is. Please welcome, Carter Anthony."

Cheers and claps erupted. I shifted my gaze to the far side and behind the curtain, only Carter didn't step out.

My body tensed as I felt a presence step up beside me. "Anytime you need help, I'll be there," Carter's deep voice said out the corner of his mouth while he waved to the audience. Then, as he walked toward Tom, he glanced back and winked.

I felt the need to vomit, pee, poop, scream, and cry all at the same time.

He couldn't have been the one who'd pulled my panties out of my ass.

Nope.

It wasn't him.

"Reagan—"

"No!" I hissed through my heavy breathing as I tried to

calm myself. "It was you," I stated in my do-not-screw-with-me tone.

"Oh, got it. You're playing dumb. Right, yep it was totally me who had my hand on your ass adjusting your panties and then patted your rump." She scoffed. "I also whispered that my helping hand was willing to do it again and then winked at you."

She quickly looked away.

Huh, guess my death glare does work sometimes.

God, how long had he been standing behind the curtain?

Shit, shit, shit. I didn't, *couldn't* think about it, or about what he heard.... Did he hear me talk about Elena? Had I said her name? She was currently sending him sultry "come screw me" eyes while he was on stage talking about how awesome his life was.

Actually, I couldn't hear what he was saying because my ears were ringing while my blood pumped frantically through my body because I was having a breakdown.

"Reagan," Brooke barked lowly.

My body jolted. "What?"

"They're calling you."

I froze. They were? Glancing at the microphone, I saw Tom glaring at me while he waved me over. Carter stood beside him smirking. At least Gerry Understock, a top sports student was smiling.

Leaning in a little toward Tom, I whispered-yelled, "What?" I rose my brows at Tom. He sighed and thumped his forehead.

"The trophy in your arms is for Gerry," Brooke supplied.

"Oh, right."

She laughed. "Get it over there before Tom strangles you."

"Reagan." Tom hurled my name at me as if he were praying it would catch me on fire.

I snorted to Brooke. "He's thought it many times, but he would never do it. He loves me too much." I started toward the microphone. In fact, I was sure Tom thought of me as his adopted kid.

Stopping in front of my adopted dad—who I just claimed, something I would tell him later when he tried to kill me—I smiled. He covered the microphone and clipped, "I'm going to staple information about assemblies to your forehead. Then maybe you'll remember what's going on."

Okay, I was his *annoying* adopted child.

"*I'm* usually down there." I gestured with my head. "Bad move on *your* part to have me up here. I get bored easily." The only way I didn't get bored was when I read or watched movies and TV shows. I'd even taken up walking on those random days nothing else satisfied me. Brooke had checked my temperature when I told her that. However, after the first few times, I realized I enjoyed it.

Gerry snorted out a laugh, until Tom scowled at him, then he quickly shut up. And Carter—the sexy mountain-of-a-man Carter—stood off to the side smirking once more. I narrowed my gaze his way; his smirk changed into a shit-eating wide grin. Did I have something on my face? God, his eyes were mesmerizing. I suddenly felt an urge to paint or draw them. Although, I still hadn't passed the stick-figure pictures, so I knew I'd totally suck at it. While I could explain the difference between a simile and metaphor, my artistic credentials sucked.

"Reagan, pass the trophy over to Carter," Tom snapped.

Shaking my head to clear my mind from stick-figures, I then nodded, "Right. Of course." I nodded again like an idiot, and stepped up to Carter, practically throwing the heavy trophy at him. I did it all without meeting his hypnotizing gaze.

"Reagan," Carter called, in his sensual voice.

Goddammit all to hell. The man was sex on legs. He knew it; heck, *everyone* knew it, and I didn't want to fall into his trap. The one where he'd undoubtedly captivate me, then *BAM,* he'd friend-zone me so fast I wouldn't know what hit me.

It was not happening. So, ignoring his call, I tapped Gerry on the arm, and said, "Congrats on your, um, award, trophy, thingy, Gerry. Top notch, young boy. Brilliant job." Shit. I needed to get out of there. I patted Gerry's arm once again and then made my getaway back to Brooke.

Facing the audience, while they listened to Tom and then Carter talk again, I whispered out the corner of my mouth, "Did I look like a total idiot that whole time?"

"Sure did."

"Thanks. I thought I had. Can you please bury me this afternoon?"

"Can do. I'll even bring wine and say something nice after you're in the ground."

"You're sweet."

"It's what best friends are for."

CHAPTER TWO

REAGAN

Of course, things couldn't get better for me. Leaning my butt against my desk while discussing my freshman class's assignment, I then cringed when I heard Wesley blow his nose for the millionth time. He sounded like a damn trumpet. What made matters worse—if him bringing his germs to school wasn't enough—was when he pulled the tissue back and then studied his mucus. Everyone knew how gross Wesley was; he didn't hide it, and more power to him for being who he wanted to be... just not when it churned my stomach.

Slamming my copy of *To Kill A Mockingbird* down, I then pointed to Wesley. "If you look at your snot one more time, I just may vomit all over you."

Students started chuckling; they were used to my

outbursts. Wesley, the little shit, lifted the tissue up with a cheeky grin on his pimply face.

"Don't do it," I warned, straightening.

"Miss," someone called.

I was too busy holding my glare on Wesley to answer. He slowly parted the folded tissue.

"I swear, my bile is rising, and it's coming for you, kid."

"Miss," was snapped a bit harsher. It was Jenifer, a grade-A student who sat in the front row closest to the door.

Closing my eyes, I dropped my head and sighed. "Someone's opened the door, right?"

"Yes." She giggled.

God, please do not let it be Tom. He was already upset with me enough. If he caught me threatening to vomit on a student, he'd be more than pissed.

"Is it the principal?" I asked, lifting my head and opening my eyes. Still, I didn't glance at the doorway until I knew if I had to make a run for it or not.

"No," Jenifer said in a swoony voice.

Finally smiling, I relaxed my stance and faced the door... then froze, but not before my smile dropped.

Shit.

Double shit.

It was Carter Anthony.

He was leaning against the doorframe with yet another smirk on his face.

I think I'd rather have Tom there instead.

"Ah... can I help you?"

Had he stumbled into the wrong room? Had he taken too many hits to the head and was lost?

Get out, get out, get out.

And suddenly I felt like yelling, "Get off my train," like the spirit in the movie *Ghost*. I clamped my mouth closed in case I did. My students would know what movie I was referencing since I made them watch it, under the guise of its relevance to understanding one of our previous topics of crafting ghost stories, but I wasn't sure Carter would know. He didn't seem like the movie watching type.

What was he doing in my classroom?

He straightened and stepped further in. His lips twitched when I widened my eyes at his approach. "You may have missed the extra information the principal gave this morning. I've been going to selected classrooms to visit to see if anyone has any questions for me."

I caught sight of Wesley opening his mouth. When I shot him a murderous glare, he snapped his lips shut. *Reminder to self: Next time Wesley makes you want to vomit, pull out the deadly glare.*

"Nope." I shook my head. "We're good in here." Did that sound rude? "Thank you, though," I added quickly. *Do not blush.*

He chuckled, and I wanted to throw something at his head, because his damn chuckle did things to my stomach. Nice things.

Never. I would never fall for his charms, his good looks, or how he's grown into his tall frame and huge body nicely. Even his sparkling eyes and sweet lips.

I was a grown woman. I had control of myself.

"Then if no one has any questions, do you mind if I stay for a while? I'd like to watch. I've never heard of a lesson from a teacher where they threatened vomiting before."

Damn. He'd heard that.

Laughing nervously, I shook my head. "Did I say vomit? I meant...." I had nothing. Why was my brain failing me now? Throwing my hands on my hips, I glared at Carter. "Anyway, we were in the middle of something, and I'd really prefer it if my class isn't interrupted."

"But, Miss, you interrupted class just the other day when your mom called," Bradly yelled.

My eyes widened. "Now isn't the time for lies, Bradly."

"But—"

"Bradly!"

My little defiant minions laughed. Carter chuckled.

Clearing my throat, I mentioned, "I'm sure Mr. Rogers, the phys ed teacher, would love to have you visit his class."

"I have a feeling you're trying to get rid of me." Carter grinned, and his head tilted to the side. "Do I know you from somewhere?"

"No!" I snorted, scoffed, and then burped. "Excuse me." I laughed. "And then there's also the FACS class. Something tasty will be cooking right about now. You should go for a taste."

Elena would also love it.

He shook his head. "Thanks for the suggestion, but I'll be fine here."

Dang it all.

"Fine," I bit out through clenched teeth. Ignoring him, though I sensed his movement to behind my desk to sit in *my* seat, I turned my attention back to the class. Wesley raised his hand. "Yes, Wesley?"

"I'd like to ask Mr. Anthony what it's like being famous."

Guess my death glare wore off on the shithead.

Clenching my jaw, I breathed deeply through my nose. "Does anyone else have questions they'd like to ask Mr. Anthony?" Half my students raised their hands. The other half were just staring at Carter like he was their favorite chew toy.

Rubbing an eye, since it started to twitch, I shifted to the side of my desk and glanced at Carter.

"Well?" I said.

"Oh, you want me to answer them?"

"Yes," I clipped.

"But I thought you didn't like—"

"*Please,* just answer them," I snapped.

Laughing, he stood and looked at Wesley. "Honestly, being famous can be a pain sometimes. No matter where I go, I have to watch what I say or do because it could end up in the media."

"But you get to bang all the chicks you want," Bradly called out.

One hand went to cover my chest—I didn't want to flash my bra—as the other shot out and up. "Bradly, the only banging we'll talk about in this class is me banging your head on your desk." Again, Carter chuckled—*shit*—and my students laughed. I winced, knowing I could be in serious doo-doo if he told anyone how sarcasm and regular threats were part of my teaching practice, but I lived dangerously. Plus, the class knew I was all talk. I would never lay a finger on them. That didn't mean I couldn't joke around. It made the day fun. More importantly, it strengthened our classroom relationship, and they knew when they had to get crack-a-lacking with work. I was lucky to teach such amazing kids.

Before the questioning continued, I added, "If anyone else says or asks something ridiculous like that again, I'll do something really drastic."

They quieted.

Carter pointed at Josiah.

"Do you ever get stressed being the quarterback?" Josiah asked.

"Actually, yes." Carter nodded. "Though, I'm sure it happens for any player really. We're a team. It's not just about me."

"What do you do after a loss?" Stacy called out.

Shifting my gaze to Carter, I caught his small smile. "What I prefer to do is go home, watch a movie with a pizza and beer."

Say what?

That sounded... so not like him. I'd heard he was one hell of a party animal. A real Casanova with women too.

"Do you have a girlfriend?" Ariel asked, and for some reason, all my kids' eyes swiveled to me quickly and then back again.

What was up with that?

Carter chuckled. "No. I don't."

"Miss doesn't have a boyfriend," Wesley called out. That kid was just asking for a nose punch.

"I do!" I yelled.

"What's his name?" Ariel questioned.

Did I say I loved my students?

I was so taking that love back.

"Ah, James?" I said slowly. And dang it for making it sound like a question.

A few of the guys snorted, some of the girls rolled their

eyes, and Carter stood, walked around the desk, and leaned his perfect ass against the edge. A smirk played at his lips. I wanted to pinch his cheeks together so he'd quit doing that.

"What's his last name?" Michael called.

Shit. A last name?

"Blunt?" I drew out.

"So you're saying your boyfriend's name is James Blunt, like that old singer guy?" Jenifer said.

Fuck.

I didn't expect anyone to know him. Evil geniuses.

I threw a hand out aimlessly and shot off a nervous laugh. "Yes. Just a coincidence." Clearing my throat, I added, "But we're getting off track. Mr. Anthony is here to answer questions, not me."

There was a knock at the door, thank God. We all turned toward it as it opened. Elena peeked her head in, scanned for a quick second before her eyes landed on her next victim. *I mean Carter*. Carter Anthony who used to date Elena. They had a history. One that could reignite as soon as she got her claws in him.

Did I care?

Nope, not at all.

I didn't.

Anyway, why would I care when I was just trying to get him to leave my room in the first place?

I narrowed my gaze as she smiled sweetly at Carter. It was a habit of mine whenever she was near. A narrowed gaze, a fisted hand, and a thought to throat punch her. Just the usual. After all, she had made my teen years hell, so of course, I had a vendetta against her.

Her past words rushed through my mind.

"Ooh, look it's fat-ass Reagan.

God, Reagan, you're going to break that poor chair with your weight.

Reagan, you stink. Did you wash between your flab?

Reagan, why don't you eat from the floor like all animals do?

I wish I didn't have to deal with such a pig in class all the time."

Laughing and mocking had always accompanied her cruel words from the people around us.

She stepped into the room, and said, "Here you are. Mr. Gallegan said you were still here." She curled her hands around his arm, leaning into him. "Why don't we head to my class?"

"But he only just got here," Wesley called.

Elena smiled up at Carter before looking at Wesley and glared. "Mr. Anthony has an important schedule, so I'm sure he needs to move on anyway."

"I was only supposed to visit the phys ed, math, and English class. I don't have time for any more," Carter explained.

I wanted to high-five him.

Elena giggled. "Oh, I'm sure you don't mind cutting *this* one short to come talk to *my* class." Her evil gaze landed on me. "Miss Wild, I didn't see you there. You don't mind if I steal him away?"

It was times like this I liked that I'd grown into my lady balls.

"Actually, Miss *Roup*." I smiled. "Mr. Anthony and *my* class were just in the middle of something. Maybe next time he visits you could have him in *your* class."

If looks could kill, I would be buried six-feet under.

The room was so damn silent, I was sure the students were holding their breaths. I also didn't miss the way Carter glanced at me with his lips tilted at the corners.

"Right. Of course. Sorry for interrupting." She was all sunshine because Carter was around. If it were just us and we weren't in the classroom, she'd be slitting my throat. The way her eyes burned told me she was at least picturing it. She laughed, and I saw her hands tighten on his arm. "Hopefully I'll get to see you before you have to leave, *Carter*," she purred his name, and then turned, swaying her hips to the door. Only the person she was doing it for wasn't looking her way. His eyes were on the floor, and he was biting his bottom lip. His reaction could be because I happened to cough out quietly "*Slut*" as she left.

When she glanced back and noticed Carter wasn't watching, she clenched her jaw, then stomped the rest of the way and closed the door quickly.

Only it came back open, and the bitch called out, "Oh, Carter." Carter looked her way. "I'm sure you remember Miss Wild from high school, right?" My body locked tight, even my butt cheeks. "Or maybe not since she is forgettable." She smiled, backed out, and closed the door once more.

I wanted to hide.

Crawl under my desk and hide.

Of course Carter wouldn't remember me because Elena was right about that. I had been forgettable. I'd been the large girl, the one who got picked on, and I was also the one who had no friends.

But I had lady balls, I reminded myself. So even with my

whole body flushing, I faced my muttering students who were glaring toward the door, and paused. They were loyal to a fault. I wondered briefly if I could give them extra credit for being able to deduce who the bitch in the room had been. Then, ignoring the man to the side of me, I said, "And that class, is what you call an awkward situation. Also, it goes to show flirting doesn't always get you what you want."

Nobody ever said I was exactly appropriate with my classes, but honestly, I think my students were better off with real, tough, and brutal life situations at times.

I preened a little when I heard some of my students talk about how they didn't like Elena as a teacher. How she bitched and moaned about other teachers in the school. And as much as I'd have loved to join in, I couldn't sink to her level and smack talk her. I never would.

In not responding to her bullshit spectacle, I hoped it showed my class it was okay to stand up for yourself in a situation where you weren't happy with what was going on. Elena wasn't better than me. Besides, it was obvious Carter didn't want to go to a cooking class.

What was also important was to move on from an awkward situation, like the man at my side finding out we used to go to school together and him not remembering me, and move on from it.

My students laughed at my comment. I grinned back and then shifted from one foot to another. Carter was too quiet, and I didn't like it.

I clapped my hands. "All right, class, since Mr. Anthony's time is short, why don't you finish the questions you have, and while you do it, I'll just finish grading these papers?"

Moving around my desk, I took my seat and realized Carter's butt was sitting on the papers I needed to grade. Great.

Instead of asking him to move, and also so I didn't have to speak to him, I quietly slid out my phone and fired a text off to Brooke while the class went back to questioning Carter.

ME:

Drinks tonight. Thank God it's Friday.

My phone vibrated.

BROOKE:

Why, what happened besides the looney act at assembly?

ME:

Carter Anthony IS IN MY CLASSROOM.

BROOKE:

BAHAHAHAHA. Enjoy, and hell yes to drinks. I want to know what else you've done.

ACKNOWLEDGMENTS

I'd love to thank you, the reader, for picking Torch up and giving him a try.

This is the first full-length novel I've written since I was diagnosed with breast cancer, lost my mum, went through treatment, and had a hip replacement. He took me a bit longer than normal since he was different to my usual biker guys, so thanks for being patient.

A massive thanks will always go to Lindsay, my alpha reader,
Becky Johnson, my amazing editor,
Amanda B, Amanda E, Christie, MJ, Maggie, and Annissia,
my beta readers,
and Christian for the brilliant cover design.